THE HALFLING'S HARVEST

S.L. ROWLAND

AETHERVALE PUBLISHING

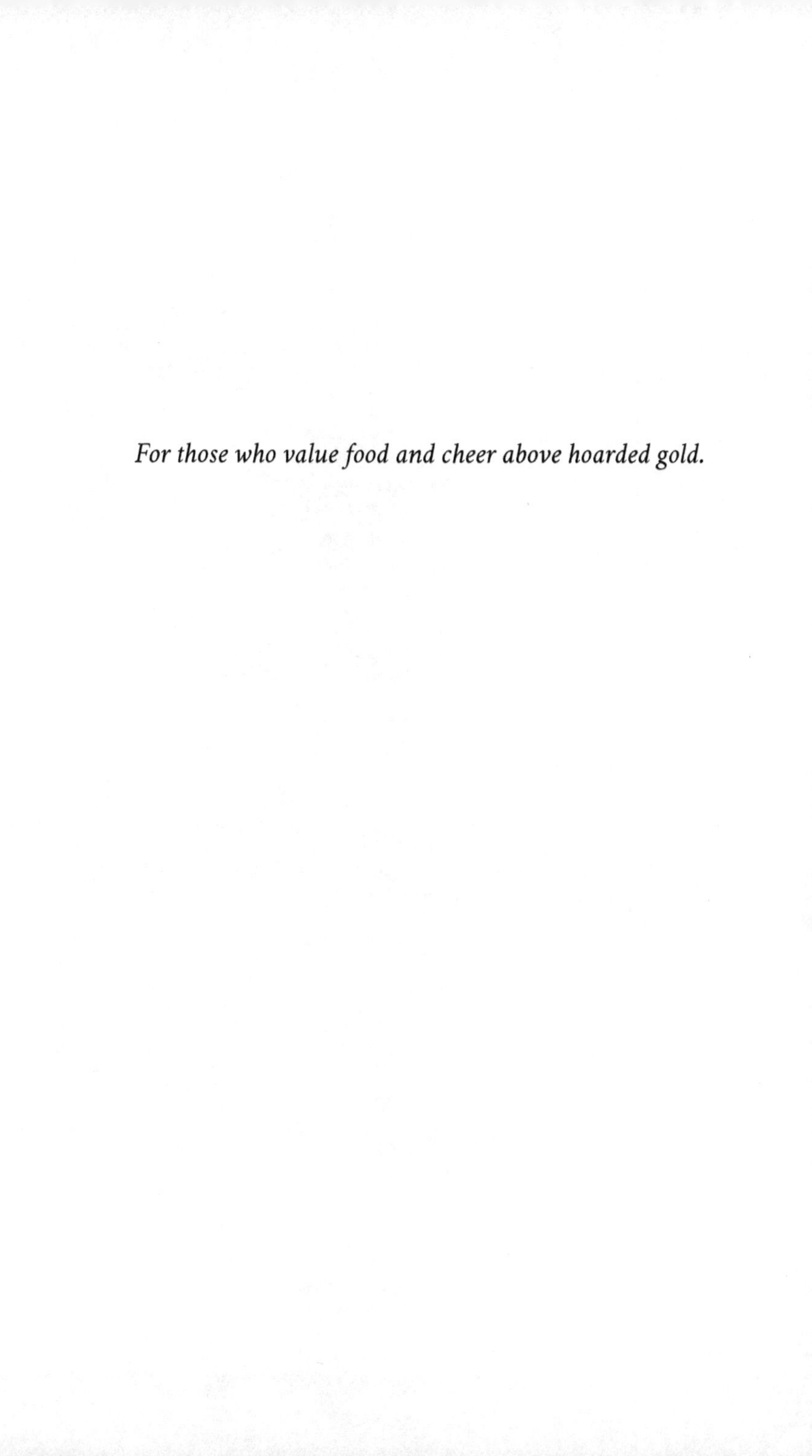

For those who value food and cheer above hoarded gold.

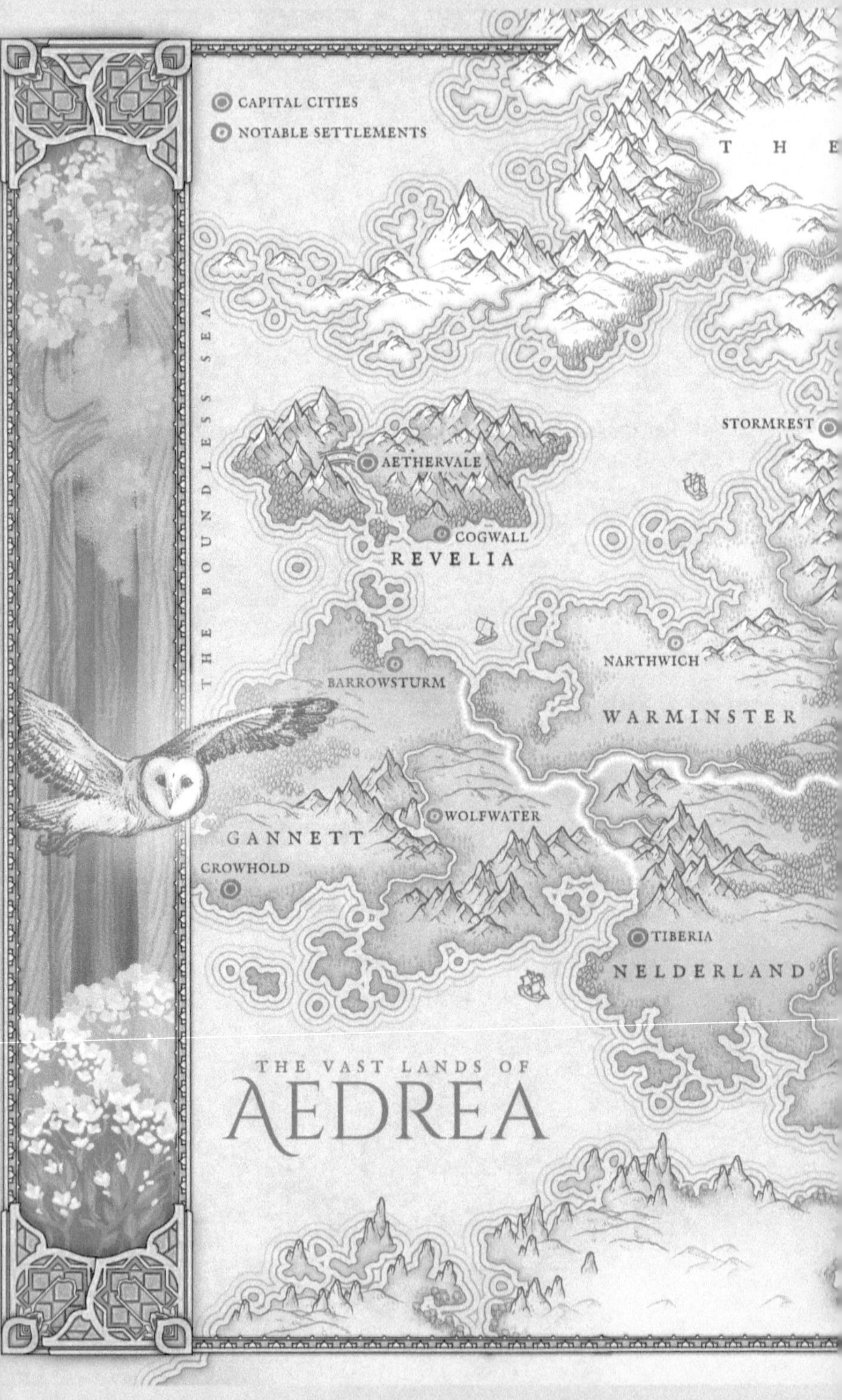

CAPITAL CITIES
NOTABLE SETTLEMENTS
THE BOUNDLESS SEA
THE
STORMREST
AETHERVALE
COGWALL
REVELIA
BARROWSTURM
NARTHWICH
WARMINSTER
WOLFWATER
GANNETT
CROWHOLD
TIBERIA
NELDERLAND
THE VAST LANDS OF
AEDREA

F R O Z E N   N O R T H
NORTHPASS
HOLLOWTON
MOUNT TOR
CASCUS
DURENDREG
SANGUIN
DRAKE CANYON
ROCKDALE
LVERPEAK
HELLS' CRAG
WHITEHAVEN
DARM
BEARMOUTH
SHIVERDAWN
HILLSIDE
WHITBLOSSUM
NIA
HONEYDALE
TYNE
VUSORA
GREENBRIAR MARSH
ASTBORNE
ICRAMEL
ERMMIR
TO THE WILDS
W A S T E L A N D S

PROLOGUE

Last Autumn

Marigold breathed in the cool autumn air. Spring, summer, and winter each had their perks, but nothing compared to the joy of fall. As the leaves changed to shades of gold and crimson, the vineyard came to life. For hundreds of years, it had been a tradition for the towns-folk to come together for the annual grape harvest in the vineyards across Tyne.

Many of Willowbrook's citizens had already arrived, but there were always a few who kept to halfling time. That was to say, they arrived when they got there.

Marigold stood at the end of a row of dreamcatcher grapes, her shears tucked in the pocket of the apron tied about her waist. She wore her thick brown hair braided to keep it more manageable during the harvest, and a wide-brimmed straw hat blocked the sun from her brown eyes and freckled cheeks. Her clothing was simple—a pair of trousers and a loose-fitting tunic.

She cleared her throat. "For those of you who haven't participated in the harvest before, this is how you'll want to cut the bunch free." She moved her hand across the vine, feeling its hardened bark before cupping a cluster of grapes in her hand. The fruit they used for wine were much smaller than the table grapes that one would find at the market. They were also much sweeter this late in the year. As she held the grapes, a wispy shoot swayed in the breeze, curling around her finger as if to say hello. "You don't need to cut the stem too high, just above the bunch."

After snipping the stem, she held the grapes for everyone to see. They were a work of art, a promise from Melora, Goddess of the Harvest, that this life was worth living. The dreamcatcher varietal came in dozens of hues from lavender to violet and pale wisteria. Their waxy skin gave them the look of colorful pearls.

She placed them into the nearest crate. "Once your crate is full, load it into the wagon. Elara will take them up the hill for the stomping. And remember, keep the varietals separate."

"Aye, get on with it, Mari." An older halfling puffed on a pipe nearly as long as his forearm. Gray curls framed his pudgy face as he blew a ring of smoke that dispersed in the breeze. "There's not a one of us that hasn't been using shears since we were knee-high to a horned rabbit."

"Is that so, Elmwood?" Marigold raised a brow. "Tell me, was it me or you who nearly lost a finger last year?"

There was laughter all around as Elmwood coughed. His face darkened several shades of red, and smoke puffed from his mouth like a sputtering chimney as he tried to speak.

He held up a finger until he regained his composure. "You can't hold that against me. It was at the harvest afterparty."

More laughter snaked through the vines, followed by chatter.

"When do we get to drink?" someone asked.

"I'm hungry, Marigold," said another.

"Look, Ma, a bunny." A young halfling chased a horned rabbit through the grass.

"I'm tired," someone complained.

"You haven't even started working."

"I'm hungry, too."

"I'm thirsty."

Marigold placed her hands on her hips. Halflings were known throughout Aedrea as a hospitable people who knew how to make the most of their lives. They loved food, drink, companionship, and above all, comfort. What they didn't love was manual labor.

She held her hand in the air and waited for the group to quiet. "The faster we harvest the grapes, the quicker we get to the fun stuff." Chatter picked up at the mention of festivities, and Marigold waved her shears until it died down. "If you're hungry, thirsty, or need a break—" She rolled her eyes at the last part. "—Locke has prepared food and drinks behind the inn." Half of the volunteers promptly left and headed in that direction. She called after them, "No alcohol until after the harvest!"

Once the volunteers had a belly full of food—a trick Marigold had learned from her father—the day passed with less complaining. "Full halflings are happy halflings," he always said. It didn't take long before songs carried through the vines as they worked, making their way across the vineyard. By early afternoon, they'd harvested enough grapes, and it was time to move uphill.

"Move it or lose it!" Elara yelled as she steered the cart, the pony slowly trudging along. The tall, blonde elf's dark sense of humor was at odds with her radiant appearance. "If you value those hairy feet of yours, you'll keep them off the path until we're through."

"Always in a hurry, this one," Elmwood grumbled as he stepped out of the way.

Marigold was thankful almost every day that Elara Moongrove was her cellar master. The elven vintner had a palate for wine on par with the halflings, and her no-nonsense work ethic meant the vineyard was in capable hands even when Marigold was preoccupied with the inn or its guests.

Elara had been the cellar master since Marigold took over the Dew Drop Inn nearly a decade prior. As the only elf residing in Willowbrook, the locals had found her curious at first, but now they bantered with her like old friends.

She was already emptying crates of emberfruit grapes into the trough when Marigold arrived. The reddish-orange fruit was the most vibrant of the four varietals grown there.

Like most of the vineyards across Tyne, honeywine was the most popular product at the Dew Drop Vineyard, but Wilbur Bramblefoot wasn't content with a single varietal. He enjoyed the spirit of winemaking. Marigold had spent countless hours listening to her father describe the intricacies of the different grapes they grew. He loved the process of aging wine made from the moonshadow grapes with their indigo skins so dark they seemed almost black at times. The pink hues of the dreamcatcher grapes provided floral notes that were unmatched, and the emberfruit offered a sweet-tartness so complex that no two grapes ever tasted the same.

As much as he loved to experiment, honey grapes were still king, and they thrived in the rolling hills across much of Tyne. They provided a unique sweetness that couldn't be found in other varietals, producing a wine so distinct that it had become synonymous with the area across Aedrea.

At the top of the hill, the inn's guests waited by the trough. Marigold's cousin, Gerty, stood with them, wearing a yellow dress that matched her straw-colored hair. Unlike the mane that Marigold had to tame, Gerty kept hers trimmed so that the short ringlets bounced with her every move. She and her brother Finn worked at the inn as housekeeper and groundskeeper, just like their parents before them.

"Gather round, gather round," Marigold called for everyone's attention. "The annual grape harvest is one of our people's most sacred traditions. It's a symbol of our community, our hospitality, and more than anything, our love for food and drink." Cheers erupted across the hill at the last part. "And what better way to show our hospitality than to let our guests begin the stomping."

"Hear, hear!" Elmwood raised his pipe in the air.

Every year during the harvest, the inn was full. People traveled from kingdoms far and wide just to experience the tradition. This year, they had human families who'd traveled from Nelderland and Warminster, a lowland dwarf from Darm, and a pair of mountain dwarves from the northern regions of Mount Tor.

The guests gathered around the trough. The hollowed-out tree had been used to stomp grapes for decades and was capable of fitting a half-dozen people with room to spare.

Marigold knelt in front of two human children. "Are you ready to get your feet dirty?"

They both giggled at the prospect of making a mess.

"Alright, take off your boots." She looked at the parents. "You too. It's a family experience. Climb on in."

"Do we need to wash our feet first?" asked the father.

"Just a rinse will be fine." Marigold winked. "The fermentation process kills off anything harmful."

The man looked at his wife and shrugged. He helped the children clean their feet in the water bucket before lifting them into the trough. Two mountain dwarves followed, and Marigold was certain she saw the twitch of a smile beneath their mighty beards. It didn't matter how strong or tough someone was, the act of crushing grapes brought out a sense of childlike wonder.

Once they were all inside, a lute strummed from somewhere in the crowd.

"That's our cue." Marigold climbed into the trough and started stomping. "You want to really get in there. Let the grapes mush between your toes."

The children laughed as they sloshed about, crushing grapes beneath their bare feet. As they stomped, juice pooled at the bottom. The two mountain dwarves were hesitant at first but then they began stomping with fervor, deep laughter bellowing between the two.

Marigold looked over the crowded hill, and there

wasn't a frown to be seen. Several more halflings had arrived with their instruments and joined in the revelry as a chorus of "Olde Merriweather" broke out. People danced to the lively tune, twirling, clapping, and laughing as folksy music filled the air.

Year after year, the harvest never failed to impress. Some of Marigold's most cherished memories were formed on days like today, surrounded by her family and friends. She only wished her father were here—the man who had instilled love in her for both the inn and vineyard. But he and her mother were off enjoying the fruits of a life well-lived.

Since retiring, they'd traveled the realm, experiencing all that life had to offer and only returning home every few years. Every so often, she'd receive a letter with detailed accounts of their exploits, and she'd read it again and again. As much as she missed them, she couldn't fault her parents for leaving. If they'd never left, Marigold would never have taken over the inn. She owed everything to her father's adventurous spirit.

After a few minutes, the children were panting from their enthusiastic stomping. The two mountain dwarves only stomped harder, staring at one another with the fierce gaze of competition.

Brothers, Marigold chuckled to herself. "Alright, alright, we can't let you two have all the fun, now can we? I'm sure you've worked up an appetite after all that work. Dinner should be ready soon."

They cleaned their grape-stained feet, and Elara took charge as Marigold led the guests down the hill for food. In their wake, the stomping began in earnest as the music picked up and halflings danced in the trough to the rhythm of the music.

"Barrels of wine are heavy, so we want to avoid having to move them uphill," Marigold explained as they walked. "We set the trough at the top of the hill so that when the pressing is over, the grape juice can drain through a hole at the bottom and flow down a gutter to the winery. Since halflings aren't known for our brawn, everything is built to be as efficient as possible." She stopped in front of a building halfway down the hill. "This is the winery. Inside, we'll store the juice in clay pots to ferment and bury them in the ground so that they stay cool. The fermentation process takes a couple of weeks and during that time, we check it daily. Sometimes, we'll add additional ingredients if we want to impart specific flavors to the wine. Once all the sediment settles, we'll transfer the wine from the pots into barrels to age. You can't tell from here—" She pointed at the stretch of ground between the winery and the inn. "—but there are tunnels that connect the two. This is how we transport the barrels to our cellar for them to age. Most of the grapes we harvested today won't be ready until next year's harvest festival, and for the moonshadow grapes, it could be years before we're ready to bottle them."

"Years?" The little girl's mouth dropped open. "That's a long time."

"It certainly is." Marigold grinned. "My father told me that good things take time. You'd be surprised what we can achieve with a little patience."

"Gods, that smells divine!" one of the dwarfs exclaimed, his eyes locked on the hog roasting on a giant spit.

"Reminds you of home, eh?" The inn's cook, Locke, looked over his shoulder as he brushed the hog with copious amounts of butter. He had his sleeves rolled up, revealing muscled forearms, and wore an apron with splotches of grease. The dwarf's black hair and beard were so dense that they shimmered in the evening sun. By trade, he was a baker but since taking over the kitchen at the inn, he now saw to all of the meals. "I spend most of my time in the kitchen but once a year, I get to roast a hog for the harvest. Have a drink, and I'll slice her up for you."

Butter sizzled as it dripped into the fire. Several barrels of wine had already been tapped, and Finn was filling carafes with honeywine and an aged red. The groundskeeper had the same curly hair as his sister, though he kept his shorter. When they were children, it had been almost impossible to tell the two apart.

"Save some for me," Elmwood called as he hurried down the hill with a carafe cradled between his hands.

Marigold narrowed her eyes at the elder halfling. "Looks like you got an early start."

"This is for the kids." He handed it to Marigold.

She raised her brows before sniffing the contents.

"Oh, don't look at me like that." Elmwood crossed his arms. "It's grape juice. Elara said she'd pull the hair from my ears if I didn't bring it to you."

Locke let out a boisterous laugh. "That sounds like her, alright."

Marigold poured herself a taste. The juice had the perfect mixture of sweet and tart that emberfruit grapes were known for. It was a bit cloudy, a far cry from the crisp, clean wine it would become in a few months.

"Elara says we've got a good crop this year," Locke

said, slicing slivers of meat from the hog. "How are you feeling about the festival?"

Marigold shook her head. "That's a conversation for another time."

"Someone's got a thorn in her foot." Elmwood gave her a knowing look. "Don't be too hard on yourself, Mari. It's not like Galvin is winning by himself. Poor timing that he brought a druid on staff the same time you took over your father's legacy."

"Put a sock in it, you old sod," Locke growled at Elmwood. "We don't need a druid to make great wine. Marigold and Elara are more than up to the task."

"I'm just saying second place is nothing to be ashamed of." The silver-haired halfling puffed his pipe. "No one thinks any less of you for it."

Locke's scowl deepened.

"Don't worry about it." Marigold patted the dwarf on the arm and forced a smile. Today was a time to celebrate, not stew on past failures. "The festival's not for a few more weeks, and it's not like we can do anything about it now. Whatever we bring will be from past seasons. Tonight, enjoy the harvest and the hog." She grabbed a carafe of wine from the table and filled the cups. "Now, tell me, who wants the good stuff?"

1. DEW DROP INN

The Following Summer

The Dew Drop Inn offered more than shelter for weary travelers to rest their heads. It was a place where they could find comfort, along with a warm meal, a relaxing drink, and friendly faces. Here, hospitality wasn't part of the job, it was a way of life.

For Marigold Bramblefoot, the inn was more than a building, it was her home. She'd scampered up and down its stairs since she was knee-high to a dire cat, or so her father always said.

In truth, it was Wilbur Bramblefoot's love of hospitality that had infected her at a young age. For over half a century, he'd owned the inn, and laughter and conversation carried through its walls at all hours of the day and long into the night on many occasions. The sounds of the inn were like a warm fire on a cold night, and they had seeped into her bones. She'd often snuck from her bed to peek through the banisters, perching like an owl and watching as strangers became friends over a glass of her father's famous wine or brandy.

Even now, she was convinced there was a magic embedded within a bottle of wine that no mage or sorcerer could ever imitate. It had the power to broker deals and cement alliances, to tether friend and foe, and bring harmony to a chaotic world.

Marigold stood at the top of the stairs, looking over the empty inn, as the heartbeat of the familiar structure pulsed against her bare feet. Gerty scurried into the dining area with a stack of plates cradled in her arms, her golden locks bobbing with each step. One by one, she placed them around the table, organizing the place settings until everything was just right. She stepped back, evaluating the table before adjusting a napkin slightly. With a nod, she disappeared back into the kitchen.

Sunlight spilled in from the windows, basking the aged timber in a warm glow. The guests were still tucked in their beds, and a snore rattled from behind a closed door. Marigold smiled at the sound. Offering travelers the comfort of a good night's sleep when they were far from home was one of the many rewards she reaped on a daily basis.

She made her way downstairs, the wooden planks of the floorboard groaning gently with each step. Unlike many of the buildings in Willowbrook, which tended to have a ground floor and deeper levels that descended into the earth and rolling hills of the area, the Dew Drop Inn was two stories tall, complete with six guest rooms, three staff quarters, a dining room, common area, library, kitchen, and a bar. It also boasted a number of hidden nooks and crannies where guests could find seclusion to read or work in private. The inn's most popular feature was the expansive cellar that ran underneath the property.

Despite the building's stature, the inn was deceptively cozy. Its welcoming embrace could be felt with every piece of carefully selected decor, from the paintings of the Bramblefoot family to the tapestries depicting wine-making and the beautiful countryside. The dark wood of the walls provided a sense of warmth and intimacy, balanced by bouquets of colorful flowers resting on the tables, and an assortment of chairs and plush throws in various sizes promised comfort to any guest no matter their stature, be it gnome, human, dwarf, or elf.

Marigold paused at the bottom of the stairs, where a sweet, buttery aroma wafted through the room. Locke was always the first to rise, the dwarven baker keen to make sure that guests awoke with ravenous appetites.

She found him in the kitchen, where a pie cooled in the open window, steam rising from the crust. Marigold closed her eyes and breathed in the heavenly scent of the buttery crust and cooked green apple. Her stomach rumbled in anticipation as she imagined the delicate balance of spices—nutmeg, clove, and just a touch of cinnamon.

She sighed and rubbed her belly. "What would I do without you, Locke?"

"Don't be silly." The dwarf looked up from his rolling pin, and the muscles in his powerful forearms relaxed. "I've tasted yer pies, and this inn isn't the only thing you inherited from yer folks."

Locke wore a white shirt with the sleeves rolled up to the elbow and an apron embroidered with the grape emblem of the inn. Both items were speckled with flour and sugar. He had the intimidating presence and deep voice of a miner, but Marigold would be hard-pressed to argue that he wasn't a halfling trapped in a dwarf's body. Flour dusted his jet-black beard, and mirth sparkled within his eyes the color of golden wheat fields.

Marigold laughed. She could always count on Locke to brighten her day.

The two had first met while Marigold was studying at Whitblossum University. It was one of the few colleges across the realm that offered studies in warmth and hospitality, and the only one in the halfling kingdom of Tyne. Locke had been an apprentice baker working across from the university at the time, and they'd become fast friends during the many hours she'd spent studying and drinking tea at the pastry shop.

She'd learned a great deal about hospitality during her year there, but everything she knew about wine had come from her father. His passion for winemaking was unri-valed throughout the town of Willowbrook, and building an inn to accompany his vineyard was how he showcased that passion to the world. As far back as Marigold could remember, taking over the inn had been her dream, and for the past ten years, that dream had become her reality. With so much to do, it had been a while since she baked anything of her own. That's why she had Locke.

Marigold eyed the pie in the window and swallowed. As kind as Locke was, she knew better than to touch his creations before he gave the okay. "The guests should be waking soon, and we have another scheduled to arrive sometime in the next few days. I have some errands to run tomorrow morning, so if you need anything from town, leave a list with Gerty and we'll take care of it."

Locke stroked his beard, leaving a fresh trail of white dust down its edges. "Hmm, I'll see what I can put together. I have a new recipe I've been meaning to try."

For a baker, Locke's workspace was meticulously maintained, even in the midst of preparation. There were bowls of chopped vegetables to one side filled with squash, tomato, onion, and mushrooms. To the other, tidy bowls of flour, eggs, and cream sat in a straight line. Vials of spices were neatly arranged in one corner, each one labeled with elegant handwriting.

With a pie in the window and a quiche on the way, the day was certainly off to a promising start.

Marigold couldn't ask for a better staff. When she'd chosen them, she'd made sure to select those with a passion for their craft that rivaled her own. Locke kept their bellies full and had invested as much of himself into this venture as she had.

"I'll be back to sample the pie shortly. First, I need to check in with Elara. I believe we have a shipment scheduled for later this—"

"Oh no, am I in trouble again?" a beguiling voice whispered in Marigold's ear at the same time as a slender hand gripped her on the shoulder.

Marigold jumped, unleashing a yelp of surprise as color rushed to her cheeks. "What did I tell you about doing that!" She swatted the elf's hand away playfully. "I swear, I'm going to put a bell around your neck so that we can hear you coming."

"I can't help that my people are naturally stealthy."

Elara grinned, and a stray lock of golden hair fell across her bright blue eye. "Speaking of bells, I'd suggest putting one on the damned cat first. Then he might actually keep the thieving rabbits away from the vineyard. They got into the honey grapes again. If we don't nip this in the bud, there won't be any for the harvest festival."

The mention of the festival dampened Marigold's spirits, but she pushed that away for another time. There were still several months before the annual celebration and a host of things requiring her attention in the meantime.

"Oh, don't be so hard on him, hon." Locke gave the elf a knowing look. "We all get old."

Elara walked behind the table and knelt, kissing Locke on the forehead. "Is that why your beard is all white?"

Locke looked down at his beard streaked with flour. "Dammit to hells."

Marigold and Elara both laughed. For someone who valued order above all else, Locke always managed to put a dash of ingredients on his person, no matter how hard he tried to avoid it.

"Hey now." Elara pressed a finger to his lips. "You better watch your tongue or people might think we've been spending too much time together."

The dwarf growled playfully. "I've never been one to care what others think."

"And that is what I love about you." A genuine smile spread across the elf's face.

Elara was, by all accounts, beautiful, but the only time Marigold ever saw her truly smile was when Locke was around. Marigold hoped to find a love like that for herself one day. The two were complete opposites in almost every way, but they somehow managed to have one of the most pure and earnest relationships she'd ever witnessed. Elara was quick-tempered, foul-mouthed, and impatient, while Locke had a heart of gold and the patience of a cleric. But they both had a love for the inn and were together responsible for two of the most important elements that kept guests returning time and again—food and wine.

"Is everything in order for the shipment today?" asked Marigold.

"Do you even need to ask?" Elara took a piece of squash from the bowl and tossed it in her mouth. In turn, Locke grunted his displeasure.

"I wouldn't be doing my job if I didn't." Marigold gestured toward the door. "Walk the grounds with me? I can't have you distracting my baker before breakfast is served."

Elara kissed Locke on the top of his bushy black hair. "See you later, handsome."

Locke wore a devilish expression as Elara exited the kitchen. Once she was out the door, he gave Marigold a smirk. "I hate to see her go, but I love to watch her leave."

"And I'd love for you to get to work." Marigold fought the urge to grin as she turned to follow the elf.

Outside, it was a crisp summer morning. Fog settled in between the rolling hills, and dew glistened upon the neat rows of grape vines that made up the vineyard. Birds chirped their morning songs, and the insects trilled.

Elara stopped, resting her hands on her hips as she let

out a sigh. "Ten years we've worked together and this never gets old."

"I couldn't imagine doing anything else, that's for sure." Marigold raised a hand, blocking out the morning sun as she surveyed the landscape. "Shall we start with the honey grapes?"

Something pressed against Marigold's leg, and she looked down to find Onyx rubbing against her calf. The dire cat was massive, with fluffy ash-colored fur that made him appear even larger than he was. When Marigold was a child, she'd witnessed him chasing away foxes and deer. Once, he'd turned back a roaming bear that had caught the scent of her mother's honey.

That was back when Onyx's fur was the same color as his namesake. Nowadays, he was long in the tooth and his black fur was tinged with gray. His chest rattled when he purred, where once it had rumbled, and his eyes were the cloudy color of tea with too much milk. Where he had once pranced through the vineyard with abandon, he now strolled its rows, often taking breaks to bask in the sun.

He'd served the vineyard faithfully for countless years, and though the horned rabbits were now more plentiful than ever, Marigold didn't have it in her heart to replace him. This vineyard was as much his as it was hers.

Every morning, he woke with the sun and patrolled the vines, albeit slowly, and he'd scamper along the paths if he saw a rabbit, never quick enough to do more than scare them.

"Well, look who it is. Coming to visit your rabbit friends, are we?" Elara pursed her lips. "Yesterday, I found him sleeping at the end of the moonshadow grapes. There was a horned rabbit munching on the vine not five feet from him."

Marigold laughed at the mental image. "He needs a lot more sleep in his old age."

Elara scoffed. "What he needs is retirement. He was past his prime when we took over the inn. I still don't know why your folks didn't take him."

"This is his home." Marigold knelt, scratching Onyx beneath his chin. Her father had offered to take the dire cat with them, but Marigold couldn't let him go. Onyx loved it here. "And he still enjoys the hunt, even if he's lost a step or two."

"Or five." Elara grinned.

As much as the elf liked to complain, Marigold knew she loved the cat. She'd watched Elara slow down and wait for Onyx to catch up more times than she could count.

They made their way down the row of honey grapes, occasionally plucking one from the vine to taste. In late summer, the grapes were still tart and acidic, a month or two away from being ready to harvest.

Elara gently released a bunch of grapes she was holding and fixed her gaze on the horizon. "We should probably start planning which wine we're going to present for the harvest festival this year."

Marigold sighed. She had loved the harvest festival as a kid, but lately, it cast a dark cloud over her every time she thought about it. Her father had won the wine tasting almost every year he'd entered, and numerous ribbons adorned the walls of the cellar.

Since Marigold had taken over, the best she managed was runner-up. Her wine was good, but Galvin Darkroot's always seemed to be better. He'd been a thorn in her side from the beginning.

Elara squeezed Marigold's shoulder. "I know it's a sore subject, but this is our year. Last year's harvest was exceptional."

"That it was, but I don't know how we'll ever compete with a druid."

Elara scoffed. "Galvin is a little weasel if I ever saw one. There's a reason he never won anything before she got there. If you ask me, there should be a separate contest for those who use magic to tend their crops."

Marigold could always count on Elara to have her back. Truthfully, Marigold had no qualms with druids. They had saved crops from droughts all across the realm and prevented famine from wreaking havoc. But ten years ago, Galvin Darkroot brought a druid on staff to help him manage the vineyard. With magical help, they grew the most ripe and flavorful grapes, and every year, Darkroot Cellars took home the blue ribbon.

Having a druid on staff meant that every vine and every grape grew to its utmost potential. There was no way to compete against that with a staff of only five. Deep down, Marigold knew there was no shame in second place, but until she won, she would always be living in the shadow of her father, the great Wilbur Bramblefoot.

Lucky for her, he hadn't raised a quitter. Marigold would continue competing no matter how many druids she faced, and she'd do it with a smile. One day, she'd win, and the taste of victory would be all the sweeter.

She plucked a grape and rolled the waxy exterior against her fingertips. "Tell me what wine you had in mind."

2. WILLOWBROOK

Sun kissed Marigold's cheeks as she and Gerty took the wagon into Willowbrook.

"Was this you?" Marigold nodded at Acorn Blossom, the pony's mane braided and adorned with flowers.

"He likes to look pretty when we go into town." Gerty grinned. "Isn't that right, Acorn?"

Acorn Blossom neighed his affirmation, along with a flick of his tail.

Marigold chuckled to herself as the wagon bumped along the dirt road. The journey itself wasn't that long, considering she could walk from the inn to town in less than an hour, but the hassle of loading the wagon and hitching a pony meant Marigold tried to limit their visits to once a week if possible. In many regards, the inn was self-sufficient, but there was always wine to deliver, and some items could only be found in town.

That's not to say that Marigold didn't enjoy her visits. Willowbrook was a beautiful town etched into the hills, a mixture of underground dwellings and quaint, cottage-style shops and inns. It was spacious and welcoming, unlike the packed cities of other kingdoms. A stream ran along the edge of town, willow trees swaying in the breeze, their branches tickling the water as halflings sat on the shores smoking pipeleaf and casting lines into the shallow water.

Unlike many human and dwarven settlements, there were no tall structures to block the expansive views of the countryside. There were no universities, alchemists, tinkers, and very few guilds. They only had one temple and bank—both operated by the Cleric's Guild. Willowbrook offered exquisitely crafted items with halfling flair, good food, great drinks, and better company.

The town would be considered small by its population, but its location between Whitblossum and Honeydale, Tyne's two largest cities, meant that travelers and tourists kept the inns full, the shops busy, and the town thriving. While much of the world was becoming more enthralled by the advancements of Runetech, in Willowbrook, things still moved at a slower pace. Sometimes, that was exactly what people needed.

After crossing the stone bridge, they entered the town, where vibrant flowers lined the streets and tea roses grew upon the walls of many buildings. They passed through Crafters Row, where they were momentarily engulfed by the steady rhythm of the blacksmith's hammer and the scent of sawdust from the woodworkers.

Marigold steered the wagon through the winding cobbled streets before pulling to a stop outside of the Hearth & Honey Bakery. Townsfolk were out and about at the local market, and the storefronts were alive and well with visitors.

The smell of freshly baked bread wafted through the windows of the bakery, and the comforting, homey aroma sent Marigold's stomach rumbling.

She turned to Gerty. "Do you have Locke's list?"

Gerty fumbled through her pockets before pulling out a piece of crumpled parchment. "Right here. I'll need to stop by the market and general store. I was also hoping to visit the herbalist for more honey cream ointment. Washing the bedding really takes a toll on my skin."

Marigold looked down at her own hands, callused from years of working in the vineyard. Maybe a little ointment would do her good. She pulled a few coins from her pocket and handed them to Gerty.

"Whatever you buy, make it two. I've got a few errands to run, but we can meet at Town Hall once we're finished."

"Sounds good, but maybe..." Gerty's eyes darted toward the bakery and back to Marigold.

Marigold bit her lip. Locke would never let her hear the end of it if he found out. Though, if he had given her a taste of the pie this morning, she might not have been so tempted.

She inhaled the welcoming aroma once again. "Fine, but not a word to Locke."

Gerty pressed a finger to her lips.

Inside, the bakery smelled so divine that Marigold had to wipe away saliva pooling at the edge of her mouth. Toasty, nut-covered loaves of bread lined the counter, and a myriad of sweet and savory pastries sat on the display shelf. Some were topped with fruits, others drizzled with glaze or caramel.

"Marigold, Gerty." The halfling woman behind the

counter smiled. "What'll it be today? I've got fresh lemon tarts, rosemary scones, and honey butter biscuits."

Marigold and Gerty exchanged a glance before bursting into laughter.

"Oh, Rosie, you know we can't resist a lemon tart." Marigold chuckled. "But we were never here."

"Of course not. And I won't be seeing you next week either." Rosie winked. "Give my best to Locke when you see him. I look forward to our pies competing again this year."

"Will do." Marigold paid for the pastries. "Don't work too hard."

Outside the shop, Marigold and Gerty sat together on a moss-covered stone. Squirrels scurried through the underbrush of a nearby tree, chittering loudly.

Marigold took a bite of the tart, and it crumbled in her mouth. The pastry was the perfect blend of sweet and sour, with a custard filling that melted as the crumbs softened. It reminded her of early mornings, following on her mother's heels as she moved around the kitchen. "This takes me back. Mom used to bake lemon tarts all the time when I was little."

"I remember." Gerty broke off a piece and ate it slowly, savoring every moment. "Finn and I would hide outside the window and sneak a few while they were cooling."

Marigold gently elbowed her in the side. "Do you know how many times I got in trouble because of you two?"

Gerty narrowed her eyes. "Hey now, we always shared with you."

Marigold laughed. "That made it worth it."

After they finished eating, Gerty disappeared among

the crowded market to fetch Locke's items, and Marigold returned to the wagon to make her rounds. The first order of business was delivering cases of wine to the local merchants who would ship them far and wide across Aedrea. Since nowhere outside of Tyne produced honey-wine, the merchants would order as much as they could. Even though the Dew Drop Vineyard was a small operation, it produced enough wine to ship out several orders per week.

Sometimes, Marigold wondered where the bottles would end up and what occasions might prompt them to be opened. Were they uncorked during grand celebrations or the small moments of everyday life? Her father often said that the best wines were the ones enjoyed with friends, and she hoped that happiness was involved wherever the bottles ended up.

Once the wine had been delivered, she traveled to the stables to buy feed and then stopped by the blacksmith for nails so that Finn could make repairs around the inn.

With her pockets full of coin, Marigold entered the bank to deposit the week's earnings. The Bank of Aedrea was one of the oldest institutions in Aedrea, and since it was owned and operated by the Order of Clerics, it had the reputation of being the safest place in the realm to store one's money and valuables.

From the outside, it looked like any other building in town, a cottage-style exterior surrounded by plants and greenery, but inside, it was a far cry from the simple and rustic aesthetic. The interior was modern and immaculate, with gold filigree that accented the walls and ceiling and polished marble floors that gleamed beneath enchanted lights.

Marigold had been to several branches across Tyne, and they always seemed to have a faint smell of mint. Since the Bank of Aedrea was the only financial institution that operated within every kingdom, it allowed Marigold's parents to travel for years at a time without needing to return home. She still wasn't sure how the bank managed to keep track of accounts across so many locations, but she supposed being an emissary of the gods had its perks.

A couple of halflings and a dwarf were already in line, so Marigold waited until a teller waved her over. She recognized the man across the counter as Hamlen, a dark-haired human who had only been working in Willowbrook for a few months. She'd seen him on her weekly visits but had never interacted with him until now.

"How may I help you today, Lady Bramblefoot?" he asked.

"Marigold is fine. I'm here to make my weekly deposit." She placed the bag of coins on the counter. "How are you liking Willowbrook so far?"

Hamlen looked up from the coins and smiled. "Can I tell you a secret?" He leaned forward before she could answer. "I'd never actually visited Tyne before the guild stationed me here. But everyone has been so nice that I may never go back."

Marigold returned his smile. "Where's home for you?"

"Stormrest, if you can believe it." He rubbed his shoulders like someone experiencing a chill. "A lot colder than these parts."

"That's quite a trek. I'm glad to see the journey was worth it for you."

Hamlen talked as he counted the coins, stacking them

in neat lines. "Everyone keeps telling me about the harvest festival coming up. It sounds like a real delight, and I can't wait to experience it myself. I've always had a fondness for wine, and they say your vineyard is one of the best around."

One of the best. Her smile faltered for a moment. "We pour our hearts into our wine, and I like to think it shows."

"Well, I hope to try some of your offerings when the time comes. If the festival is half as exciting as everyone says, I'm in for a treat." Hamlen made a note on his ledger and leaned forward to give Marigold a receipt with her balance. "I'll be rooting for you, Lady Bramble—er, Marigold."

"I appreciate it, Hamlen." She tapped him on the arm. "You're going to fit in just fine around here. And if you ever want to try our wines before the harvest festival, stop by the vineyard anytime."

The last item on Marigold's agenda was Town Hall, the beating heart of Willowbrook. If someone needed a permit, a request, records, or somewhere to catch the latest news or gossip, Town Hall was the place to be. The front door opened into an arched hallway. On one side, there was a noticeboard pinned with job offers, upcoming meetings, events, items for sale, and even a few stained recipes someone had decided to share. On the other, plaques and paintings stretched the length of the hall. Polished wood floors gleamed in the light of the candle sconces leading to an octagonal dome in the building's center.

Marigold stopped by the noticeboard, where a bright orange flyer with black text caught her eye.

Willowbrook's 577th Annual Harvest Festival

Come join in one of the town's most historic traditions!

Featuring:
Music
Dancing
Singing
Drinking
Storytelling
Pumpkin Carving
Wreath Making
Corn Maze
Food and Wine Tastings
And much more!

With Contests For:
Pie Eating
Apple Bobbing
Best Local Pipeleaf
Best Local Wine
Largest Pumpkin
Largest Vegetable (non-pumpkin)

Location: *Willowbrook Town Square*

Marigold was focused on the flyer when someone

bumped into her side. She stumbled as parchment fluttered through the air and scrolls toppled to the wooden floor.

"Oh, my! I'm so sorry. I didn't see you there." A blue-haired gnome looked up as she struggled to gather her belongings, stuffing scrolls into a canvas satchel.

Marigold knelt to help, gathering sheets of stray parchment scribbled with notes. She reached for the closest sheet at the same time as the gnome, and their hands touched. For a moment, they crouched in silence like deer caught in the glow of lamplight. Marigold forgot all about the parchment, her attention focused on the gnome before her.

Large, round spectacles took up the majority of the gnome's face, the lavender lenses complementing the dusty-pink complexion of her skin. She had a button nose and wore her hair in a messy bun. Several strands of sapphire hair dangled across her forehead.

"Er..." The gnome's cheeks flushed as she stared at Marigold, their hands still touching.

"Right, uh, sorry." Marigold pulled back her hand before offering the papers she had gathered. "Here you go."

As the gnome shuffled the parchment and put them away, Marigold took in the rest of her assailant's appearance. The two of them were of similar height. Halflings and gnomes would have been difficult to differentiate if not for the jewel-toned skin and vibrantly colored hair of the latter. She had a slender frame and wore a red tunic embroidered with gold thread, and forest green-trousers were tucked into her boots. On her back was a bulging pack stuffed with even more scrolls and who knew what else. She had a book with a travel strap slung over one shoulder and several small journals tucked into her waistband.

Marigold couldn't begin to imagine what one person would need so many papers and scrolls for unless perhaps she was a traveling bard working on an epic poem or one of those census takers that rolled through town once a decade.

"Sorry again," the gnome apologized as she stuffed the parchment into her satchel with ink-stained fingers. "I should have been paying better attention."

"Don't worry about it." Marigold offered her a smile. "Looks like you're on important business."

"In a sense. To know the past is to understand the future," she said as if reciting the phrase from memory. She brushed a strand of hair behind her ear and adjusted the pack on her shoulders. "I'm in town doing research for the Gnomish Historical Society. I couldn't find the library, so I was coming to Town Hall for help."

"Ah, you've come to the right place, then. Town Hall has a robust record system detailing our histories for generations. We don't have an official library, but many of the local families are known to hoard books and have personal libraries in their homes. What is it you're researching?"

The gnome's face lit up at the question, the same way Marigold's father's did when he talked about wine. When someone truly loved something, it radiated through their eyes.

"I've been tasked with researching the halfling tradition of the harvest festival. I traveled to Whitblossum beforehand, but I was told that if I wanted to truly experience what it was like, I needed to find a smaller town, so here I am. I'll be staying for several months to research the full experience."

"In that case, I feel we need a proper introduction." She extended her hand. "I'm Marigold."

"Poppy. Pleased to meet you, Marigold."

They shook hands, and the softness of Poppy's touch sharpened Marigold's awareness of her own rough, calloused skin. The vineyard had etched its mark on her hands, and all she could think about was how desperately she needed some of Gerty's honey cream ointment. "I can show you to the archives if you'd like."

"That'd be wonderful."

They walked down the hall and into the atrium where the main offices were located. It was filled with people—mostly halflings but a few dwarves and a couple of humans whose heads came precariously close to bumping into the candle chandeliers. Normally, people would be scattered around the building in meetings or private conversations, but this time, everyone was gathered around the mayor's office focused on whatever was happening inside. The crowd also happened to be blocking access to the stairwell that led to the archives.

Marigold paused to see what the fuss was all about. Whatever had the entirety of Town Hall enraptured had to be interesting. She stood on her tiptoes in an attempt to get a better view, but it was impossible to see past the crowd. She could see Mayor Sweetwater gesturing and laughing, but a human blocked her view of who or what had him so excited.

There was more laughter and then the crowd began to

part. Marigold's mood instantly soured when she saw who the mayor had been talking to.

Galvin Darkroot walked side-by-side with the mayor, chatting like old friends as they passed through. Galvin had dark, beady eyes, an upturned nose that matched his pompous attitude, and the smile of a cat— the kind where you could never know if he was laughing with you or at you. For a nemesis, he was certainly dressed for the part. Where most halflings who worked the earth wore simple clothing, he wore suits of fine fabric with elaborate brooches and gaudy jewelry. Even his shoes were polished to a shine.

Behind them, Tansy Ironvale, the human druid Galvin had hired to tend his vineyard, towered above the two halflings. Her expression was stoic as she followed along, and her clothing was lavish, nothing like the depictions of druids in the fairy tales Marigold read as a child.

Marigold had nothing against the finer things in life, or those who enjoyed the fruits of their labor, but to her, Galvin Darkroot was a fraud. Someone who had taken one of her people's most sacred traditions and exploited it.

He sought profit above all, and the worst part was that thanks to the druid, he was succeeding. He could do less work and still produce a superior product.

A pink hand wrapped around Marigold's arm, pulling her from her thoughts.

"Are you okay?" Concern was etched into Poppy's brow.

"Yes, sorry." She took a deep breath. "He and I have a… history."

"Oh." Poppy grimaced. "This must be awkward."

"Not like that. I mean—"

"Is that Marigold Bramblefoot I see?" Galvin grinned like a wolf as he approached. "I am so looking forward to the harvest festival this year. I was just telling the mayor about the newest upgrade we've made to the cellar."

Mayor Sweetwater stopped next to Galvin as the rest of the people began returning to their business. His graying hair was neatly parted, and while not as extravagantly dressed as his two companions, he wore a green vest of fine quality, its breast adorned with a golden brooch. "Revelia really does have some of the most fascinating technology." He rubbed his hands together excitedly. "Our people have never been much for enchantments, but I do appreciate gnomish ingenuity." He gestured to Marigold. "You should really look into ordering a chiller for your cellar as well."

"A chiller?" Marigold raised a brow.

"It's Runetech," Poppy inserted herself into the conversation. "Our master enchanters are able to carve frost runes into metal boxes and trap the cold air inside. It allows you to store food and drink at cooler temperatures so they last longer. Some of them are even able to freeze water into ice. They've really taken off in some of the larger cities and come in all shapes and sizes."

"I donated one to Town Hall as a gesture of goodwill." Galvin grinned. "If you've never tried a glass of chilled honeywine, let me tell you, you are missing out."

Marigold forced a smile. She'd had honeywine that had chilled in the cold air on a winter day, so she knew he was right, but there was no way she was giving him the satisfaction. "I think I'll pass."

"Of course." Galvin laughed. "You know, if you weren't

so stuck in the past, you might actually win the wine tasting one of these days. You're a talented winemaker, Marigold. Imagine what you could do if you didn't have to fight against nature."

"Some of us take pride in the old ways." Marigold clenched her fist to keep from lashing out. "Enjoy your chiller. I need to show Poppy the archives."

"See you around." Galvin waggled his gilded fingers as Marigold and Poppy descended the stairwell.

Marigold was still fuming when they made it underground to a chamber similar to the one above. Enchanted lights lined the walls, casting the room in a warm glow. While most of Willowbrook's buildings still used candles for light, the archives were an exception. Enchanted lights didn't burn, which was safer for storing documents, and they were one of the more affordable forms of enchanted items. Marigold imagined something like a chiller would cost a month of the inn's income. Darkroot Cellars might be able to afford it, but it was out of reach for the Dew Drop Inn.

"He seems like a real peach." Poppy gestured toward the ceiling.

"More like an ass." Marigold smirked. "He wasn't always, but like I said, we have a history."

"Sounds like an interesting one."

"A story for another time." Marigold led Poppy to a table supporting several massive books. "These are the directories. There's one for each hallway, and they should all be sorted alphabetically except for the most recent. That one will be sorted by the date it was archived. When that tunnel is full, it will all be re-catalogued. Since you're looking for the history of the harvest festival, probably best to save that one for last."

Poppy nodded her understanding. "Thanks for your help. And sorry again for bumping into you." She smiled as she ran her fingers over the embossed text of the cover. "Hopefully, I'll see you around."

"I'd like that." Marigold bit her lip, not wanting to leave but knowing that Gerty was probably already waiting for her. "Take care, Poppy. I hope you find what you're looking for."

3. AN UNEXPECTED GUEST

After the guests were served a dinner of roasted rosemary chicken, stuffed baked potatoes, and herbed carrots, Marigold retreated to the kitchen to eat her dinner with Locke and Elara. Not even the blueberry pie resting on the counter could pull Marigold from her slump. Her glass of dreamcatcher wine sat untouched as she pushed her carrots around her plate, still ruminating on her interaction with Galvin.

"Something on yer mind, Mari?" Locke crossed his arms and sat back in his chair. "You've barely touched yer dinner. If I didn't know better, I'd be offended."

Marigold sighed. "I ran into Galvin at Town Hall today."

Elara's face instantly turned to a scowl. "What'd that little weasel say to you this time?" She pointed a slender finger like a dagger as she spoke. "Let me hear it, and I'll go over there right now and give him a piece of my mind."

"No need for that." Marigold smiled at the elf's ferocity. "He didn't even say anything that bad. He actually complimented me, if you can believe it. Said I was a talented winemaker, and that if I wasn't so stuck in the past, I might actually win."

Elara rolled her eyes. "I'd like to stick him with something."

Locke patted Elara on the arm. "Let's not be too hasty, dear. What was it that prompted this exchange?"

"He donated a chiller to Town Hall."

"Of course he did." Elara shook her head.

Locke wore a confused expression as he looked from Elara to Marigold. "What's a chiller?"

"Runetech." Elara tapped her wine glass with a fingernail. "I had a guest ask me if we served chilled wine a few weeks back. When I looked at her like she had a mushroom growing out of her forehead, she elaborated. It's some kind of gnomish contraption that can keep things cold. Like a movable ice house. She said they were popular in the human kingdoms."

Locke's eyes lit up. "A chiller..." His voice trailed off, and Marigold could see the wheels turning in his mind as he stroked his beard, imagining all of its uses. "If I had one of those, I could make pies in batches and store them through the week. I could prep ahead of time. I could make iced cream. I could—"

"Don't get your hopes up, Locke." Marigold pursed her lips. "I don't think a chiller's in our budget anytime soon."

The dwarf's enthusiasm faded, and he took a gulp of his wine.

"So Galvin donated a chiller to Town Hall. Why's that got you in such a fuss?" asked Elara.

"It's just..." Marigold's brow furrowed as she tried to find the words. "It's not that he can buy one for himself, and it's not that his vineyard is doing well enough to give one away. It's knowing that if we gave up our morals, we could have all of that, too."

Elara laughed.

"What's so funny?" asked Marigold.

"I hate to burst your bubble, but druids aren't just growing on trees. They're rare, and most of them have little desire for business. Mages like to keep their hands in the coffers, but not druids. They'll help us through a drought or tough times, but most care more about nature than a sack full of coin. Any druid who'd willingly go into business with you is not one you'd want to work with."

Marigold shrugged. "Maybe you're right."

"I am right, Mari. Now eat your food before you hurt Locke's feelings."

Thankfully for Marigold, no children were staying at the inn this evening, and most adults didn't require a bedtime story, so after the chores were done, she sat on the front porch in her father's old rocking chair, listening to crickets chirp and watching the fireflies flicker across the vineyard. Onyx lay on his side nearby, heavy snores rattling with each breath.

Elara and Locke had retired for the evening and Gerty was tidying the downstairs, giving Marigold a moment of peace before she turned in. She sipped on a glass of dreamcatcher wine, finishing the last of the bottle from dinner.

It was hard to be upset when enjoying the fruits of their labor. The white wine had a lovely floral nose with notes of apple blossom and honeysuckle, and a crisp refreshing palate that offered just a hint of sweetness. It was delicious, and whether or not it had been chilled wouldn't change that. How Galvin chose to conduct himself didn't concern Marigold or her vineyard, so until the harvest festival arrived, she'd do her best to put him out of her mind.

She downed the last of the wine and took a deep breath, inhaling the cool night air. Tomorrow would be a new day and with it came infinite possibilities.

The next morning, Marigold lost herself in the daily routine of the inn. After a quick chat with Locke regarding the day's menu, she helped Finn milk the goats and gathered eggs from the henhouse. Then it was time to serve breakfast, after which she reminded Gerty to replace the table flowers. For Marigold, managing the inn meant getting her feet dirty and lending a helping hand where it was needed.

Teatime came and went before she settled down in her office to prepare for any upcoming reservations. For most of the year, the inn had plenty of vacancies. Once the harvest season was upon them, many of the guests would stay for weeks at a time to experience the festivities. It was rare to be fully booked this early in the season. Most nights, they had at least three of the six rooms occupied by travelers, but this week, they'd been at full capacity minus one room that had been reserved.

Marigold had received a letter earlier in the week with advanced payment to hold a room for a Perida Deepspring, but the reservation gave no additional information on exactly when the person would be arriving or if anyone would be accompanying them. Payment was payment, however, so she'd hold the room whether they showed up or not.

After lunch, she met with Elara in the cellar to go over next week's shipment, and then it was time to give the guests a tour of the vineyard.

That was always one of her favorite tasks, showing guests how wine was made and all the work that went into every bottle. Depending on the time of year, she might lead them up the hill for apple picking or down by the water to watch the fish migrating upstream. Every tour ended with a tasting in the cellar, where they'd sip different varietals paired with an assortment of fruits and cheeses that would showcase the wines' unique flavor profiles.

By the time afternoon tea was served, Marigold was ready for a quiet moment to herself.

After bringing biscuits to the table, Locke sat talking to a female dwarf who was traveling to Honeydale to see about a blacksmith position. The two had grown up in neighboring towns outside of Hillside.

No sooner had Marigold planned her escape when a knock came at the door. Gerty rushed to set the teapot down, but Marigold waved her off.

"Don't worry, I'll get it." She opened the door with a smile. "Welcome to the Dew Drop Inn, where good times are only a sip away." Marigold extended her hand and promptly froze when she saw a blue-haired gnome standing before her. "Poppy! What are you doing here?"

"Good to see you, too." Poppy grinned, setting her

traveling case on the porch. "I didn't know you worked here."

"I don't. Well, I mean, I do. I just…" Her cheeks flushed, and she let her hand fall to her side. "What I mean to say is that I'm the owner."

"Winemaker and inn owner." Poppy nodded approvingly. "Is there anything you don't do?"

"Win wine tastings at the harvest festival." Marigold laughed nervously. She wasn't normally one to disparage herself, but she felt uncharacteristically flustered.

"You're an interesting person." Poppy chuckled. "So, do I get to check in or do you normally make your guests sleep on the porch?"

"Oh, Poppy, I'm so sorry, but we're actually fully booked." It was then that she noticed a traveling trunk behind Poppy and the carriage that had delivered the gnome pulling onto the main road. "If you hurry, maybe you can wave them down."

Poppy looked over her shoulder but didn't seem the least bit concerned.

Marigold frowned as the carriage disappeared over the hill. "I suppose I can take you back to town later this evening, if you don't mind waiting."

"That won't be necessary," Poppy said calmly.

"You can't possibly carry that trunk back to town by yourself."

"Of course not. Can you imagine?" Poppy laughed.

Marigold closed her eyes and massaged her eyelids with her fingers. The gnome had seemed a bit eccentric at Town Hall, but Marigold was beginning to wonder if there was something off about her.

Locke's heavy footsteps thudded behind Marigold as

he joined her at the door. He narrowed his eyes as he looked from Marigold to Poppy. "Everything okay here?"

"Everything's fine." Marigold patted the surly dwarf on the back. "I was just explaining to Poppy here that we are fully booked for the night."

Locke crossed his arms. Even though he was a big softy, he had an intimidating appearance.

Poppy's smile widened. "I think there's been a misunderstanding."

Locke huffed. "Seems that way."

"I have a reservation."

Marigold gulped. She could feel her heart rate climbing with every awkward moment that passed. "Are you sure it wasn't somewhere else? The only reservation we have is for a Perida Deepspring."

Poppy extended her hand, smudges of ink darkening her fingertips. "At your service."

Marigold blinked several times as the pieces began to fit together. "You… You're Perida Deepspring?"

"Perida Poppinton Deepspring, but only when I'm in trouble. My friends call me Poppy." She reached into the pocket of her cloak and removed a small card, handing it to Marigold.

After wiping her sweaty palms on her tunic, Marigold accepted the card. It was made of thick cardstock, and the details were printed in gilded letters. On the back, there was a crest of a quill and magnifying glass crossed over a stack of books.

Perida Deepspring
Historian
Gnomish Historical Society

"Oh, Poppy. Why didn't you say so?" Marigold

returned the card, her cheeks still flushed from the whole situation. "Let me help you with your trunk."

"I'll be in the kitchen," Locke grumbled as he turned to walk away.

Marigold swayed from the weight as she carried the trunk indoors, where guests were scattered about the room. Two dwarves and a halfling sat at the dining table, deep in conversation as they enjoyed Locke's delicious gingersnap and shortbread biscuits with their afternoon tea. Two more halflings sat in the far corner, one reading a book and the other sipping a mug of tea.

"What do you have in here, bricks?" Marigold set the trunk down with a thud at the foot of the stairs.

"Just a few books and journals." Poppy smirked. "I wasn't sure how many journals I'd need to make it until winter, so I came prepared."

Marigold flexed her hands. "You know we have a general store in town, right?"

"I know that *now*." Poppy set her pack in the corner and grabbed the handle on the end of the trunk. "Here, let me help you. Where will I be staying for the foreseeable future?"

"Now, now." Gerty rushed over, patting Poppy on the arm. "That won't be necessary. Allow me."

"I don't mind." Poppy's grip held firm. "Honestly."

"I must insist. You're a guest of the Dew Drop Inn." Gerty wedged herself in front of the trunk until Poppy was forced to either let go or the two were going to get very comfortable with one another. "We take hospitality seriously around here."

Marigold's heart raced as the two argued over who would help carry the trunk. It wasn't uncommon for guests to stay extended periods, especially during the harvest season, but the incident at the door had really thrown her for a loop. She needed time to gather her bearings, but that wasn't a luxury she was afforded at the moment. "You're planning to stay here through the harvest festival?"

Poppy had the room reserved for the week, but there had been no arrangements made past that.

"As long as you don't kick me out." Poppy released her grip on the trunk. "This is a lovely inn, by the way. It has such a welcoming atmosphere."

"We try to make it a home away from home." Marigold recognized that the trunk wasn't moving any time soon and stepped away. Gerty gathered the same and returned to teatime. "I've seen enough inns that have a bar, some tables, and not much else. My father wanted to build something different, somewhere people could relax and mingle in comfort."

Marigold took a great deal of pride in the ambiance that the inn offered, from the oak bar with its glossy finish that gleamed beneath the candlelight chandelier to the hearth, which crackled merrily during the cooler months. Everything from the rustic furniture to the carefully selected tapestries and countless small details said this was more than a place to sleep.

The shelves behind the bar were filled with bottles of wine and spirits, and a small cask of ale rested on the counter. Across from the bar, a massive dining table sat in the center of the room, capable of seating anywhere from eight to twenty, depending on the size of those doing the sitting. Right now, it was topped with platters of biscuits and vases filled with yellow daffodils that gave a touch of brightness to the dark walnut wood.

Beyond the table was the lounge area, with a sofa and two comfy chairs in front of the hearth, smaller tables for work or conversation, and additional seating scattered about. There was no shortage of comfortable locations to curl up and read a book or ruminate over a glass of wine or a hot cup of tea. During the annual harvest, the bottom floor could fit forty to fifty people with room to spare.

Poppy looked around the room as if searching for something. "If I'm not mistaken, there's a library on the premises?"

"You're not mistaken. It's on the second floor." Marigold gestured up the stairs. "My father was a collector of books. Sometimes, he would trade bottles of wine with our guests to add to his collection."

Gerty returned with the teapot after making her rounds. "Can I offer you some tea?"

"Tea sounds lovely, but I think I should get settled in first." The gnome put on her pack, adjusting the straps on her shoulders. "Perhaps a cup in the library later, if it's not too much trouble."

"No trouble at all." Gerty set the tea on the table and grabbed one end of the trunk.

She and Marigold carried it up the stairs to the room reserved for Poppy. It was cozy, with exposed wooden beams in the ceiling that gave the room a rustic charm, and a circular window with a view of the vineyard. With the curtains pulled back, the afternoon sunlight cast the bed in a warm glow. The bedframe was carved from oak, with ornamental bedposts, and was covered with a patch-work quilt and hand-stitched pillows. A chest of drawers took up a majority of the wall next to the bed, and a sturdy desk sat in the corner.

Marigold and Gerty placed the trunk at the end of the bed.

"What do you think?" asked Marigold.

Poppy ran her fingers across the quilt. "This is perfect."

"There are more blankets in here if you get cold." Marigold opened the chest of drawers. "Dinner will be in a few hours, and the library is at the end of the hall. If you need anything else, just ask." She turned to leave.

"Marigold," Poppy called after her.

"Yes?" There was something in the gnome's voice that gave her pause.

"I know I can be a bit scatterbrained at times. My mom used to say that if I wasn't reading, I had a tendency to unravel like a pixie in heat." She smiled sheepishly. "I'm happy our paths have crossed again, and I look forward to seeing you around."

"Me too, Poppy. Let us know if you need anything." Marigold closed the door behind her. For a moment, she just stood there, staring at the pattern of the wood. What a strange morning it had been.

4. THE CELLAR

For the next three days, Marigold saw very little of Poppy. The gnome spent most of her waking hours in the library with her nose buried in a book. She took meals in her room, always with several books, journals, or scrolls spread across the desk. One night, a guest complained that there was a creature scurrying through the walls, but upon further investigation, it had only been Poppy working, her quill scratching vociferously against the parchment in the wee hours.

Marigold was beginning to think she'd offended the gnome, but then on the fourth day, Poppy showed up for dinner with a wide grin.

She took a seat next to a gray-bearded dwarf just as Marigold was bringing a bowl of seasoned green beans to the table. "You were right about the library. Your father has amassed quite a collection."

"More than most of us could read in a lifetime." Marigold set the beans next to a plate of buttery scones. "How's your research coming along?"

"Quite well." Poppy raised her glass of wine to the dwarf and they clinked them together before she returned her attention to Marigold. "Between your library and the archives at Town Hall, I should be able to form a good basis for my research. What I really need are some primary accounts. I suppose I'll go into town for interviews in the coming days."

"Hmm." Marigold tapped her chin. "Would journals count as primary sources?"

"That depends—" Poppy took a sip of her wine. "—on whether or not the journals describe first-hand accounts or if they're a retelling of events that were told to the author."

"I still have Father's old work journals in the cellar. I've never been much of a writer, but he kept track of everything." Marigold smiled at the memory of her sitting on a keg while her father scribbled down the day's events. "He'd write down the weather, reports on the vines, and how the grapes tasted. Once the wine was barreled, he'd make notes of the tasting process and how he chose which bottles to age or ship out. He was very meticulous."

Poppy's eyes widened, and her hands vibrated with excitement. "That sounds like exactly what I need!" She spun around on the bench, ready to abandon her meal in the name of research. "Can I see them now?"

Marigold laughed at the gnome's enthusiasm. "How about after dinner? I can give you a tour of the cellar and show you his journals."

Poppy clapped her hands together like a young halfling at the sweets shop. "Oh, that would be lovely. Thank you so much!"

While the guests ate their dinner, Marigold returned

to the kitchen. Elara hovered over Locke, massaging his shoulders while he sat in a chair, slumped over in absolute bliss.

"That's the spot," he groaned. "Just a little deeper. Oh, yes, that's the spot, hon. Yer hands are magical."

Finn sat at the small table, watching with a mixture of intrigue and revulsion.

Marigold cleared her throat, and Locke looked up, suddenly aware that he was being watched.

"Heh." He smiled devilishly. "If you've never had an elvish massage, yer missing out."

Finn blinked several times. "If you're like this with a massage, I'm glad you two have the cottage to yourself."

Locke reached over and pulled the plate of food away from Finn. "I could always make you work for that meal." Locke's smile transitioned from devilish to menacing in a flash. "Yer hands look strong enough, and my lower back is killing me."

"What I mean—" Finn looked to Marigold for help, but she only shrugged. "—is that you two work so hard that you deserve somewhere to relax away from the inn."

"That's the spirit, laddie." Locke slid the plate back.

Elara winked at Finn. "Nice save."

Marigold took a seat across from Locke. "I'll be showing Poppy around the cellar after dinner. She wants to see Father's old journals." She looked up at Elara, who was now digging into Locke's shoulder with her elbow. "Do you mind if I show her your notes on last year's harvest?"

"Help yourself." She wedged her elbow until Locke's eyes rolled into his head and he groaned in relief.

Elara kissed the top of Locke's head, and the dwarf sat up, heavy breaths wracking his body.

Finn stared with an open mouth but didn't utter a word. He stood, taking his plate with him. "It's a lovely night. I think I'll eat on the porch."

"I don't see what the big deal is. It's just a massage," Elara said as she took Finn's empty seat. "So our little gnome finally leaves the library, and now she wants to read old journals in the cellar. Does she ever have any fun?"

Marigold laughed. "When your job is your passion, is there a difference between work and play?"

Elara's brow furrowed as she pondered the question. "I suppose she's not that different from us in that regard."

After dessert was served and the plates were cleared, Marigold escorted Poppy down to the cellar. It was located directly beneath the inn, with tunnels that expanded beyond the structure's borders to the winery uphill.

Cool, damp air greeted them as they descended. An earthy scent lingered in the air—a mixture of aged wood, wet stone, and the aroma of fermented grapes that had seeped into the walls over the years.

"Breathe it in." Marigold took a deep breath that sank into her core. "This is the smell of history and tradition."

Poppy did as she was instructed, inhaling the musty air. "I love it. It reminds me of the gnomish catacombs in Cogwall."

A mosaic of stone tiles covered the floor, and densely

packed bricks formed the walls and arched ceiling. Enchanted lights were spaced overhead so that they cast a warm glow over the multitude of wine barrels. The cellar was the only place on the property that had these magical upgrades. Marigold's father had chosen to install the glowstones so they could move barrels without the need for torchlight. They still had lanterns for use when needed, but the glowstones provided enough light to work by. They had been expensive, but they burned constantly and could last many years before the runes needed to be recharged.

A sea of blue ribbons dotted the wall, speckled with a few pieces of red and silver, serving as a reminder of the Dew Drop Vineyard's storied history—both an inspiration and an albatross Marigold could never escape.

Rows of barrels sat in neat lines, each one marked with charcoal to denote the varietal and the year it was harvested. Slabs of wood were wedged securely underneath each one to keep them from rolling away.

"Most of our white wines are aged one to three years," Marigold explained as they walked. "Occasionally, we may age dreamcatcher barrels for up to five years if we want the vintage to take on a more nutty and oaky profile. Like most people, wine mellows as it ages. The longer we let it sit, the more the citrus notes fade, and the wine becomes something entirely different."

Poppy had her journal open, jotting down notes as Marigold described the various wines and what they might taste like once they were ready to be bottled.

"I promise there won't be a test at the end," Marigold teased.

"You never know what small detail might come in

handy." Poppy tapped the journal with her finger. "I've found it pays to be thorough."

They stopped in front of several barrels that were covered in dust and cobwebs. "For our moonshadow grapes, we age them for at least five years, but these three have been down here for a decade." Marigold pointed to the back of the row, where a dozen or so smaller casks sat on shelves. "Those are our fortified wines. They're also made with moonshadow grapes, but with those, we mix the wine with brandy during the fermentation process." She turned to Poppy. "Tell me, Miss Scholar, do you know why?"

Poppy frowned as she contemplated. "To make it stronger?"

Marigold nodded. "That's part of it. The brandywine stops the fermentation process, leaving the resulting wine both stronger and sweeter, hence we call it fortified wine. We don't produce a lot, but it's great as an after-dinner drink or a nightcap."

The last row contained casks in various sizes, all smaller than the standard wine barrels.

"This is where we experiment." Marigold grinned as she walked down the row. "Oftentimes, there's leftover juice from the harvest, not enough to fill another barrel but too much to let go to waste. So what we do is blend the different varietals together, creating something completely new. Sometimes it's good, other times—" She grimaced. "—not so much, but it's always a fun experiment. You never know how it's going to taste."

"That sounds delightful."

Marigold pointed to a barrel labeled "Dreams of Ember Honey." Below the label, it was marked with the varietals, the percentage of each, and the year it was aged. "This one is a blend of fifty percent dreamcatcher and twenty-five percent of both emberfruit and honey grapes. It's been aging for two years, and I'm excited to bottle it soon."

At the end of the wine barrels, they came upon the bottling station, where shelves and crates were filled with bottled wine. Hundreds of additional empty bottles were stacked in crates against the wall, waiting to be used. The station was a simple design. It contained a platform with a lever that hoisted barrels above a filtration system that funneled wine into bottles. Across from the machine, there was a second tunnel for wagons to unload bottles or take deliveries into town.

"That's about it for the cellar. Most of the action happens uphill at the winery, but this is the final touch. We bottle the wine, label it, and send it off to be shipped across Aedrea."

Poppy took a deep breath. "I never realized how complicated winemaking was. You put a lot of work into it."

"Eh." Marigold shrugged. "It's complicated and simple at the same time. A lot of it comes down to intuition and patience. Knowing when to harvest, how long to ferment, and when to wait."

"Not that different from life, is it?" Poppy stuffed her journal in her satchel and looked around the cellar.

Marigold chuckled to herself. The gnome was endearing in her own way. At times, she was steady and focused, nose buried in her books. Other times, she was like a squirrel, always searching for the next nut.

"Let me show you to the office." Marigold gestured

toward the far end, where the cellar narrowed into a tunnel.

To one side, there was a rustic bar that served as the tasting area—a thick slab of dark walnut over a stone base with barstools in front. Wine bottles and glasses sat on a shelf behind it. Most of the wine tastings happened upstairs in the inn, but whenever the staff gave a tour of the vineyard and winery, it always ended with a tasting in the cellar.

Opposite the bar, an elaborately designed door stood ajar. Elegant filigree and grape clusters had been carved into the wood, and a circle of purple-and-green stained glass was set in the center. There was an office nestled on the other side with an enchanted light glowing overhead. The layout was simple. It had a table covered in invoices and ledgers, several stools, and shelves stuffed with small crates of journals, receipts, and notes lined the walls.

"This is where you'll find the history of our vineyard." Marigold swept her arms through the air and was suddenly aware of how cozy the space was. Somehow, it never felt this small when it was her and Elara in here. She pointed to the topmost crates, which were covered in a thick layer of dust. "These crates are receipts, invoices, and notes that go back at least fifty years. They're all sorted chronologically. You're welcome to peruse them, but I don't know how much value you'll gain from my father's shorthand of shipments."

Underneath the table, there were more crates filled with papers stuffed in a haphazard manner. "It's easy enough to tell Elara's records from my father's. With Locke's steadfast desire to give everything order, I don't know how he stands the elf."

Poppy shrugged. "Some say that opposites attract."

"In their case, it must be true." She laughed as she pulled a stool over to the shelf and grabbed a crate from a few rows up. "These are my father's journals." She pulled one out and flipped through the pages. "He loved to write. You probably saw some of the family journals in the library, and he was just as earnest with the vineyard. It was like a child to him in many ways. Kind of like the sibling I never had."

Like father, like daughter. She offered the journal to Poppy.

"It must be nice to have those memories to go back to." Poppy held her hand to the cover like it was a priceless artifact. "We live in a world where clerics can heal wounds in a breath, where mages can conjure fire from thin air or call upon the earth to move at their command, but wouldn't it be nice if we could capture life's special moments and see them again?"

"That does sound lovely."

"This is as close as we can get." Poppy opened the journal. "Artists can capture the essence of something, but this… These are your father's memories. They're etched in time for eternity."

Marigold's throat tightened, and she struggled to swallow. All these years, she'd had her father's journals and had never viewed them in that way.

She watched Poppy as the gnome read through the text, noticing her eyes as they darted across the page and the way her lips moved as she silently mouthed the words.

Marigold's cheeks flushed with heat. "Is it me or is it hot in here?" She took a deep breath. "What do you say we have a glass of wine and then I'll leave you to your research?"

Poppy closed the journal. "That would be wonderful."

Marigold poured them each a glass, and they sipped honeywine while flipping through the old notebook. It had been years since Marigold had taken a moment to appreciate the countless pages of her father's passion. Reading his detailed accounts of tasks as simple as pruning a vine reminded her of why she'd followed in his footsteps. Winemaking was never about winning a contest, it was the joy of the process.

One glass turned into another, and soon, two empty bottles sat on the old timber, while gnome and halfling swayed contentedly on their stools.

Marigold lifted an empty bottle, turning it upside-down as a few final drops fell into her glass. "My father always said there was a story at the bottom of every bottle. I want to thank you for this one."

"Zuh worl' is movin' fasser and fasser eez days." Poppy slurred her words as she tilted her empty glass, giggling when nothing came out. "Sums-times we jus' needs a be remine-ned ter slowdown."

"You didn't tell me you were a lightweight." Marigold laughed. She was feeling the wine as well, but she still had her wits about her. "Let me help you to your room."

The two stumbled upstairs, where most everyone had retired for the night, save for a lone halfling in front of the hearth smoking his pipe. Poppy tripped on a stair to the second level, nearly falling, but Marigold was there to catch her.

Once they made it to Poppy's room, Marigold eased the gnome onto the bed. She mumbled unintelligibly before falling into a deep sleep. Marigold removed Poppy's boots, placing them by the door, and covered the gnome with a blanket.

As she was leaving, Marigold stood by the door for a moment, watching Poppy's chest rise and fall with each breath. With a long sigh, she pulled the door shut.

Moonlight shone through the open windows of the hallway on the cloudless night, casting the world in a silver glow. Marigold's head was still spinning as she made it to the library, pulling one of her father's personal journals from the shelf.

She collapsed in one of the high-backed chairs, pulled a blanket across her lap, and opened the book to a random page.

I'll never tire of days like today. Mari joined me in the vineyard, babbling about as she followed me through the rows on the unsteady feet of a newborn foal. Twice she planted on her rear and cried out, only for Onyx to nuzzle his great black head against her cheek and turn the cries to laughter.

Gardenia was hesitant about the cat at first, but I believe he and Mari will be a pair for the ages. Together...

Marigold's eyes drooped shut, and the journal slid from her fingers as sleep finally claimed her, too.

5. FABLES

Marigold shivered as she stepped into the cold water of the stream. On warm afternoons, the sensation was a welcome relief that could soothe achy feet, but this early in the day, dew still blanketed the meadow, and fog shrouded the valleys in mystery.

Goosebumps prickled along Marigold's arms as she crouched, reaching into the water to unearth a stone the size of her head. A creature darted from underneath, obscured by the cloud of silt flowing downstream, and Marigold's muscles tensed with the effort of pulling the heavy stone above the water.

"Too round." It wasn't a question, but she still looked to Finn for confirmation before dropping it back into the stream.

He stood a few paces upstream, wearing nothing but a pair of short overalls. Finn was bent over, his arms submerged to the elbow as he searched the streambed. His face contorted and he groaned, straightening his back as he lifted the stone.

"This one will do." Finn grinned, his cheeks a rosy-red as he leaned back, showcasing his prize to Marigold.

The stone was a wide rectangle, slate gray and worn flat by the passage of time. Finn splashed his way toward the bank, where Onyx lay sprawled in the morning sunlight. "Only about thirty more of these and we'll be done."

He dropped the stone on the ground next to the wheelbarrow. The dire cat raised his head at the thud, only momentarily concerned by the disturbance.

Marigold fared better on her second attempt, pulling a triangle-shaped stone that was flat enough to use for the new garden path. Building a stone walkway from the inn to the garden had been on her to-do list for several months, and they were finally making time for it. It was a tedious process, searching for stones and then wheeling them from the stream to the inn, and since it was a luxury more than a necessity, it had been pushed back in favor of more pressing matters.

Between the inn and the winery, there was always something in need of repair around the property. Marigold kept Finn busy with the groundskeeping, gardening, attending the farm animals, and managing the stable.

His and Gerty's parents had worked at the inn for nearly as long as Marigold's parents had owned it. When Marigold finally took over, they decided it was time to retire as well. The elder Bramblefoots set to traveling the realm, and the Meadowlarks settled down in town. Finn and Gerty's parents had always embraced more traditional halfling values, where the height of adventure was experimenting with a new recipe in the kitchen.

Marigold and Finn traversed the stream for hours searching for the perfect stones. The process required a great deal of trial and error. Each rock needed to be wide enough to walk on but flat enough that it wouldn't be a tripping hazard. If one was too round or too thin, then back into the stream it would go.

By noon, the sun beamed upon their shoulders as they worked beneath a cloudless sky. The heat, mixed with the intensity of manual labor, had Marigold's tunic stained with sweat. She cupped her hands, thankful for the cool water as she splashed her face and neck. Finn was less graceful, choosing to lay in the stream to cool off.

After they'd gathered enough pieces for the path, she and Finn took turns pushing the wheelbarrow across the field to the inn. They unloaded the rocks not far from the garden, near a picnic area with several tables, a firepit, and a grill.

Several times a month, Locke would roast meats and vegetables on the grill and serve the guests outdoors. Nothing as big as the harvest hog, but he knew his way around an open flame. Today, he'd brought Marigold and Finn a plate of sandwiches, sliced apples, and cheese, along with a pitcher of water mixed with sliced lemons.

Marigold collapsed on the picnic table, chugging her water. "Now I remember why I've been putting this off."

"You're telling me." Finn wiped his brow and leaned back against the table, releasing a deep sigh as he spread his arms. "I'm glad to have the extra pair of hands."

They ate lunch without a word, content to recover their energy in silence, minus the groans of delight as they devoured the crisp bacon, lettuce, and tomato sandwiches. Locke was a wizard in the kitchen, and he'd slathered a creamy sauce on the bread that managed to somehow accentuate both the sweetness of the tomato and the smokiness of the bacon.

Onyx approached, and his chest rumbled as he nuzzled Marigold's legs. After scratching him beneath the chin, she offered the dire cat a sliver of cheese. Satisfied with the offering, Onyx curled around her feet.

A towering apple tree cast shade over the picnic area, its branches filled with tart green apples. Marigold was looking forward to the cool weather just around the bend, and the ripe apples that followed, providing Locke with fresh fruit for his autumn recipes—apple pies and glazed cakes, cinnamon-sprinkled slices, and fresh cider.

"You two look beat."

Marigold looked up as Elara took a seat across the table.

The elf was so light on her feet that most people never heard her approaching. "Our shipment is already sorted for tomorrow, so I suppose I can lend you a hand."

Finn pressed his hands together and bowed slightly. "I don't care what anyone says. You are a blessing from the gods."

"Don't I know it." Elara smirked, never one to shy away from a compliment. She glanced at the stones stacked neatly beside the wheelbarrow. "I was wondering when you'd get around to this."

"It was now or never." Marigold finished the last of her lemon water and stood, taking in the project area.

The guests frequented the picnic tables and firepit often enough that they'd worn a path through the grass. It wasn't a bad thing, but a stone path would give the area a more fitting aesthetic.

Elara grinned at Marigold as she positioned a piece of stone.

"What?" Marigold recognized that look. It meant Elara had some gossip she wanted to share.

The elf beamed wider. "I heard you were up late last night."

Heat rushed to Marigold's cheeks. "Let me guess. Gerty?"

"You know she can't keep a secret," Finn said as he laid a stone.

"So it was true." Elara laughed. "Locke was right."

"Right about what?" Marigold focused on the rock she was laying to avoid the elf's gaze.

"He said he had a feeling." Elara crouched in front of Marigold, lowering her head to meet the halfling's eyes. "Something about the way you two were floundering at the door."

"Floundering?" Marigold choked on her saliva and went into a coughing frenzy as she relived those awkward moments. Luckily, the brief fit gave credence to her blushing cheeks. "That was just a misunderstanding. There's nothing going on between us." She cleared her throat, and Onyx looked up, the sound likely reminiscent of a nasty hairball. "Poppy's research is an opportunity for more people to learn about our traditions. If more people are willing to travel across the realm to visit our towns and vineyards, it's better for all of us. I was showing her some of Father's old journals, and she had one too many glasses of wine. So, I did what any respectable inn owner would do and helped her up the stairs. Nothing more to it than that."

Elara raised a brow, inspecting Marigold with the

same intensity as she did a grape on her morning walks. "If you say so."

The elf seemed satisfied with the answer, so the conversation shifted to the routine talk of the inn as they worked. They placed stones strategically along the path, leaving a few inches of space between each one for grass to grow. In time, the tiles would sink into the earth, adding to the charming appeal of the inn.

With Elara's help, they laid the stone in a fraction of the time it had taken to gather it. Once the path was complete, Marigold returned to the stream to rinse away the sweat before dinner.

For dinner, Locke cooked a hearty beef stew served in bread bowls and topped with sprigs of parsley. That particular meal always went over well with the guests, especially children who took great joy in its destructive nature as they ripped the bowl apart.

This evening, there were a number of children staying at the inn. When Marigold was a child, she cherished the days when other children visited. It always meant her father would tell a bedtime story in front of the hearth, which somehow felt more exciting than being read to in bed. Marigold had kept the tradition alive since she'd taken over.

After a dessert of sticky toffee pudding, she instructed the children to meet her in the common area at nightfall. And so it was that as the crickets began their nightly lullaby and the owls hooted in the distance, they gathered around the hearth for a bedtime story. Three young halflings sat on the floor, giddy with anticipation, and a human teenager slouched in one of the larger chairs. The girl was traveling with her father to Greenbriar Marsh on mercantile business.

Parents watched from the table, where Gerty made her rounds refilling wine. Poppy started to make for the stairs, but Marigold waved her over.

"This story is one of my favorites. You should stay for a bit and listen to it," Marigold said before taking her position in front of the hearth.

"I do love a good book," Poppy said, finding a cozy chair near the wall and pulling a blanket over her lap.

Marigold held a tome, its orange binding faded from years of use. "Tell me..." She ran her fingers across the cover, feeling the embossed leather that made out the title of *Grimaldi's Fables*. "—have any of you ever wondered why there are so many stars in the night sky?"

The three halflings raised their hands, giggling to one another as they spouted off guesses of fireflies and gemstones trapped in the sky.

"Those are all good theories, but tonight you'll learn the story of Seluna and the Guiding Tree." Marigold opened the book and began reading. "Long ago, when the world was young and the gods had only begun to make their imprint across Aedrea, Soris forged the sun from his inner light and hung it in the sky so that it might warm the land. The days that followed were bright and full of life, but at night, the skies were an endless void. Creatures hid in their caves and burrows, flowers closed their blooms, and all across Aedrea, no halfling or human dared to leave their home."

The three halflings had their hands interlocked, and even the teenager sat up in her seat to listen.

"Shrouded in darkness, even the gods grew quiet. Seluna asked her brother to forge a second light to push back the darkness, but he refused, saying that all things required balance. An eternal daylight would throw the world into even greater chaos. 'Even the day has shade,' she argued. 'Why shouldn't the night offer guidance?'

"Soris would not be moved, so without the aid of her brother, Seluna traveled to Durendreg, where dwarven glaziers crafted a mirror the size of a lake, so big that it was called the moon because of its monstrous size. Seluna pulled from her power, enchanting the glass so that it might gather light throughout the day and glow like a lantern through the night. She hung the mirror in the sky, and as the sun set, the moon reflected a silver glow across the land. For the first time, creatures left their burrows, and some found they preferred the gentle cover of night.

"For an age, Seluna walked the earth, the moon serving as a beacon to those who needed its light. She grew to know the hoot of the owls and the call of the wolves, but there was a part of her that felt wanting. For the night sky was vast, and the Moon could only reflect what it was given. Its position was ever shifting and though she'd given the world light in the darkness, it still lacked guidance. One night, while walking the rolling hills of Tyne, she came upon a gnarled tree upon a hill. Its crooked branches had been hung with lanterns so that travelers might find their way home.

"Seluna pressed her palm to the tree and spoke, 'Beautiful tree, how I wish that your branches could light the night sky.' The tree rustled its leaves in response, 'I would love nothing more than to light the heavens, but I am rooted to the earth, and my light is not my own. What is there to do?'

"Seluna pondered on the tree's words for a day, before returning to its place upon the hill. 'Tonight, if you wish, you shall bear fruit that will glitter across the night sky.' She once again pressed her palm to the tree, this time, infusing it with her inner light.

"Though her light was not as strong as her brother's, it turned the tree's branches to silver, and fruit sprouted into bursts of starry light. The stars danced and twirled, many of them breaking free and leaping into the sky. One by one, they climbed the moonbeams, taking their place among the heavens, where they glittered and flickered, sparkling against the darkness. But, because the tree was kind, it made sure to save some of its stars, keeping just enough to light the hill so that travelers might always find their way home in the dark.

"Seluna was so touched by the kindness within the tree that she drew a map among the stars so that no matter where they were, travelers could always find their way home."

It was a silly story, but Marigold had loved it as a child. Every time she'd heard it, she would find the highest windows in the inn and look out upon the moon-kissed hills, searching for the Guiding Tree.

Marigold closed the book. "Thanks to Seluna and the Guiding Tree, we never have to worry about getting lost. If we look to the stars, they will always guide us home."

6. ROGUES & DRIFTERS

As the weeks passed, the warmth of summer began to cede its hold on the land to the approaching autumn. The nights grew cooler, and the apple trees speckled their branches with yellow and orange. Harvest season was approaching, and with it, the busiest time of year for the Dew Drop Inn.

Marigold sat at her desk, going over invoices and making lists to ensure that the inn was prepared for the upcoming influx of guests. That meant more feed and seed for horses, soap for additional baths, and firewood for the hearth, among a myriad of other items that kept the inn running smoothly.

Once the harvest season arrived, not only were there more guests but more visitors as well. The local farmers supplied the market with apples and pumpkins, but there was something special about pairing a stroll through the hills with a glass of wine that the market couldn't match. Hand-picking apples from a tree or searching through the patch for that perfect pumpkin was an experience, and those kinds of memories could last a lifetime.

After finishing the admin work, Marigold made her rounds, checking in with the staff and ensuring the guests were content. She spotted a familiar roguish adventurer wrapping the leftover bread from lunch and stuffing it in his satchel. Garrick had been a regular over the years, stopping by once or twice a season between quests. Locke enjoyed the man's tales of adventure and always sent him packing with a few provisions for the road.

Garrick extended a hand tattooed with scars from battles and bar fights. "Always a pleasure, Marigold." The politeness of his words was at odds with his gravelly voice.

"Likewise." She accepted his firm handshake and grabbed a bottle from the bar. "Care for some wine before you go?"

"I've never been one to turn down a drink." His mouth curled in a mischievous smile. "Especially one as fine as yours."

Marigold laughed at the man's rambunctious spirit as she poured them both a glass of honeywine. "Where are you off to this time?"

"Greenbriar Marsh." He raised his glass, and they toasted one another. "There's an infestation of bog rats in one of the towns, and I'm going to cull the horde. Apparently, there was an incident involving an alchemist, and now the bloody bastards are the size of cats. They're terrorizing the town and people are afraid to leave their homes, so the mayor sent a raven to every guild outpost for a hundred miles asking for help. It takes a particular brand of adventurer to take on giant rodents."

Marigold's eyes widened. "I don't envy you on this one."

Garrick grinned. "Oh, I'm quite looking forward to it." He downed the rest of his wine in a single gulp and tossed the satchel over his shoulder. "Give my best to the staff, and twice to Gerty." He winked. "Mark my words, I'll make a dishonest woman of her one day."

Marigold laughed. "I'll be sure to let her know. Take care of yourself out there."

After Garrick departed, Marigold went upstairs to help change the bedding in his room. Gerty had already opened the window, folded the blankets, and removed the pillowcases.

Marigold grinned as she helped pull the sheet from the bed. "Garrick certainly has a thing for you."

"He has a way about him, that's for sure." Gerty clenched the sheet between her fingers and bit her lip as she disappeared into some far-off memory. "I know he's a scoundrel. Probably has a woman in every city from here to Crowhold, but when he sets those smoldering brown eyes on you, it's like you're the only person in the world."

"Wait..." Marigold let the end of the sheet drop to the floor. "Don't tell me you're actually considering it."

Gerty shrugged, and her cheeks flushed. She wore a sheepish smile. "There's nothing wrong with having a little fun."

A loud thud echoed from down the hall, followed by a stream of curses.

"Speaking of fun." Gerty waggled her brows as Marigold left to investigate.

She found Poppy in the library perched near the top of the sliding ladder. Several books had taken a tumble and lay haphazardly on the hardwood floor while another sat precariously on the topmost shelf just out of the gnome's reach. Poppy dangled from the ladder like an acrobat, one hand on the siderail and the other inches from the book. She certainly had a knack for creating chaos.

"You're gonna fall and break your neck," Marigold called from the doorway as she tried to contain her laughter.

Poppy grimaced as she reached again, the ladder shaking as her fingers barely grazed the book's spine.

She let out a sigh of defeat. "The wheels on the ladder got stuck. I was already up here, and I thought I might be able to reach the book I wanted, but all I managed to do was make a mess."

"Here, let me help you." Marigold crossed the room and grabbed the ladder with both hands. "Hold on tight. I'm gonna slide you over." Poppy clung to the ladder, and Marigold slowly inched it across the floor. "I should have mentioned that you can only slide the ladder from the bottom, otherwise it has a tendency to get stuck."

"I can see that now." Poppy grabbed the book, tucking it under her arm before carefully descending. "Thanks for your help. And sorry for the mess."

"No problem. I've been meaning to grease those wheels for a while now." Marigold helped gather the fallen books and placed them on the table. "How's the research coming?"

"Really well." Poppy's eyes flared with excitement. "I'm going into town shortly to interview some of the locals."

"Need a ride?" Marigold rested her hand on the ladder. "I can have Finn ready a wagon for you."

"No need for that." Poppy banished the idea with a

swipe of her hand. "We're not that far from town, and I could use the exercise. I've been spending a lot of time hunched over a desk and walking gives my ideas time to marinate."

Marigold couldn't argue with the logic. She often wandered the property when she needed to clear her mind or make sense of something. And while a wagon could make the trip to town in about half an hour, if Poppy wasn't lugging around all of her books and journals, the two-mile walk wouldn't take much longer. Plus, there were some beautiful views of the countryside along the way.

"Alright then." She nodded to Poppy and then made for the door. "If you change your mind, let one of us know."

Later that afternoon, Marigold was working the downstairs bar, serving wine to a pair of halflings passing through on business when she heard the sound of a lute strumming outside. She tilted her head, listening as the music grew louder until footsteps padded against the porch.

The door swung open, and a halfling woman jingled as she stepped inside. She wore a voluminous yellow skirt that had likely once been of fine quality, though now it was stained and tattered, with colorful patches holding it together in places. A floral bodice topped a loose-fitting green blouse tucked into her skirt, and she had an orange patterned scarf wrapped about her head that kept a mane of wild, honey-brown hair somewhat contained. Jewelry chimed with each step from the many necklaces and hoop earrings she wore, and her fingers glittered as she stroked a lute that had more nicks and chips than a dartboard at the Brown Boar Tavern.

Marigold was so enthralled by the woman's unexpected appearance that she could only stare for a moment. She'd heard of the Dandyfolk before, not named for their fashion sense but the way they drifted through life like dandelion seeds in the wind. Her father often told the story of how a trio had wandered in on a stormy night and serenaded the guests in exchange for a bed and a hot meal, but it wasn't often that one came through Willowbrook.

"Greetings, salutations, and blessings from the Breeze." The woman strummed the lute again and then bowed low.

"Welcome to the Dew Drop Inn." Marigold stepped out from behind the bar. "How can I help you?"

The bangles on the halfling's wrist jingled as she tucked a strand of loose hair into her scarf. "I'm but a humble traveler upon the winds of life. For a meal and a night's rest, I can provide the inn with an evening of entertainment."

"That sounds like a fine trade." Marigold nodded. With Garrick gone, the inn had two empty rooms for the night.

She'd always found the Dandyfolk interesting, and more than that, she'd been taught to lead with kindness and to respect lifestyles and points of view that differed from her own. Her father believed that there was always something to learn from those who saw the world in a different way, and by running an inn, they could meet people from all walks of life.

"Can I interest you in a drink?" Marigold gestured toward the bar.

The halfling tapped the body of her instrument. "Only if I can play you a song first."

"By all means." Marigold took a seat next to the other two halflings. "I'm Marigold, by the way."

"Bella." She set her satchel in a nearby chair and rested her backside against the dining table. "Bella Wildsong of the Dandyfolk."

Marigold wondered if Wildsong was her given name or one she'd chosen for herself. Either way, it was fitting since the Dandyfolk were a group of free-spirited wanderers known for their bright clothing, gaudy jewelry, and flighty nature. Most of the time, they traveled alone or in small groups, except for every few years when they would unite for a celebration known as the Gathering of the Breeze. If the stories were true, the Gathering never took place in the same location twice. Sometimes, it was held deep within a forest; other times, the Dandyfolk would appear in the heart of a town or city, filling the streets with music. The celebration would last for several days before vanishing as suddenly as it had appeared.

Bella plucked the strings of her lute, humming along as she tuned the instrument. "This one is called *The Giving Spirit*."

She strummed the lute a few times and then jumped into a spirited tune.

"A cup of tea, a loaf of bread,
A gentle place to rest one's head,
There's no place I'd rather be,

Than surrounded by good company!

A pint of ale, a cozy seat,
A hearth to warm our hands and feet,
The more you give, the more you find,
That joy abounds when you are kind!

So give a smile, spread some cheer,
Share your love with all those near!
Raise a glass and sing along,
With open hearts, we all belong!

From one who walks along the Breeze,
May we brighten one another's days!"

Bella played a second verse, and the two halflings at the bar swayed along with the music, joining in the chorus and shouting "give a smile, spread some cheer" as they clinked their wine glasses. The bard's every word dripped with a folksy comfort that felt like home, and Marigold was so enraptured by Bella's mesmerizing voice that she didn't notice the growing audience until the song ended and applause filled the room.

Behind her, Locke leaned against the doorframe of the kitchen, flour-speckled arms crossed over his apron. Elara stood behind him with a hand on the dwarf's shoulder. Finn and Gerty were whispering to one another at the end of the hallway, and two more guests leaned against the railing at the top of the stairs.

Marigold smiled. There was nothing like music to bring people together. Well, except for wine.

Hiring a traveling bard was always a roll of the dice. In the bigger cities, guild cards were commonly required to play the more preeminent establishments, but in the smaller towns, many taverns would take what they could get. Sometimes, the bards were talented; other times, they were little more than vagabonds with an instrument.

"You have a lovely voice," Marigold said as she offered Bella a glass of wine. "I look forward to hearing more."

"Thank you." The bard accepted the wine with a gracious nod. "There's nothing more divine than bringing others together. We are all a part of the Breeze, whether we realize it or not."

"Cheers to that." The nearest halfling raised his glass. "Always a pleasure to be serenaded by the Dandyfolk." He nudged his elbow against his partner. "Did I ever tell you about the time I stumbled upon the Gathering in Wolfwater?"

"You're pulling my toes." The other halfling frowned. "You attended the Gathering?"

"By Lyrianna's grace, I did." The first halfling held his hand in the air. "I was an apprentice back then, barely had hair on my feet, when the old gaffer told me I'd be joining him on a trip to Wolfwater. Was my first time ever leaving Tyne, and the world seemed awfully big at that point. I still remember how we could hear the music from across Wolfwater Lake long before we made it to the city. When we finally arrived, there were more tents outside the city gates than there were homes in my village. For three days, every time we stepped into the streets, the Dandyfolk blessed us with music. It's something I'll never forget." He turned to Bella. "Would you like to join us?"

"I'd love to." The bard's arm jingled as she tucked another wayward strand of hair into her scarf. "The greatest joys of traveling are the people we meet along the way."

Marigold stood and offered Bella her seat. For the next couple of hours, the Dandyfolk chatted and laughed with the two halflings.

Like a fly on the wall, Marigold listened as they connected over travels and a lifetime of experiences, occasionally offering her own input. They talked about music, traveling, small towns, and big cities. There were many great things about owning an inn, but it was always a special time when strangers from different walks of life came together under her roof. Even if the guests had nothing else in common, for those few moments, they shared an experience.

Sometimes, those experiences became something more. With a little luck, they might become memories.

By late afternoon, the inn was fully occupied, with the final room booked by a human couple traveling to the elvish city of Icramel. Since the quickest way to reach the elven lands was by ship from Greenbriar Marsh, Marigold hoped that Garrick and the other adventurers would be able to deal with the plague of bog rats before the duo arrived.

A couple of hours later, the guests had all gathered downstairs, lured by the smell of roasted meat. Marigold and Gerty set the table as the guests chatted with one another, and it was no surprise that Bella was the center of attention, hounded with questions by curious travelers. Poppy had a journal out, jotting down notes as the Dandyfolk bard described her escapades across Aedrea.

Judging by the fragments Marigold overheard, they were all in for an interesting evening.

For dinner, Locke had cooked an herbed venison pie along with mashed potatoes, roasted leeks, and cranberry jam. The flaky pastry was filled with chunks of tender venison, mushrooms, onions, and a litany of herbs and spices, all in a rich brown gravy. It was so beautiful that Marigold took a moment to appreciate the golden buttery crust before finally cutting into it.

She opened a bottle of moonshadow wine to pair with the meal, its rich and robust profile a perfect complement to the hearty dish. Once everyone had been served, she returned to the kitchen, where a second pie waited for the staff.

"This smells delicious, Locke." Marigold's stomach rumbled as she took a seat, and she inhaled the savory aroma. "You've really outdone yourself tonight."

The dwarf grinned as he sliced into the pie, dividing it into five portions. "It's not every day we have a Dandyfolk among us."

Finn looked over his shoulder at the door and sighed. "I could listen to her sing for hours. She has the voice of a siren."

"And equally as likely to lure you to your doom." Elara smirked as she stole a piece of meat.

Locke raised a brow. "What do you know of the Dandyfolk?"

Elara placed a slender hand on top of the dwarf's and squeezed. "Oh, sweet Locke. I'm just looking out for him." She turned to face Finn. "I spent a summer traveling with a troupe of Dandyfolk in my younger days. Trust me. That is not a carriage you want to ride. It'll leave you bumped and bruised."

Marigold dropped her spoon, and it clanked against the plate. "You spent a summer with the Dandyfolk? How have I never heard of this?"

"What?" Elara scooped herself a generous helping of pie. "I had a life before we met, you know."

Locke looked at the elf with disbelief. "You are a magnificent and mysterious creature."

"Oh, hush." Elara rolled her eyes. "Like you never had any misadventures. Don't forget the night I drank your brother under the table at The Dancing Tankard. He told me plenty of tales from your younger days."

"That scoundrel." Locke laughed, pounding his fist on the table. "He always was a blabbermouth."

"How did I ever become friends with such miscreants?" Marigold chuckled.

"Because you see the good in people, Mari." Locke's joyous tone turned serious. "You always have."

"Some might even say you're a good influence on us." Elara's gaze was a touch more mischievous. "Who knows what nefarious adventures we might have had if not for you to rein us in."

Marigold blushed at the compliment.

Locke and Elara were her two closest friends. Sure, Elara could be rowdy at times and Locke had a temper when pushed too far, but the truth was that there wasn't a negative thing to say about either of them. They had their faults, but they were good people to their cores.

The kitchen door opened, and Gerty entered with an empty dish.

Marigold was thankful for the distraction. "How is everyone?"

"Happy as a dragon with its hoard." Gerty placed the dish on the counter. "They all seem pretty excited about tonight."

"Tell them to hurry up, then." Finn rubbed his hands together. "I, for one, am ready to get this party started."

Locke groaned. "Patience, laddie. Patience. A wise owl waits for the moon to rise."

"Save it, Locke." Gerty narrowed her eyes at Finn. "No one has ever accused my brother of being wise."

"Wisdom is earned, not given." Finn crossed his arms and sat back in his chair. "And I intend to learn from experience."

"Well, I'll be damned." Elara gave him a look of surprise. "There might be hope for you yet."

They all bickered playfully until the guests had finished eating. As Marigold helped clear the plates and minimal leftovers, she moved a little quicker than usual. Finn wasn't the only one looking forward to the evening's festivities.

Marigold stepped onto the porch and breathed in the cool autumn air. Fireflies flickered across the vineyard, its rolling hills cast in a silver glow. In a couple of months, their twinkling lights and the comforting chirp of crickets would cease, and the owls and wolves would lay claim to the night.

She scanned the area before her for signs of Bella. After dinner, the bard had gone for a walk to stretch her legs, and she still hadn't returned. Some of the guests were growing restless, worrying they'd miss the opportunity to hear a Dandyfolk sing. Not Poppy, though. Marigold could see the curious gnome through the window, her head buried in a book.

As Marigold went in search of Bella, she noticed Onyx had disappeared as well. The dire cat was probably trailing the Dandyfolk on her evening adventure.

Marigold checked behind the inn, but there was no sign of the bard beneath the apple tree, sitting area, or garden. She was about to head uphill toward the winery when she heard humming coming from within a row of vines.

Like a sailor toward a siren, Marigold followed the sound, mesmerized by its beauty. Even though there were no words, the song called to her with its melody. She found Bella sitting on the ground at the end of a row of honey grapes, surrounded by horned rabbits, their pearlescent horns gleaming in the moonlight. Her eyes were closed as she hummed, and Onyx leaned against the Dandyfolk, nuzzling her with his giant head.

The dire cat approached Marigold, letting out a hoarse meow of acknowledgment as he threaded between her legs.

For a moment, Marigold closed her eyes and listened. There was something so soothing about the bard's voice that she'd never heard at any festival or tavern. Tension left her shoulders, and if not for the waiting guests, she would have sat among the vines for as long as Bella kept singing.

When the song ended, Marigold finally spoke. "Don't let Elara see you singing to the rabbits. She's been waging war against them for years with very little help from Onyx here."

Bella opened her eyes, not the least bit surprised. "We have a tendency to do that, don't we?"

"Do what?"

"Lay claim to the world as if it doesn't belong to all." Bella plucked a grape from the vine and offered it to the closest rabbit. The creature hopped over, taking the offering before scurrying away. "Life is a circle but too often, we try to make it a square."

Marigold furrowed her brow. "I'm not sure I catch your meaning."

"There are few who do." Bella chuckled. "Most think that Aedrea was made to be conquered, but we're all connected. From the grapes to the rabbits to the stars in the sky. You may have planted these grapes, but they're not truly yours. They grow for themselves, uncaring of who eats their fruit as long as the seeds are spread."

"I see your point—" Marigold nodded. "—but I think there is more nuance to it than that. Society has evolved, and it continues to evolve whether we wish it or not. We learned to build houses to protect us from storms, to farm so that we don't starve, to make wine so that we might enjoy the pleasures of life. It would be nice if the rabbits could roam freely across the vineyard, but unfortunately, they like to dine on the leaves more often than the grapes. If we let them run unchecked, the vines would slowly wither and eventually produce no fruit."

"So you are their guardian, then?" Bella smiled. "The protectors of the vine."

"I've never thought of it like that, but in a way, yes. We care for and protect the vines so that they can grow strong and produce the best fruit." Marigold knelt, scratching Onyx behind the ears until he purred like a roaring hearth. "I believe it's important to remember that we're all connected, but sometimes, it falls to us to maintain order and balance."

Bella grinned. "There are many Dandyfolk who feel the same way."

Marigold gave her a look of surprise. "Really?"

"Absolutely." She traced her fingers across one of the vines. "We do more than sing and play music, you know? At every Gathering, there are wonderful discussions of what we've learned during our travels. The Breeze is not a strict path, it is an understanding that whatever path we take will leave a mark on the world."

Onyx flopped in the dirt and gently pawed at Marigold's pant leg. She ignored him as she pondered the Dandyfolk's words. "What mark do you hope to leave?"

"I hope to bring people together with my music."

"You've certainly done that." Marigold offered her hand to Bella. "There's an audience waiting for you at the inn."

Bella took Marigold's hand. Once she was standing, she didn't let go. "I'm glad we had this moment."

"Me, too." She met Bella's gaze. "You're more than what I expected."

The bard released her grip and shook the dirt from her skirt, which drew Onyx's attention. "People tend to be if you give them a chance."

Back at the inn, Bella tuned her lute in front of the hearth. There was a palpable excitement as guests sat around the room, the light from the candelabrum overhead dancing along the rustic walls. Drinks flowed as Elara worked the bar, pouring wine and serving ale from a mini keg. Locke sat across from her, enjoying a large tankard of ale imported from the dwarven city of Hillside. With the kitchen cleaned and the evening snacks prepared and waiting to be served, he could finally relax.

Marigold found Poppy sitting alone on a sofa, her head buried in a book. "Mind if I join you?" she asked as she offered the gnome a glass of wine.

Poppy looked up, a wide grin spreading across her face as she accepted the glass. "By all means." She closed her book and patted the sofa. Once Marigold sat, Poppy leaned in and whispered, "Can you believe it? I've heard stories of the Dandyfolk, but I've never met one myself. There's an entire department at the Historical Society dedicated to studying their culture."

"Really?" Marigold raised a brow. "A whole department?"

"Well, it's one person, Professor Allin Palerock, but he is the preeminent scholar on Dandyfolk studies. He's traveled all across Aedrea gathering research and collecting their stories." Poppy tapped the journal in her lap. "I've taken a few notes for him from our conversations at dinner."

Marigold laughed. "Of course you have."

"I wonder if she'd be willing to give me an interview?" Poppy pressed a finger to her chin as she pondered.

Marigold turned to face the gnome. "Poppy, I say this with the utmost respect for your work ethic, but how about you take the night off? You've been working nonstop since I met you. Don't you ever take time to just enjoy yourself?"

"Take a night off?" The gnome wore a confused expression. "But there's so much to learn. And I enjoy what I do. I thought you, of all people, would understand that."

"Oh, I do. Believe me. I love my job, and I love this inn." Marigold leaned back into the comfort of the sofa. "But sometimes, you need to step away from it. I promise that when you do, you'll appreciate it that much more."

"You really think so?"

"I do." Marigold took a sip of her wine. "Do you mind if I share a little advice?"

"Uh, sure." Poppy fidgeted with the sleeve of her tunic.

"You are probably one of the most hardworking people I've ever met." Marigold set her glass down, taking a moment to choose her words carefully. "You can learn everything there is to know about the history of the harvest festival through books and interviews, but if you want to fully understand it, then it's something you need to experience. The harvest festival is more than a list of events and contest winners. It's a celebration of unity and thankfulness. There's an excitement that courses through our veins as the season ends and we prepare to enjoy the fruits of our labors. I hope you keep that in mind as you tell our story."

"You're right." Poppy placed her journal on the table next to her. "I had a professor at university who told me something similar. She said that research without understanding was like missing the forest because you're too busy looking at the trees."

"Sounds like a wise professor."

"She was." Poppy raised her glass. "To Professor Greatvane and her infinite wisdom."

"I'll drink to that." Marigold clinked her glass against Poppy's.

Bella took a few more minutes to tune her lute. Once the bard was happy, she tapped the soundboard, gathering everyone's attention.

"My name is Bella Wildsong, and I'm so blessed to be here with you tonight." She strummed the lute, and a gentle melody settled over the audience. "No matter where you are heading as you journey through the Breeze of life, tonight, our paths have crossed. So raise a glass, enjoy one another's company, and though it may be dark at times, remember we have the power to brighten one another's days."

Her first song was a repeat of *The Giving Spirit* that she'd sung upon her arrival. The inn came alive with each verse, including a few new ones she hadn't sung earlier. Guests joined in at the appropriate parts, and by the end, their chorus echoed off the rafters.

Bella held their spirits high with lively tunes, and Elara kept the drinks flowing while Gerty brought out a platter of cured meats, cheeses, and crackers. Marigold was grateful for their help so that she could take her own advice for one evening.

Joy and laughter were abundant, and after the third song, several pieces of furniture were moved to make room for dancing. The two older halflings who had been at the bar when Bella arrived kicked off their shoes and danced side-by-side, swinging their elbows as they kicked and stomped a folksy dance that was common among their generation.

Finn and Gerty soon had the crowd enraptured with their own dance moves as they showcased years of practice. When they were children, the two had competed in many local dance competitions. Finn twirled his sister, and the frills of Gerty's dress flared as she spun to the delight of the crowd.

Once the song ended, they took a bow, and Bella switched to a more melancholy tune about elvish lovers. Her voice held so much emotion that Marigold felt a pang in her heart as the story unfolded. Off to the side, Elara and Locke slow-danced, the dwarf resting his head against the elf's chest as they swayed back and forth.

"Those two." Poppy gazed longingly at the couple. "They seem so in love."

"They are. They're lucky to have found one another." Marigold's gaze settled on Poppy, and her pulse quickened at the sight of candles reflecting in the gnome's purple eyes. She swallowed hard, wondering if her next question might be too intrusive. "Is there anyone waiting for you back home?"

Poppy chuckled. "No, but if you asked my mother, she'd say I was married to my books."

Marigold let out a nervous laugh. "It does seem that way at times."

"Oh, hush." Poppy gently elbowed Marigold in the arm. "I don't think you have too much room to judge."

"No judgment." Marigold raised both hands in defense. "Only an observation."

The song ended, and another more spirited tune began as Marigold's cousins approached.

Gerty frowned, one hand on her hip. "Are you two going to dance or sit there like bumps on a log?"

Finn extended a hand to Poppy, but she sat back, shaking her head vigorously. "No, no, no. Marigold can attest, I was born with two left feet."

"Nonsense." Finn stepped closer, his hand still

extended. "There's no such thing as bad dancing. Come on, I'll help you get started."

Poppy looked at Marigold with a terrified expression, but she just patted the gnome on the shoulder and laughed, taking Gerty's hand. "He's right. Just think of it as another opportunity to learn something."

Poppy sputtered a complaint before reluctantly taking Finn's hand. Marigold and Gerty interlocked their elbows and began skipping in a circle. Marigold was thankful for the distraction from their awkward conversation.

"Things look like they're going well." Gerty grinned as they switched arms and spun the opposite way.

Marigold rolled her eyes. "Will you stop it?"

They let go of one another, squaring off as they danced from one foot to another with the rhythm of the music.

"What?" Gerty shrugged as she feigned innocence.

"You know what." Marigold took Gerty's elbow as they spun again. "There's nothing going on."

"It's cute." Gerty's grin widened. "I've never seen you so nervous around someone."

"I'm not nervous, I'm—"

"Switch!" Finn called as he released Poppy's arm and hooked elbows with his sister, leaving Marigold and Poppy standing there awkwardly. "Come on, you two. Dance!" Finn cackled as he waggled his eyebrows.

Marigold cheeks flushed as she offered her elbow to Poppy.

"Sorry if I step on your toes." Poppy smiled sheepishly.

"Don't worry about it." Marigold began to skip. "That's the key to dancing, do it like no one's watching."

As they twirled, she was keenly aware of the warmth

radiating between their bodies. Marigold focused on Bella's voice, anything to take her mind off the sensation.

By the next song, Poppy had relaxed a little, and the look of nervous terror was replaced by something else—joy. She occasionally stumbled, or stepped too close, but she seemed to have taken Marigold's words to heart.

The next couple of hours passed in a blur as they laughed and danced and drank. Finn taught Poppy several of the easier dances, and before they knew it, Bella announced her final song.

"It's been a pleasure to share my music with you tonight, but the Breeze goes ever onward, and so must I. I'll leave you with a final song. This one is titled, *The Road, It Calls to Me.*"

She strummed the lute slowly, and all around the room, people paired off.

"You were right again." Poppy stood in front of Marigold and offered her hand. "It was nice to take the night off."

Marigold took Poppy's hand, resting her other on the gnome's side. They swayed like cattails in the summer breeze as Bella sang.

"The road calls to me like an old friend's song, its melody worn by time;

Though I've rested my head in many a place, no hearth have I called mine.

For there's a call that stirs my soul, a whisper of lands untrod;

And I chase the wind that guides me, a leaf among the forest.

. . .

Oh, onward, onward! Through hill and hollow, where shadows fall and new dawns rise;

With well-worn boots and tales in tow, beneath the boundless, changing skies.

I follow the stars or the mountain's crest, and each day find a new place to rest;

The realm is wide, with paths unknown; and as I walk, the road calls on.

Through valleys deep and peaks so high, where rivers sing and forests sigh,

I press ahead with foot and song, though none may know me passing by;

For there's a joy in the Dandy life, for a bard who wanders far and wide,

And every face, some strange, some dear, they mark the journey year by year.

Oh, onward, onward! Through hill and hollow, where shadows fall and new dawns rise;

With well-worn boots and tales in tow, beneath the boundless, changing skies.

I follow the stars or the mountain's crest, and each day find a new place to rest;

The realm is wide, with paths unknown; and as I walk, the road calls on.

. . .

Sometimes in the firelight's glow, I glimpse those I've left behind,
Their memories etched forever in this wandering heart of mine.
But still, I take that fateful step, for lands untraveled lie ahead;
The road may part, the bonds may break, but never will my travels end.

Oh, onward, onward! Through hill and hollow, where shadows fall and new dawns rise;
With well-worn boots and tales in tow, beneath the boundless, changing skies.
The road calls on, my spirit sways, to wander ever, across the Breeze.
The road calls on, my spirit sways, to wander ever, across the Breeze."

Marigold and Poppy held onto one another as the music faded. For a brief moment, nothing else existed. And then the applause of the group came crashing in as Bella placed her lute to the side and bowed.

Their hands released, and Marigold let out a shaky breath, wondering what exactly she'd gotten herself into.

8. A PERFECT DAY

When Marigold made her weekly deliveries a few days later, Bella's performance was the talk of the town. Everyone she spoke to wanted to know what it was like to witness the Dandyfolk perform. Marigold didn't need to ask how they all heard about the performance. Gerty had come to town a day prior. Her cousin was a lot of things, but tight-lipped wasn't one of them.

Marigold endured the deluge of questions. Some, like the mayor, took the time to recount their own interactions with a Dandyfolk, and the trip ended up taking twice as long as usual.

She let out a long sigh when she finally rejoined Gerty in the wagon. "You really love to gossip, don't you?"

Gerty smiled sheepishly. "It was either tell them about the performance or tell them about the gnome you can't seem to get enough of."

Marigold's cheeks flushed bright red. "Gertrude Meadowlark, how many times do I have to tell you?"

"There's nothing going on." Gerty bobbled her head as

she mocked her cousin's words. "I think we both know that's not true."

"You are incorrigible, you know that?" Marigold flicked the reins, and the wagon began to move.

Gerty scoffed. "I'll have you know a lot of people think I am a delight."

The two bickered and teased one another the entire ride home. When they finally arrived at the inn, they found a cloaked figure standing on the porch. At the foot of the steps, a massive horse was tied to the hitching post. The golden mount had a mane and hooves as dark as night, and its powerful body rippled with muscle every time it moved. Large satchels hung to each side of the mighty beast, and Onyx sat in the grass, sniffing the creature's hooves.

Comparing the stranger's horse to Acorn Blossom was like comparing Onyx to a house cat.

Marigold handed the reins to Gerty and climbed down from the wagon. The cloaked figure raised a hand in acknowledgment but didn't remove the hood as they descended the steps to meet Marigold. All she could see beneath the cowl was a pointed chin and a few strands of dark hair. Several dark metal rings adorned their fingers, and the gray cloak protruded about the hips concealing what had to be swords. They had a long, curved bow carved from white wood fastened across their back. By the look of them, this was another adventurer headed toward their next quest, and judging by the overflowing satchels, they were in for a long haul.

"I'm Marigold Bramblefoot, owner of the Dew Drop Inn." She smiled. "How can I help you?"

The stranger cleared their throat. "I need a room for the night and somewhere to rest my horse."

Although the voice was deep, there was a feminine quality to it, as if they were purposely concealing it. This wasn't the first time a guest had attempted to hide their identity. Over the years, the inn had roomed many travelers who wanted their privacy. If all they needed were a bed and a warm meal, then so be it.

"We can accommodate that. Follow me inside, and I'll have Finn take your horse to the stable." Marigold opened the door for the stranger to step inside. "What should I call you two?" She'd found long ago that in situations like these, that question went a lot better than asking for their name.

The stranger paused in front of the door. "Call me Seeker. The horse is Nighthoof."

"Very well, Seeker. Right this way."

Marigold helped the mysterious traveler settle in and for the rest of the evening, Seeker voluntarily stayed in their room. At dinner, they ate their meal away from the other guests, sitting by the window with their hood pulled low. The candles in the chandelier overhead cast long shadows that gave them an even more mysterious appearance.

Locke leaned against the doorway to the kitchen, his arms crossed as he watched from afar as spoonfuls of stew disappeared beneath the shadowy hood. "Strange folk, adventurers."

Marigold shrugged. "Who are we to judge? I'm sure it can't be easy fighting monsters day in and day out."

Finn peeked around Locke from inside the kitchen. "I'll have you know they don't just fight monsters. There's enough variety in quests to make a living without ever lifting a blade."

Locke frowned over his shoulder. "How would you know, laddie?"

"Hey, I know things." Finn scowled at the dwarf. "Besides, I see the quests posted on the notice board every time I go into town."

"Will you lot give it a rest?" Elara called from deeper in the kitchen. "Stop ogling the poor fellow and let them eat in peace."

Locke grunted as he turned around. "It's not like they could see me with their hood pulled down to the floor, anyways."

The next morning, Seeker left before the rooster had time to crow. As mysteriously as they'd arrived, the inscrutable traveler was gone. Maybe they were an adventurer, but Marigold would likely never know for sure. What she did know was that if someone was hiding who they were, they usually had a good reason. The inn was often full of people content to share their news and travels, but sometimes, she wondered about the ones who drifted by. What stories might they tell if given the chance? What adventures waited on the horizon?

Marigold was still pondering Seeker and Nighthoof's destination when she stepped outside into the crisp morning air. Onyx wandered over, climbing the steps and leaving a trail of large, wet pawprints in his wake. The dire cat's chest rumbled as he nuzzled against Marigold's thigh. Somehow, he could always sense her presence despite his cloudy eyes.

Across the vineyard, a layer of dew glistened in the early morning light, and through the hills, apples speckled the trees like rubies, calling for someone to capture their treasures.

Marigold rubbed her hands together. One of the best things about being the boss was that occasionally, she could shirk her responsibilities and follow her own desires. She knelt, scratching Onyx underneath his chin. "What do you say we have ourselves a little adventure?"

Onyx answered with a husky meow that cracked halfway through.

Today was a perfect day for apple picking, and it wasn't as if the pursuit was complete frivolity. Locke would use the apples for pies, pork roasts, apple cider, and a dozen other things.

Marigold grabbed baskets from the shed before remembering she'd left her water skin inside. She found Poppy standing on the front porch, holding a cup of hot tea as she looked over the vineyard.

Poppy smiled when she noticed Marigold. "You're up and at it, aren't you?"

"The first to the river drinks the clearest water." Marigold stopped at the bottom of the stairs and placed a hand on her hip. "What has you up so early?"

Usually, Marigold didn't see Poppy until at least noon, so it was surprising to find her up at this hour. Her hair was even messier than usual, and she had her robe pulled tight to fight the morning chill, its navy fabric accentuating the gnome's pinkish skin.

Poppy took a sip from the steaming mug. "I've never

been much of an early riser, but I thought I would finally try this brunch I've been hearing so much about."

"You're right on time, then. Gerty should be setting the table soon."

"I thought maybe it was just a coincidence at first, but it feels like it's always time to eat around here. Every interview I've scheduled has been either just before or right after mealtime." Poppy shook her head as she looked in the direction of town. "Halflings sure do love to eat, don't they?"

"That we do." Marigold laughed.

"Back home, I'm always so caught up in my work that I usually only do two meals a day, if I'm lucky." She lifted her cup of tea in Marigold's direction and nodded. "But thanks to your advice, I'm trying to embrace more of my time here. Still, I can't say I've paid much attention to when the meals are served."

"You're in luck. Here, let me show you something." Marigold climbed the stairs and opened the door for Poppy. Inside, she led the gnome to a sign hanging on the wall between the bar and kitchen entrance.

Traditional Halfling Meal Times
** Breakfast: early morning **
Brunch: mid-morning
Morning Tea: late morning
** Lunch: noon **
Afternoon Tea: mid-afternoon
** Dinner: early evening **
Supper: late evening
Night Cap: before bed

The sign had an elegant script surrounded by paintings of flowers and fruits.

Poppy's mouth was agape. "You really eat that often?"

Marigold shrugged. "Sometimes, but they're more like guidelines than hard rules. Like most of the realm, we eat when we're hungry. Breakfast, lunch, and dinner are the main meals, so unless it's a holiday, the others are optional, and usually a bit lighter."

"Wow." Poppy set her teacup on the bar. "It's like a whole new world."

The door to the kitchen swung open and Gerty exited carrying a platter of toasts, jams, and sliced fruits.

"Speaking of food, Locke makes some of the best jams." Marigold stepped aside, gesturing to the food as her cousin passed. "His apple jam is particularly special. Maybe I can twist his arm to make some once I'm back from the orchard."

"Wait, you're going apple picking today?" There was an excitement in the gnome's eyes. "Would you mind if I joined you?"

Marigold stared at the gnome. Poppy had been so enthralled with her work since she'd arrived that the question caught Marigold completely off guard. It seemed the gnome had truly taken her advice to heart. Poppy lingered uncomfortably as several guests moved from the common area to the table.

"I'm sorry." She cast her gaze downward, picking up her teacup. "I didn't mean to intrude. Maybe some other time."

"No, no." Marigold grabbed Poppy on the arm. "Sorry, it's not that. You're more than welcome to join me. I was just surprised is all. I figured you'd be working." She released the gnome's arm. "I've got a few things I can busy myself with. Enjoy your brunch, and you can meet me out back whenever you're ready."

"Alright." Poppy grinned. "See you then!"

By the time brunch was over, the morning chill had faded, leaving behind a gorgeous day. The sun beamed from a clear blue sky, and birds chirped all around as a gentle breeze rolled through the whispering vines. Marigold was checking on the chicken coop when she heard Poppy approaching. The gnome had changed into a pair of tan trousers and a form-fitting red tunic. She was almost unrecognizable without an armful of books and her reading spectacles.

"No journals?" Marigold teased.

Poppy pulled a small notebook about the size of her hand from her pocket and grinned. "Just in case. A scholar without a journal is like an adventurer without a sword."

"It'd be a tragedy if you learned something without writing it down." Marigold smirked.

Poppy crossed her arms and huffed. "You joke, but that's not a theory I'm prepared to test just yet."

"Alright, Professor Poppy." Marigold handed her a basket. "Let's see what today has in store for us."

They followed a path to the orchard but didn't make it far before Marigold spotted a group of horned rabbits gathered at the edge of the garden, nibbling on the prickly leaves of the squash. As usual, Onyx ignored them, forcing Marigold to chase the creatures away. She stomped hard and yelled until the rabbits bolted into the hills.

"There was a time when Onyx would have chased a rabbit from here to town," Marigold said as they continued.

"I bet." Poppy bent down and stroked the dire cat along the spine. "I'm sure he was a formidable force in his prime. Just look at those paws."

Onyx turned around, nuzzling her hand before plopping on his side.

"He was." Marigold gave him a pat on the head as she passed. "I think if there was trouble, he still could be. The rabbits are annoying, but truthfully, they don't harm much."

"Isn't there something you could use to keep them away? Like a potion or ward?" asked Poppy.

"We have wards for keeping out deer and other creatures. We even have one for protecting the chicken coop from foxes, but for whatever reason, horned rabbits are unaffected. Dad said it was something about their horns that could mitigate magical effects."

Poppy pulled out her journal and jotted down a quick note. "What?" she asked when she saw Marigold grinning. "That's a good fact to know."

"Oh, nothing." Marigold chuckled. Wine wasn't made in a day, and some habits died slowly. "Have you ever picked apples before?"

"From a produce stand." Poppy grinned. "We don't have many orchards in the city."

Marigold stopped next to a tree that was dotted with apples. "It's pretty simple. You want to pick the red ones. If they have any yellow, then they'll need a few more days to ripen. You'll want to take the apple and grab it like this." She reached for an apple, clamping it with her fingertips.

"Then give it a gentle twist. If it comes free, it's ready. If you have to tug at it, then it's not ripe yet and you'll need to find another."

"Sounds easy enough." Poppy twisted her first apple, and when it didn't give, she moved to the next. The second popped free with a soft snap. She showed it to Marigold. "How's this?"

"Looks good. Just remember, apple picking isn't about speed or quantity. It's about quality."

They continued through the orchard, taking their time to select the most vibrant fruit.

"I haven't had a chance to ask you recently." Marigold set her basket down so that she could reach a higher branch. "How's your research coming along?"

"Really well. Your father's notebooks have been invaluable for learning about the winemaking process, and the townspeople have been so welcoming. It's fascinating to hear them recount their favorite moments over the years."

"That's wonderful. Pretty soon, you'll be able to see what all the fuss is about." Some of the trees already had hints of yellow and orange, and that meant it would only be a few weeks before it was time to harvest the grapes.

They continued onward until Marigold found one of her favorite trees. It was located at the top of a hill, and any apple that fell would roll into the valley. If it was an especially windy day, there would sometimes be piles of fruit at the bottom.

She stopped and pointed to a branch sagging with bright red apples. "Anyone can grab low-hanging fruit, but these...these are the dragon's hoard."

Poppy swallowed hard and took a step back. "How are we supposed to reach them?"

Marigold's lip curled at the edge. "How do you think?"

The gnome's eyes widened. "You saw me in the library. I don't think I'd be a very good climber."

"Don't worry, I'll toss them to you. I've been climbing these trees since I could walk." Marigold wrapped her hand around the lowest limb and hoisted herself up, climbing from one branch to another, being careful to keep one foot steady at all times. She'd climbed these trees a thousand times and knew them like the back of her hand. Once she made it to the limb she wanted, a thick one that grew horizontally, she straddled it and slowly scooted toward the apple-laden branches.

"Be careful!" Poppy called, concern evident on her face. She wore the expression of someone who had taken numerous falls in their life.

"I'll be fine." Marigold scooted further out, only a couple of feet from her prize. She took a moment to appreciate the view. There was a certain thrill to climbing high and seeing the world like a bird among the branches. Wrapping one arm around the limb to anchor herself, Marigold leaned forward until she could reach the branch loaded with deliciously red apples. "Ready?"

"I guess."

Marigold shook the branch, and two apples fell. Poppy yelped as she tried to catch them both. One bounced off her hand and the other hit her in the chest before rolling down the hill.

"Dammit!" Poppy cursed as she chased after the fallen apples like a cat after a string. She charged down the hill and almost caught one before it hit a bump and launched into the air.

Marigold cackled at the sight, laughing so hard that she needed to grab the branch for support. The moment she put her weight on it, there was a crack. She tried to steady herself, but the limb sagged under her weight. Momentum carried her forward as she tumbled headfirst through the smaller branches.

Panic flared in that brief moment as she fell, replaced by an unyielding pain as she hit the ground with a thud. She gasped for air as lightning shot through her arm and up her shoulder, white-hot and debilitating. Poppy yelled something, but it came across as warbled and distorted. Marigold tried to sit up, and her vision darkened at the edges, stars dancing in the darkness like fireflies. She rolled onto her back, and a fresh wave of pain shot through her arm.

As she lay there, the apple tree swirled overhead.

9. AN APPLE A DAY KEEPS THE CLERIC AT BAY

Marigold took deep breaths in an attempt to control her spinning vision. It felt as if she were trapped on a ship during a raging storm, her body heaving one way then another.

"Gods, Marigold! Are you okay?" Poppy hovered over the halfling, her voice full of panic. "That was quite a fall."

"I'm fine," Marigold mumbled. She tried to sit up again. "Just need to—" Her head spun, and she collapsed back to the ground.

"It's okay. It's okay." Poppy's voice quivered. "I'm here. Tell me, where does it hurt?"

A warm hand cradled Marigold's cheek as Poppy knelt beside her, the gnome's purple eyes brimming with tears. Despite the pain, all Marigold could think was how beautiful they looked, like polished marbles against a cloudless sky.

"My arm." Marigold winced as she tried to raise it. "I landed on my arm."

Poppy grimaced as she inspected the injury. "Your

elbow is swollen pretty bad and there's already bruising. I think you may have broken it." She squeezed Marigold's good hand. "We're going to need to get you to a cleric but just sit there for a minute until the shock wears off. You're going to be fine."

Marigold closed her eyes, taking careful breaths as the pain ebbed and flowed. She could hear Poppy's shaky breathing, but the gnome never let go of Marigold's hand. She could only imagine what it must have felt like watching her fall from the tree.

"Hey." She squeezed Poppy's fingers. "Can I ask you something?"

Poppy sniffled. "Sure, what is it?"

"Why the harvest festival?"

"What do you mean?"

"What made you want to research it?"

"Um." Poppy stared at the ground for a moment, and then her gaze drifted over the rolling hills. "I don't know, really. Gnomes aren't exactly known for taking time to enjoy things. We're a people fueled by innovation. Reading about it, the harvest festival seemed so different from my life in Aethervale. I think deep down, a part of me wanted to know what that was like."

For several minutes, they waited beneath the broken branches of the apple tree until Marigold could sit up safely. Poppy helped the halfling to her feet, and they began the slow trek back to the inn. Poppy talked the entire way, telling stories of the different locations she'd traveled to for research. Marigold could barely process most of it, but she was grateful that the gnome was trying to take her mind off the pain.

Elara was working in the vineyard when they

returned, Onyx trailing at her heels. She noticed Marigold —one arm wrapped around Poppy and the other hanging limply at her side—and took off at a full sprint. Marigold had never seen the elf move so fast as she ran toward them.

"Shit, Marigold, what in Melora's name happened to you?" Elara's normally stoic face was etched with concern.

"She fell from a tree," Poppy offered. "I think she has a broken arm."

"Seven hells!" The elf threw her arms in the air. "What were you climbing a tree for?"

"Apples." Marigold chuckled, followed by a grimace as a jolt of pain shot through her arm. "Oh, no."

"What is it?" Elara asked, inspecting the halfling for more injuries.

Marigold winced as she looked over her shoulder toward the orchard. "We forgot the apples."

"To hells with the apples. I swear." Elara shook her head. "Come on. Let's get you to town."

Finn steered the wagon toward Willowbrook, and Marigold's arm throbbed with every bump in the road. The last time she'd needed a cleric was years ago, back when she'd smashed her finger with a hammer while repairing a post in the vineyard. That pain had been intense, but it was nothing compared to what she was experiencing now.

Poppy held Marigold's hand between her ink-stained fingers. It was a comforting gesture, and the warmth of their skin touching helped to take her mind off the discomfort. When Elara had told Poppy that she should stay behind, the gnome refused, arguing she'd run behind the wagon if she had to. In the end, Elara conceded to let Poppy take her place.

There were plenty of people out and about when they crossed the bridge into town. The temple was located near the town center, a few blocks away from Town Hall, forcing them to pass the market as it was closing down for the afternoon. Several heads craned in their direction as the wagon passed. Marigold avoided their gazes. No doubt Gerty would fill them in on all the details the first chance she got.

They arrived at the temple, and Finn helped Marigold from the wagon. The stone building looked slightly out of place with its massive bell tower and elaborate stained-glass windows. Unlike the bank, the Order of Clerics hadn't tried to match the facade of the temple to its surroundings.

Inside, the walls were a drab, dreary gray that served to accentuate the vibrant windows. A sunburst-shaped mosaic of stained glass blazed with color from the afternoon light. There were rows of pews on each side of the central aisle. It led to a dais where a statue of Melora, Goddess of the Harvest, towered above them. Though the gods depicted in the temples across the realm varied, Melora was a fitting one for Willowbrook. She was tall and full-figured with wild hair adorned with flowers, and even though she was carved from stone, the sculptor had managed to infuse her with movement. Power and grace radiated from the statue as she cradled a lamb against her chest, her dress blowing behind her in the breeze. At her feet, an overflowing cornucopia represented her bountiful harvest.

A hooded cleric stirred from the front row as they entered, closing the book he was reading. He had dark features and a braided beard that draped over his chest.

"Blessed harvest to you. How may I be of service?" The voice was deep, reminding Marigold of Locke.

"She fell from a tree while picking apples," Poppy answered. "We think her arm might be broken."

"I thought an apple a day was supposed to keep the cleric at bay." He let out a boisterous laugh.

Marigold snorted at the cheesy humor, then hissed as a fresh wave of pain shot through her arm.

"Sorry, sorry. I'll save the jokes for later." He extended his arm. "May I?"

Marigold nodded, and the cleric lifted her sleeve, revealing an elbow that was swollen and bruised. He muttered prayers as his hand hovered a couple of inches above her skin.

"It's a fracture all right, but nothing Korin can't handle. Luckily for you, this wasn't a full break, so a mending like this should only take about an hour." He gestured toward the pew. "Have a seat."

Finn tapped Marigold on the shoulder. "These things always make me queasy. If you don't need me, I'm gonna wait outside until you're finished."

Marigold nodded again and took a seat next to the cleric. Poppy sat beside her, her eyes more alert than Marigold had ever seen them. Korin placed his open palm over the injury, and Marigold winced at the touch.

"Don't worry, miss. That'll be the worst of it." He

began praying, and a golden glow emanated from the cleric's palm.

Ethereal energy blanketed Marigold's elbow, radiating warmth that felt like taking a hot bath. She sighed at the relief, resting her back against the pew.

"You know," Poppy whispered as Korin worked, "I thought I was supposed to be the clumsy one."

"I've climbed that tree hundreds of times. Never so much as slipped." Marigold patted Poppy on the leg. "I'm lucky you were there."

The time passed quicker than she'd expected, and once the mending was finished, Korin tapped Marigold on the arm. "That should do it."

The halfling flexed her elbow. When it didn't hurt, she clenched and unclenched her hand several times. No pain or lingering effects. It was as if the fall had never happened. "Thank you, Korin." She extended her hand.

"My pleasure." Korin shook it. "I've only been stationed in Willowbrook for a couple of weeks now, so I'm not familiar with the townsfolk. What's your name?"

"Marigold, I'm the owner of the Dew Drop Inn and Vineyard."

"I've heard of that one. They say you make some of the best honeywine around."

"You should stop by for a tasting sometime. It's the least I can do after today."

Korin chuckled. "I don't do this for the accolades, but I might take you up on that."

"Consider it my little way of welcoming you to town." She smiled. "Where was it you were stationed before Willowbrook?"

"Vusora. Nice enough place but the trees are a little too empowered for my taste."

"Empowered?" Marigold raised a brow. "Like tree-walkers?" She'd read stories of the tree creatures that could uproot themselves and travel across forests.

"Not quite." Korin shook his head. "Let's just say that these liked to talk, and I don't think they were too fond of having a dwarf in their midst. They'd creak and groan all through the night. It was so bad that I had to stuff my ears to get any sleep."

Poppy reached in her pocket for her journal but then thought better of it, forcing Marigold to conceal a laugh.

"Well, I'm glad that you ended up here." She tested out the movement in her arm again. "I hope to see you around."

The cleric returned to the pew, opening his book as Marigold and Poppy exited the temple. Outside, Finn waited by the wagon.

He held up both hands. "Please, I'm glad you're healed, but I don't need to hear any of the gory details."

"What do you think goes on in there?" Marigold exchanged a glance with Poppy, who wore an equally puzzled expression. "Finn, have you never needed a mending?"

"Nope, I have a hearty constitution." Finn flexed his arm and patted the biceps, as if that explained it. "Gerty broke her arm once, and to hear her tell it, the mending was worse than the fall. I have no intention of watching someone's bones get rearranged."

Marigold forced a cough to keep from laughing. If Gerty's prank had lasted this long, she wouldn't be the one to ruin it.

They all climbed into the wagon and began the journey home. While it might not have been the perfect day Marigold imagined, it hadn't been half-bad, considering the company.

In the days that followed Marigold's accident, the vineyard was busier than it had been in months. The injury had served as a reminder to the townsfolk that apple-picking season had arrived, so they were flocking to the Dew Drop Inn for a day of fun and wine tastings.

Elmwood sat in a chair by the garden, puffing on a pipe the length of his arm. He was one of the oldest halflings in Willowbrook, and his gray hair curled in ringlets around his pudgy face. He'd brought a gaggle of his great-grandchildren to the orchard, where he promptly left them to their own devices.

"I guess there really is no such thing as bad publicity," he said as a giant circle of gray smoke dissipated into the air above his head.

"You would know, wouldn't you." Elara hammered a stake into the ground at the beginning of the trail. The sign attached read, 'No climbing the trees.'

"When you live as long as I have, you learn that the

opinion of others rarely matters." Elmwood set the pipe aside and took a sip of his wine.

Marigold pointed at the sign. "Is that really necessary?"

"I don't know, Marigold." Elara gave her a stern look. "But it would be a shame if someone broke a bone because they were being careless."

"It was an accident." Marigold held out her arm. "Look. Good as new."

Elara pursed her lips. "Still, I'd rather not charter any more trips to the cleric on our account. We're already playing with fate with Elmwood here."

The elder halfling scoffed. "You nearly cut off your finger one time, and it's all they talk about."

Marigold ignored his comment. "Fine, leave the sign. But it's not as if we can enforce it anyways." She gestured across the sprawling countryside. "There are only five of us to manage the entire property. And speaking of which, I need to get back to the inn. Will you check on the customers in the cellar once you're finished here?"

Elara nodded, giving the stake one final hammer before leaving.

Back at the inn, Gerty was in the midst of setting the table. The earthy scent of Locke's famous stuffed mushroom caps wafted from the kitchen, and a halfling couple had already taken their seats at the table in anticipation.

Marigold couldn't blame them. Her mouth had started watering the moment she stepped inside. The meal was always a symphony of flavors and textures, from the creamy blend of herbs, garlic, and melted cheese to the toasted breadcrumbs that offered the perfect crunchy complement. Every bite was an experience, and her stomach growled just thinking about it.

Poppy stepped out from the hallway at the top of the stairs, her pack once again bulging like a turtle shell. She wore a red tunic and green trousers, similar to what she'd been wearing the day they first encountered one another in town. Her lavender spectacles were folded and tucked into the collar of her tunic.

She waved at Marigold as she descended. "How's your arm?"

"I haven't climbed any more trees, so still good." Marigold smiled. "Staying for lunch?"

"Not today." Poppy shook her head. "More interviews. I'm meeting someone at Crust & Crumble, so I think we'll eat there. I'll be back for dinner, though."

"That place is lovely." Marigold cupped a hand over her mouth and whispered, "Don't tell Locke, but they have the best chicken pot pie in town."

"Your secret is safe with me." Poppy winked. "See you later."

Marigold watched as Poppy left. Since the accident, the two hadn't spent much time together, and Poppy was once again burying herself in her work. Although things had returned to normal the day after, Marigold still felt the echo of warmth from Poppy's hand against hers. In those moments after she'd fallen, when the world was nothing but pain and panic, she'd found comfort in the gnome's touch. Part of her wanted to lose herself in that comfort, but Poppy had only been concerned with Marigold's safety.

She was a friend, nothing more, and that would have to do.

Marigold was in her office sorting through invoices when Finn entered in a panic. He flung open the door, eyes wide as he took quick, heavy breaths.

"You need to come outside, now. Onyx has lost his mind." He disappeared without explanation, his footsteps thundering across the floor.

She hurried out the front door, where a man was fending off Onyx with a staff down the driveway. The dire cat's ears were flattened, and his hackles raised as he hissed at the man. His tail twitched violently as he spat again.

The man was tall, with long white hair and an equally long beard. He stood in front of a wagon, and though he had his staff raised defensively, he didn't seem worried by the dire cat's aggression.

"Onyx, back!" Marigold called, but the cat held firm, a deep growl emanating from his chest. "What has gotten into you?"

She gently petted Onyx on the side, and his growl deepened. He was so tense it was like petting a wine barrel.

The man kept his staff extended like a spear, as if the gnarled piece of wood could stop the dire cat if it chose to pounce.

Beneath the wide-brimmed hat with a tall pointed crown, the man's piercing blue eyes were focused on Onyx. Smoke trailed from the end of a long pipe hanging loosely in his mouth, and a long, silky white beard fell to his belly. He had an equally luscious mane that draped down the back of flowing blue robes. His clothing was of fine quality, embroidered with silver thread that depicted elaborate patterns about the shoulders and sleeves, and a leather belt cinched his robes at the waist.

Onyx let out another deep growl as something squirmed within the satchel at the man's side.

"Sir..." Marigold stepped forward, her palms raised. "I think whatever you have in your bag is upsetting the cat."

"Astute observation." His voice was calm, but his gaze never left Onyx. "Now, what do you say we make peace so that I can check in for the evening? I'm an old man and would greatly enjoy getting off my feet and into a warm bath."

By this point, a crowd had gathered on the porch. Elara and Locke were standing behind Onyx.

"What's in the bag?" Locke crossed his flour-covered arms.

"Wizard business." The man's eyes flitted to the dwarf. "AKA, none of yours."

Locke's mustache twitched, and his eyes narrowed before he met Marigold's gaze. She shook her head. Anger would only add fuel to the already tense situation.

"Sir, with all due respect, if whatever's in the bag is upsetting Onyx, then I'm not sure you should be bringing it into the inn."

The man took a step back and lowered his staff. He pinched the bridge of his nose, letting out a sigh that went on much longer than it should have. "Fine." He opened the satchel and pulled out a bundle of small twigs, holding them out for everyone to see. "Happy?"

Onyx hissed again, revealing a mouthful of dangerous teeth.

"What is it, boy?" Marigold gave him a pet, but he was as rigid as forged iron.

Elara scoffed. "I think the cat has finally lost his mind."

"Not now, Elara." While Onyx might be more lackadaisical in his old age, he was still as sharp as ever. If he was acting like this, there had to be a reason.

Without warning, the twigs within the man's palm twitched, and their ends took on a violet glow. They hovered in the air, rearranging until they transformed into a stick figure. It had a bulbous piece of wood for its head, slender twigs that formed its arms and legs, and a slightly thicker stem for its torso.

Marigold's jaw dropped. There was a mage in her yard. An actual mage.

The small stick figure raised its arm, shaking a wooden fist in Onyx's direction.

"This is Splinter." The mage lifted his hand for everyone to see. "He's one of my traveling companions. Now, if it's all the same to you, I'd like to settle in now."

Onyx growled, and Splinter retreated into the wizard's sleeve, draping the fabric around him like a cloak. The two dark knots shifted on the creature's head, giving the appearance of eyes as they peeked from within the robe.

"What is it exactly?" Marigold took a step closer. Onyx followed at her heels, hackles still raised.

The mage's face softened as he watched the curious creature. "They go by many names across the realm. Golemites, thaumatons, aetherformed, arcane constructs. They're all different ways of saying the same thing—an inanimate object that has been given sentience by magical means."

That explained a lot. Onyx must have been able to sense the magic radiating from sticks hidden in the satchel. That still didn't explain why he was so upset, though. Marigold had witnessed him lying in the grass, surrounded by horned rabbits without so much as raising a paw.

"Onyx doesn't usually get this riled up." She looked down at the dire cat. "Would it be okay if he sniffed Splinter? It might help to ease his distrust."

"I suppose." The mage lifted his hand so that Splinter could climb onto his shoulder, where the little construct concealed himself within stands of white hair. "Give me a moment to grab something from my cart."

Upon closer inspection, the wagon was actually a merchant cart. It had columns of drawers on one side, a canopy over the top, and two cupboard doors on the other side. The strange part was that there were no handles for pulling the thing or anywhere to hitch an animal. Marigold had no idea how he'd managed to move the cart.

The wizard opened a cupboard door and placed his satchel inside. After rummaging around for a moment, he removed a metal cage. It was dome-shaped with thin wire bars and a circular base, much like a bird cage. Inside, there was a small chest and a little swing that hung from the top.

He took Splinter from his shoulder, and the golem jumped inside the cage.

Marigold wasn't sure when it happened, but Onyx had relaxed. His body was still tense as he clung closely by her side, but his hackles had lowered and his ears were in their normal position. He seemed more curious than hostile.

The mage set the cage on the ground, and Marigold and Onyx slowly approached. Upon seeing the dire cat,

Splinter crawled inside the chest, pulling the lid closed from within, leaving only his little twig fingers clenched around the opening so that there was a slit to see through.

If he could see. It was clear that the construct had some level of awareness, but Marigold wasn't sure how any of this worked.

Onyx sniffed at the cage with heavy breaths.

"He's a very perceptive cat." The mage knelt, and Onyx approached, sniffing the wizard's robes. "Most can't sense the presence of my constructs."

"He may be old, but he still has a fire inside him." Marigold gave Elara a knowing look, and the elf rolled her eyes. "In his younger years, he patrolled this entire property."

After deciding the mage wasn't a threat, Onyx returned his attention to the cage. Splinter had opened the chest, though he still crouched inside. The dire cat lay on the ground, head low as he watched curiously.

Splinter hesitated, then climbed from the chest.

"It's okay. Go ahead," the mage urged the construct onward. Splinter approached with caution until it was inches from Onyx's massive head.

The construct reached through the bars and touched the dire cat's nose. Onyx licked Splinter's hand, and the poor construct abandoned its form, clattering into a pile of twigs.

Marigold gasped, but the wizard only chuckled. A moment later, the sticks glowed with violet energy and rearranged themselves once again. This time, Splinter walked to the edge of the cage, gently stroking Onyx's fur until a rumbling purr vibrated through the cat.

"I apologize for my curtness earlier. I'm a little weary

from traveling." The mage stood. "I trust that we can put this behind us now."

Marigold nodded, and the mage lifted the cage off the ground, hanging it from a hook on the frame beneath the canopy of his wagon.

Onyx rolled on his back and pawed at Marigold's boot, about as concerned with the construct as he was with the horned rabbits.

"Sorry about all of this, Mister..." In the chaos, Marigold had never asked the man's name.

"Aldric. Aldric Oldheim. I'll be staying at your inn through the harvest festival. One of my contacts should have made a reservation for me several months back."

"Oldheim?" Marigold wore a surprised expression. Several months back, Mayor Sweetwater's assistant had stopped by the inn to make a reservation for an alchemist, but he'd made no mention of a mage. "You're the alchemist for this year's firelight display?"

The firelight show was always one of the highlights of the festival. And since there was no Alchemist's Guild in Willowbrook, the alchemists were always recruited from the cities. Marigold wondered if the mayor knew he'd hired a mage capable of bringing sticks to life.

"I dabble with alchemy." Aldric snapped his fingers, and the cart started rolling of its own accord. "It's a hard life being a construct mage with a limited radius. All of my golems fail once I'm out of range, so I've been forced to find other avenues for income."

Hopefully, Aldric knew what he was doing. While the vibrant explosives were beautiful when they burst into colorful patterns across the sky, they could be dangerous in the wrong hands. Ever since the incident in Eastborne, the guild required special certifications and permits to buy some of the raw materials.

"Isn't there a Mage's Guild to help you find jobs for your particular abilities?" Marigold asked. If it was anything like the other trade guilds, they should help with job postings.

"Mage's Guild." Aldric scoffed, gesturing wildly with his pipe as he spoke. "I'd sooner run into the wilds than be beholden to that group of spineless boggles. It's all politics, and the elemental mages get all the glory. Never mind that the whole lot of them are overrated. All show and no substance."

Marigold gulped. She hadn't meant to broach such a touchy subject. Apparently, there was a lot of tension among the magically inclined.

"Would you like me to help you with the cart?" Finn smiled nervously, his gaze flitting to the self-driving cart. "I can store it by the stables."

"No need." Aldric puffed his pipe and waited for the cart to catch up. "I'll leave her parked out front. There are enough enchantments on ol' Bertha here to hold off a band of goblins."

Finn looked to Marigold for confirmation, but she just shrugged. Her experiences with mages were limited to what she'd read in books. She'd seen several from afar, and had even gone to a few performances while studying in Whitblossum, but she'd never interacted with one on this level before.

The cart rolled beside the porch, and there was a clank as several rods descended and anchored to the ground.

"Alright, everyone, show's over." Elara held the front door open as the guests funneled inside. She met

Marigold's gaze and waggled her brows as a mischievous grin tugged at her lips.

Marigold laughed. Considering there was a mage, a twig construct, and a self-driving cart in their midst, she had a feeling the show was just getting started.

11. TRUE MAGIC

Marigold sat in her office watching ribbons of steam waft from her afternoon tea. For a quaint little inn, it certainly had been an exciting few weeks. Between a gnome historian studying halfling culture, a Dandyfolk serenading them for an evening, a broken arm, and now a mage staying throughout the harvest season, she wondered if her father had ever experienced this much hullabaloo in such a short period of time.

If nothing else, the Dew Drop Inn would be the talk of Willowbrook, at least until the festival. Gerty was probably already gathering her talking points as she prepared Aldric a bath.

Marigold took a sip of tea and savored the smooth, nutty flavor as she opened her father's journal. A touch of sweetness from the wildflower honey lingered on her tongue as she found her place. Since that evening with Poppy in the cellar, she'd taken to reading an entry or two each day. At first, it had been strange to read about the winery from her father's point of view, but after a while, it felt more like a conversation. They had shared so many similar experiences over the years, and the pages were filled with hard-earned wisdom. Marigold often found herself nodding along or shaking her head as her father described the challenges of running an inn and vineyard. She wondered what he would think of their eclectic guests of late.

Elara knocked on the doorframe. "Busy?"

"Just ruminating." Marigold closed the journal. "Everything okay?"

"Everything is fine. I was on my way to find you earlier when all of the chaos happened." Her brow furrowed. "I've never seen Onyx act like that. There's more fight left in him than I thought."

"Yeah, it was strange, but at least no one got hurt. I'm not sure even Elmwood could spin that story into a positive." Marigold sipped her tea. "What was it you wanted to talk about?"

"I think we'll be ready to harvest in a couple of weeks. We should probably post a notice in town on your next trip to let everyone know."

"I'll add it to the list."

Elara turned to leave but then paused. "Actually, there is one more thing. Have you given any more thought to which wine we should enter in this year's festival?"

That was the one thing she'd been purposefully putting off. Choosing which wine to enter in the annual tasting competition was a reminder of all her past failures. Ten years of them. Her chest tightened just thinking about it.

Marigold sighed. "Not yet, but I'll get around to it."

"Hey." Elara smiled. "This year is going to be different. I can feel it."

For dinner, Locke served fish stew with saffron and leeks. The dish was perfect for the warmer months since it wasn't too heavy, and with fall around the corner, this was probably the last time it would be served until next spring.

Despite the recipe's simplicity, the stew was layered and complex. Local fish offered a fresh, slightly sweet flavor that paired well with the floral and earthy notes of the saffron. Unlike regular onions, the leeks brought a milder essence—similar to a sweet onion—that didn't overpower the other ingredients.

Locke stood just inside the doorframe of the kitchen, looking content as he listened to the sounds of slurping and spoons scraping against bowls.

Marigold patted the dwarf on the shoulder. "If their empty bowls are any indication, you've outdone yourself again."

"I can't take all the credit on this one. I learned this recipe from an old dwarven fisherman." Locke stroked his beard. "Typically, it uses saltwater fish for their natural brininess, but I make my own salt brine to replicate the flavor."

After dinner, most of the guests lingered about downstairs. That in itself wasn't an uncommon occurrence, since guests would often read, play games, or have a drink at the bar, but tonight, the energy was different from usual, and it was pretty easy to tell why.

Aldric sat in a wingback chair near the fire, smoking his pipe and knitting a scarf, oblivious to the atmosphere around him. After taking a bath to wash off the dust from traveling, the mage had changed into a purple silk gown patterned with yellow moons and stars. He reminded Marigold of the depictions of mages in the fairy tales she'd read as a child. There was a far-off look in Aldric's eyes as his long, slender fingers worked with practiced precision. Splinter nestled in the chair next to the mage, the end of the gray scarf tucked over the construct like a blanket.

Marigold knew precious little about golems, constructs, or whatever someone chose to call them, but now she wondered if they required sleep, and more than that, how much awareness they actually had. Splinter had seemed perceptive enough earlier, enough to be fearful of Onyx, and there was a strange understanding etched into his wooden face as the dark knots that mimicked eyes expanded and contracted.

Her gaze swept across the rest of the room as she polished a glass. Poppy lay on a sofa with a book open across her chest. Every so often, she'd glance at Aldric. There was no doubt she had a million questions burning inside of her. At a nearby table, a human and halfling played a game of checkers, and they also seemed distracted by the mage's presence.

The only guests not focused on the mage were a dwarven family sitting on the floor in front of the hearth. The mother and father sat across from one another, watching their child with adoration as she played with a stuffed bear between them. The girl couldn't be more than a year or two, yet she already had a generous amount of fuzz across her cheeks.

She squeezed the bear to her chest and mumbled incoherently before flinging the stuffed toy with all the strength her little body could muster. The bear soared over Aldric's head, lodging between the back of his chair and the wall.

The girl let out a squeal of delight and waddled over to the mage. She leaned against his leg, babbling as she reached toward the toy above his head.

Splinter poked Aldric in the side, and the mage snapped back to reality. He watched the girl with curiosity. "Well, hello to you, too."

"Apologies, Mr. Oldheim, sir." The girl's father wore a worried expression. "She doesn't know her own strength yet."

Aldric set the scarf aside, covering Splinter in yarn. "She has quite the arm on her."

"That she does." The dwarf beamed with pride. "Her grandpappy was a boulder-tosser for the mining company. It's in her blood."

Aldric reached over his shoulder to grab the bear. His brow furrowed as he examined the toy. "Would you mind if I altered the bear? Nothing permanent, of course."

The father exchanged a look with his wife, then nodded. "Help yerself."

The mage placed the bear on his knee, and the girl's eyes lit up with excitement. A stream of gibberish flowed from her mouth.

"Do you want to see something special?" Aldric asked.

Her tiny hands reached for the bear.

Aldric held up a finger. "Not yet, little one. Give me one moment."

The girl's mother scooted closer, gathering the child in her arms while the mage worked.

He held the bear about the midsection, and it was as if all the life had been sucked from the room as everyone watched expectantly. A soft glow of violet energy emanated from his hands and quickly seeped into the stuffed animal, infusing its brown fabric with a similar aura.

Marigold found herself captivated by the display. Poppy abandoned all pretense of reading her book and sat on the edge of the sofa.

Aldric placed the bear on the floor, and it fell forward, slumping like Elmwood after one too many drinks. Aside from the babbling child and crackling fire, the room was silent.

The bear twitched, and the mother gasped, her grip tightening around her child protectively. The bear's head moved as the toy sat up. It looked around the room with its button eyes, as if it was taking it all in. After a moment, the bear stood, and in a similar fashion to the child, it waddled toward her.

The girl giggled with excitement, clapping her hands together as the bear wrapped its soft arms around her foot.

Aldric smiled. "The enchantment will fade in a day or two, but it should provide plenty of entertainment in the meantime."

The father's mouth was agape as he watched the toy move of its own accord. "Thank you, sir," he finally managed to say as he nodded his appreciation.

For the next little while, the bear roamed the downstairs with the girl following its every move. Splinter joined the parade, somehow knowledgeable enough to stay just out of the young dwarf's reach.

Eventually, the guests made their way upstairs for the night, except for Aldric who continued to knit by the fire. Locke and Elara sat at the bar with Marigold as she cleaned up.

Locke raised a brow as he watched Aldric. "Is he knitting a scarf for a giant?"

Marigold had wondered herself. The thing was long enough to fill the mage's lap and still drape to the floor.

"Who knows, maybe he'll turn it into a snake." Elara grinned as she trailed a finger down Locke's forearm in a snake-like pattern.

Locke grunted. "Don't even joke about that. You know I don't like snakes." He downed the last of his ale and slid the mug to Marigold. "Time to call it a night. See you in the morning, Mari."

"Good night, Locke."

Elara stood to join him. She reached across the bar, placing a hand on top of Marigold's. "About earlier... I don't mean to put any added pressure on you."

"I know." Marigold squeezed the elf's hand. "You're right, though. We need to decide soon."

"Just don't overthink it. I'll see you tomorrow."

Don't overthink it. Marigold shook her head and sighed. After ten years of going in circles, it was hard not to. Should she stick to something traditional, like honeywine, or try something bold and unexpected, like a blend? Whatever she chose, it would have to compete against Darkroot Cellars.

She was so engrossed in her thoughts that she didn't notice Aldric had left his seat by the fire until a barstool grated against the floor in front of her.

"Mind if I have a nightcap?" he asked as he set Splinter on the counter. The construct walked the length of the bar, examining all of the glassware and bar tools.

"Not at all." Marigold smiled at how cute the little stickman was as he picked up a piece of cork. "What can I get for you?"

Aldric shrugged. "You're the expert. You tell me."

"Well, it depends on what you like." She gestured at the bottles lining the shelf. "Anything catch your eye?"

"I've never been too concerned with outward appearances. It's what's on the inside that matters." He winked. "That goes for wine and for people."

Marigold grinned. "I like that." She tapped her chin as she looked at their selection. "Let's see, then. Honeywine is our traditional halfling wine. It's on the sweeter side. The emberfruit is more citrusy, while the dreamcatcher has more floral notes and a crisp finish. We have a couple of blends as well, and if you like something rich and robust, there's always the moonshadow varietal. Personally, I'd go with a fortified wine. It's a little heavier, but it goes down smooth, perfect for a nightcap."

"Fortified wine it is."

Marigold poured two glasses and slid one across the bar. "That was very nice, what you did for the little girl earlier."

Aldric swirled the fortified wine and sniffed the glass. "We could all use a little magic in our lives from time to time."

"I'll drink to that." Marigold clinked her glass against

the mage's and took a sip. There was a hint of spice to the fortified wine, but the most prominent flavors were ripe, dark fruits. It was much more full-bodied than even the most robust moonshadow wine, almost syrupy in its consistency, but the natural acidity brought the wine full circle, and left it with a rich, refreshing finish. "Is that why you also do the firelights?"

"Hmm. I'd never considered that. Maybe on some level. What I do know is that there are forces in this world that push and pull us in different directions. Forces beyond our understanding." Aldric tilted his head as if he was seeing Marigold in a new light. "Mages may have power, but they're not the only ones capable of magic. It's all around us if you know where to look. Tell me, is there anything more spectacular than a child's laughter? Have you ever watched the stars with the one you loved, or drifted to sleep upon their chest while listening to a rainstorm lullaby? True magic can't be conjured." He downed the rest of his drink and then held out his hand so Splinter could climb into his palm. "Thanks for the nightcap. It's time for me to rest these old bones. Good night."

"Good night, Aldric." Marigold finished her wine and wiped down the bar a final time. The mage's words replayed in her mind.

On her way to bed, she stopped outside Poppy's room, listening to the scratch of a quill on the other side of the door as the gnome worked late into the night. Marigold closed her eyes, remembering Poppy's hands around hers as they rode into town. Her stomach fluttered at the memory.

Maybe Aldric was right.

She swallowed hard and knocked gently on the door.

The quill silenced, followed by soft footsteps before the door swung open.

"Marigold?" Poppy had on a cream-colored nightgown. She wore a surprised expression as she met the halfling's eyes. "Everything alright?"

"Everything's fine." Heat rushed to Marigold's cheeks. "I heard you working, so I thought I would ask you something before I forgot."

"What is it?"

Marigold's heart raced as she gathered her courage. "I was thinking of picking a pumpkin tomorrow, and I, uh, I wanted to see if you'd like to join me?"

"Pumpkin picking?" Poppy grinned. "That sounds delightful. As long as there are no trees involved."

"I promise." Marigold placed a hand over her heart. "I, Marigold Bramblefoot, will not climb any pumpkin trees tomorrow."

Poppy laughed. "That's good enough for me."

"Alright then, see you tomorrow."

The door closed, and Marigold leaned against the wall. Her entire body tingled with nervous excitement.

"That wasn't so hard, was it?" she whispered to herself. Now, if she could only channel some of that confidence for the harvest festival, she might finally decide on a wine to enter.

12. MYSTERIOUS HAPPENINGS

The next morning, Marigold hummed with excitement as she toured the grounds with Elara. Onyx trailed behind them, his paws wet with dew as they walked each row of the vineyard checking stems, assessing the grapes' texture and color, and tasting their sweetness. All of this in order to gauge how soon they would need to be harvested.

There was no hard rule on when to harvest, and most of it came down to a vintner's intuition. White grapes tended to be harvested first, usually followed by red grapes a week or so later. There were certain varietals—like gnomish icewine or those used for dessert wines—that would stay on the vine a little longer to gather the maximum amount of sweetness, but those weren't commonly grown in Tyne.

"You seem awfully chipper this morning," Elara said, taking a bite of a honey grape and puckering as she let the juice settle in her mouth. "What did you do now?"

"I didn't do anything." Marigold tried to fight the heat

rushing to her cheeks but it was no use. "I'm a happy, happy halfling. It's kind of what we're known for."

"Is that so?" Elara burst out laughing, and strands of golden hair fluttered in the breeze. "I'd say you're known for your ravenous appetites and lackadaisical attitudes. More than that, I know you, and I know when you're hiding something."

Marigold pretended to focus on the vine in front of her. Nothing ever got past Elara. The elf was as perceptive as a griffin.

A grape thunked against Marigold's chest, and she looked up to see Elara with her hands on her hips.

"Well?"

"Fine." Marigold feigned annoyance, but she couldn't hide the smile. "I was talking to Aldric last night after you all went to bed. He's a bit out there, but there's a surprising amount of wisdom in his words. The short version is that he got me thinking, and so I asked Poppy if she wanted to go pick a pumpkin with me today."

Elara wore a devilish grin. "So you're finally ready to admit it?"

"Admit what?" Marigold covered her mouth to hide the blossoming smile.

"Marigold Bramblefoot, I swear. Admit you like her or I'll have Gerty yell it across town."

"Fine, fine." Marigold threw her hands in the air. "Fine. I like her. I like Poppy. Are you happy?"

"So happy." The elf wrapped her arms around Marigold and squeezed. "What was it the old kook said to get you in your feelings?"

Marigold chuckled. "Something about how the real magic was all around us."

"You're as bad as Locke, I swear." Elara cackled. "How did I find myself surrounded by such softies?"

Marigold reached and tapped a finger at Elara's chest. "Because deep down in that cold elven heart of yours, there's a warm, gooey center."

They finished with the honey and emberfruit grapes and were about to start on the dreamcatcher when Elara came to a stop.

"You have got to be shitting me." She frowned as she ran her hand along a vine that had been stripped of all its fruit.

Marigold mirrored the elf's expression. This was odd. A ten-foot section had been picked clean, removing the grapes and leaving the stems behind. It wasn't that the fruit was gone, but the way in which they'd been removed. Somehow, the grapes had been detached from the bunch without breaking a single stem. The skeletal clusters still hung on the vine, and grape seeds littered the ground below. It was as if they'd been plucked one grape at a time, eaten, and then the seeds were spat onto the ground.

Marigold stared at the vine, equally perplexed. "How is this possible?"

"Damned rabbits." Elara scowled at Onyx as he sunbathed in the grass.

"I don't think so." Marigold knelt, examining the lowest leaves on the vine. They were untouched. "Rabbits have an appetite for the leaves, not the fruit, and these haven't been touched. Look. Plus, that wouldn't explain how the grapes were removed from the stems without damaging anything else. There's not even any flesh left on the stems. This doesn't make any sense."

"You're right." Elara sighed. "Could it have been birds or some rowdy kids in search of a snack?"

Marigold shrugged. "Birds usually eat the seeds, too, and if this was the work of troublemakers, why not take the cluster and run? It must have taken hours to pick the grapes off individually like this."

Elara snapped an empty cluster from the vine and examined it. "There's some kind of residue on here." She held it up to the sunlight. "It's faint, but it kind of shimmers, almost like a snail trail. Do you think the wards are failing?"

"Strange." Marigold squinted at the empty cluster. They had wards around the property for keeping out pests during the fruiting season. Even if it were snails, she'd never seen them behave in such a strange manner. The few times they'd invaded the garden, their damage was always sporadic, leaving a trail of holes and slime. Whatever had done this had been precise, picking the row clean without damaging the vines. She tried to make sense of the damage, but to no avail. "I don't think it's snails, but if you see Finn before I do, have him pay the wardmaster a visit to make sure everything is still working properly."

Marigold was still pondering the mystery later that afternoon as she swept the front porch. It wasn't the first time there'd been a mysterious occurrence around the inn. There was the time a guest thought they saw spirits roaming the vineyard, but those had turned out to be nothing more than a flock of wisps. Or the time an apple tree burst into flames when a fire sprite made a home inside its hollow. Her personal favorite was when she'd tried to convince her parents that the attic was haunted so they wouldn't discover the baby opossum she and Finn were trying to keep as a pet.

Whatever was happening to the grapes, there had to be a logical explanation.

She heard the sound of wagon wheels a moment before Aldric appeared around the corner of the inn. The mage puffed his pipe, leaving a trail of smoke in his wake as the enchanted cart rolled behind him. She waved to him, and he stopped, raising his staff in acknowledgment. Splinter poked his head out of Aldric's satchel, offering a salute.

"Off to town?" Marigold asked.

"Having dinner with the mayor to discuss the festival."

Marigold leaned on the broom handle. "We can always give you a ride into town if you need it."

"Appreciated, but not necessary. I need to bring ol' Bertha along to pick up a few supplies while I'm there. Besides, I have this." He tapped the front of the cart with his staff, and something shifted within, wood groaning as a seat emerged at the front. "For when I'm feeling lazy."

Marigold chuckled. "That cart is a wonder."

"Perks of the job." Aldric winked and set off for town.

As the cart rolled away, Marigold went back inside. Poppy was already waiting downstairs, her nose buried in a book. She wore the same flattering tan trousers and red tunic from their last outing.

For a moment, Marigold watched the gnome. Her purple eyes flitted across the page, and strands of sapphire hair fell upon her dusty-pink skin. Whatever Poppy was reading must have been captivating, because she didn't acknowledge Marigold's presence even when the halfling was standing right beside her.

"Hey there," Marigold whispered.

Poppy tensed, clutching the book to her chest. "Oh, hi." She let out a shallow breath. "You startled me." She sat up, closed the book, and placed it on the table. "I get lost in my own world sometimes."

"Must be pretty interesting to have you so engrossed." Marigold grinned. "Ready for our next adventure?"

Poppy removed her spectacles, folding the frames, and setting them on top of the book. "Hopefully, this quest is a little more laid-back than the last one."

"We can hope, but you know what they say." Marigold waggled her brows. "A proper adventurer must always be prepared for the unexpected."

"I should probably go grab my sword, then."

"Don't worry." Marigold pulled a pair of shears from her apron. "These will protect us."

"My hero!" Poppy placed both hands over her heart. "In that case, I think we're ready."

"My lady." Marigold bent forward, mimicking the motions of a knight as she offered the gnome her hand. After a day of mystery, it was time for a little magic.

13. SPIRIT LANTERNS

Marigold and Poppy walked among the pumpkins, dried leaves crunching beneath their boots.

The patch was located on the western edge of the property, serving as a natural border between the Dew Drop Vineyard and the neighboring farmlands of the Hilltopper family. At this point in the season, most of the greenery had shriveled into brown stalks, leaving the countryside dotted with orange, yellow, white, and the occasional blue pumpkin.

"Want to know something interesting?" asked Marigold.

"Always." Poppy pressed her hands together as if she were in for a surprise.

Marigold loved the childlike excitement that radiated from the gnome any time she could learn something new. When so many people were stubborn or set in their ways, it was an endearing quality.

"Before my father first bought the property, it was all mostly farmland, and the pumpkin patch served as a barrier between the two farms. The thing is, both families had worked the lands for so long that neither one could remember who actually planted the patch to begin with." She pointed at the neighboring farm. "That's the Hilltopper farm. The family liked the idea of having a winery within walking distance, so instead of fighting over this piece of land, they came to a compromise with my parents. As a gesture of goodwill, the Hilltoppers offered to maintain the patch. They would sell pumpkins at the market, and in exchange, we could pick as many as we wanted for us and our guests."

"Really? I don't think anyone back home would be so generous." Poppy knelt, grabbing a pumpkin by the stem. "City folk are a different breed. They're liable to— Ouch!" She dropped the pumpkin, and it hit the ground with a thud. "What the hells?" Poppy grimaced as she kissed her fingers. "You didn't tell me they bite."

"Sorry!" Marigold fought to keep from laughing. Not at the gnome's pain, but at her expression of betrayal. "I'm sorry. It's not funny. It's just—" Marigold held a fist to her mouth, tears brimming in her eyes. "—your face. It caught me off guard."

"I'm glad my pain can amuse you." Poppy narrowed her eyes, but there was a playfulness to her tone.

"I'm sorry." Marigold wiped a tear away. "It's really not funny."

"It's fine." Poppy was grinning now, her eyes wrinkled at the edges. "I was once kicked out of a lecture because I couldn't stop laughing at the way the light gleamed off the professor's head."

"I bet that was a sad day for you."

"It really was." Poppy frowned. "I missed a lecture on

the fall of Hells' Crag. And let me tell you, that is a fascinating subject."

Marigold pulled a pair of gloves from her apron and offered them to Poppy. "I should have given you these to start with. Some of the stems can be prickly."

"I knew I should have researched beforehand." Poppy rubbed her fingers together. When she was satisfied that they no longer hurt, she put on the gloves. "So, how does one properly select a pumpkin? I've never picked one before."

Marigold grabbed a nearby pumpkin by the stem, her calloused fingers unaware of the prickly spurs. "It depends on what you want to use it for. There are probably a dozen varietals throughout the patch with different colors, thicknesses, and flavor profiles. Some can be baked whole, others are great for pies or mixing with ale." She held the pumpkin for Poppy to see. It was white with faded green ribs that looked like stripes. "The first thing you want to check for is firmness. Especially the bottom."

"Who doesn't love a firm bottom?" Poppy smirked.

Marigold's cheeks flushed. She swallowed the lump in her throat and tried to ignore her spiking pulse by patting the pumpkin on the side. "Once you have a nice firm pumpkin—" She cleared her throat. "—you'll want to give it a little tap, like this." She tapped the pumpkin, and a hollow sound rang out. "Give it a try."

Poppy repeated the action, tapping the pumpkin several times until she created a similar sound.

"When it comes to color, you generally want one that's a solid color from top to bottom. Except for these guys." Marigold picked up an orange pumpkin that was speckled with green, wart-like lumps. "These are called warty goblins. Despite its grotesque appearance, they are surprisingly sweet." She set it down and moved on to a traditional orange pumpkin. "Make sure there aren't any soft spots or blemishes. Then, you check at the stem. Dark brown is the best but dark green works too. The pumpkin's shape isn't that important, but it can play a role depending on what you're using it for. The round ones are easier to carve for spirit lanterns, and they also tend to have more seeds for roasting. The oddly shaped ones are nice for decorating, but they can be a pain to carve."

"What's a spirit lantern?" Poppy wore a curious expression.

Marigold raised a brow. "You've never heard of a spirit lantern?"

The gnome shook her head.

"Hmm. I was going to give whatever we picked to Locke for a pie, but now I have an even better idea." Marigold placed the pumpkin on the ground and clapped her hands. "It must be your lucky day, Poppy Deepspring, because there's no better way to learn something than with your own two hands."

Poppy raised a finger. "Well, actually, there are several schools of thought on the subject."

"Remember what I said about experiences?" Marigold wagged her finger in challenge. "This is your chance to embrace one of the oldest halfling traditions. Pretty soon, there'll be a spirit lantern outside of every home from Honeydale to Hillside. Trust me, it'll be fun."

"Alright, professor." Poppy looked out over the patch. "Where do we start?"

"First, we need to find the right pumpkins. You're going to be carving it, so I suggest picking one of the rounder ones. But in the end, it's all about finding one that speaks to you."

Poppy frowned. "But I still don't know what a spirit lantern is."

"That'll be covered in the second part of the lesson."

As they walked the patch turning pumpkins this way and that to check for bruises and coloring, the sun crept toward the horizon, casting their diminutive frames as giant shadows across the field. They searched until they both found a pumpkin they were happy with. Marigold's was a tall, orange oval with a stem that curled into a wispy end like a lizard tail. Poppy chose a ghost pumpkin. It was white with a bulky base and had a thick, dark green stem.

Marigold gave Poppy an approving look. "Those make for great spirit lanterns."

The gnome patted the bottom as she held her pumpkin up. "Nice and firm, see?"

Luckily for Marigold, the fading daylight concealed her blushing cheeks.

When they arrived back at the inn, the sun had completely set. The night sky was overcast, blocking out the moon and stars, and an evening breeze passed through the trees as Marigold set her pumpkin on a table near the firepit.

She smiled to herself. A windy night was perfect for telling a spooky story.

Poppy placed her pumpkin next to Marigold's. "It's pretty dark. I guess we'll have to carve them tomorrow."

"Nonsense." Marigold tossed a few logs into the pit

from the nearby pile. "There's nothing better than carving a spirit lantern by firelight."

Once she had the fire roaring, Marigold went inside to gather carving knives, spoons, and bowls for the pumpkin seeds and innards.

When she returned, she sat across from Poppy, momentarily mesmerized by the flames dancing in the gnome's eyes as she organized her bowl and utensils.

Poppy leaned forward. "Do I finally get to learn about the mysterious spirit lanterns?"

"I'll explain the process first, and then I'll tell you about the origin. How's that sound?"

"Why must you torture me?" The gnome bit her lip.

Marigold gulped. There was something incredibly attractive about the act, and she had to force her mind away from more dangerous thoughts. She rolled her pumpkin across the table until it was sitting in front of her. "First, we'll cut a hole around the stem so that it can serve as a lid." She stabbed her knife into the top of the gourd, making Poppy jump as the bowls rattled. "Make it wide enough to fit your hand and spoon inside, because things are about to get messy."

She carved a circle while Poppy did the same. Once the hole was cut, they removed the top. Strands of pumpkin flesh and seeds clung to the bottom of the lid, so Marigold sliced them off and tossed them in the bowl.

"Now, you want to scrape out as much of the pulp as possible. The fleshy part can be used for pies and purees, and the seeds are great for roasting. The thinner you make the walls, the better it will be when we start the next part."

Poppy looked up as she scooped. "You're a good teacher, you know that?"

"Really?" Marigold leaned back in surprise.

"I know I've been teasing you, but you're very thorough and detail-oriented. For someone who has spent a lifetime learning, I appreciate it."

"Well, thanks." Marigold stared at her pumpkin.

"You're not good with compliments, are you?" There was a softness to the gnome's voice.

Marigold met her eyes. "What gave it away?"

"I think you know." Poppy chuckled. "But it's okay, pobody's nerfect."

Marigold snorted. "Pobody's nerfect. I've never heard that one before."

"Some scholarly humor for you." Poppy smiled. "We say it whenever someone makes an error or misquotes something."

They worked in silence for a moment, the sounds of the night mixing with scraping spoons and pulp sloshing into piles. Once the insides were empty, Marigold held up her knife.

"Now comes the fun part." She waved the blade, and it flickered with the fire's reflection. "This is where we carve faces into the side of the pumpkins to ward off the dead."

Poppy tilted her head like Onyx when he heard a strange sound.

Marigold laughed. "What?"

"Oh, nothing. I just never took you as the superstitious type."

Marigold grinned. "Halflings aren't a very superstitious people, at least not by dwarven standards, but we do have a few eccentricities, spirit lanterns being one of them."

"Okay…" Poppy nodded. "Do I get the full story now?"

"Soon." Marigold stuck out her tongue. "Just a few tips to get you started. I find it works best if you draw the face on before you start carving. That way you ensure you have enough room to fit all the features. Other than that, it's up to your imagination. The scarier the better."

Marigold took the smallest knife and used it to etch the outline into the pumpkin. As she and Poppy worked, Marigold began the story of the spirit lanterns.

"Long ago, when Aedrea was still young and the gods walked the realm, there were no such things as seasons. Wherever Melora traveled, flowers blossomed and trees bore fruit in the wake of the Goddess of the Harvest." Marigold paused to admire the outline she'd etched with its angular eyes and a mouth of sharp teeth. She scratched two nostril holes into the pumpkin and continued. "Her brother Umbrus, the God of Gloom, resided in the shadow realm. It was his responsibility to guide lost souls through the long night and into the underworld. Together, the siblings brought balance through life and death."

Poppy looked up, smiled, and then focused on her pumpkin. She wore the same expression of concentration that Marigold often saw when the gnome was making notes or writing in her journal.

Marigold stuck her knife into the pumpkin and started carving. "One day, Umbrus tired of a life between worlds, so he struck a bargain with Melora. For most of the year, he would fulfill his duties as usual, but for a season, he wished to walk upon the mortal plane. Melora knew the toll that his presence would take on the world, for everywhere that Umbrus went, a chill followed. If he walked the earth, crops would wither, and the days would grow shorter as the gloom grasped for its god. Melora warned her followers of the incoming cold and darkness, and in preparation, they would store what they could to survive the winter. This became known as the harvest. Now, every year, when Umbrus walks among the living, a cold descends upon the realm, and the nights grow longer. With no one to guide them to the underworld, the spirits become restless wanderers, and as the trees go barren and leaves turn to dust under autumn boots, the dead roam, waiting for the first sprout that will reclaim the spring and send them to their next life."

Poppy froze, her knife buried halfway into the pumpkin. "Is this a ghost story?"

Marigold shrugged, her grin covered by shadow as she continued to carve. "With nowhere to go, the spirits drift through the darkness, their whispers carried by the wind. In the cold discontent, their spectral bodies search for warmth. If you ever hear a scratch against your window in the dead of night, or the rustle of branches beneath a starless sky, it's the spirits begging for the glow of the hearth."

"Spooky." Poppy looked over her shoulder as something rustled in the garden. "You actually tell this story to children?"

Marigold forced her smile away. She was used to the sounds of the vineyard at night, but they could be unsettling to city folk. "Children get a simpler version, but I thought you would enjoy the full experience. You know, for research."

"Lucky me." Poppy laughed nervously as she returned her attention to the pumpkin.

Marigold admired her own. She was no great artist, but the lack of symmetry could add to the frightful effect. "Thanks to Melora's warning, my ancestors devised a plan to protect our homes by using lanterns to ward our doors from the roaming spirits. We carve the pumpkins and place a candle inside so that when the spirits look upon their glowing, monstrous faces, they're frightened and turn away."

Poppy crossed her arms. "You don't actually think—" There was a chilling creak as a branch scraped against the shed. Her gaze narrowed as she stared over her shoulder into the darkness. "Real funny."

A breeze passed overhead, and the tree groaned as its branches shook and rustled.

"What? It wasn't me." Marigold scanned their surroundings, but the cloudy sky made the night darker than usual. "Maybe the spirits have something to say."

She stood, holding the end of a long candle to the fire until it lit. She used it to light a smaller candle inside the pumpkin, igniting the lantern's features and giving life to its monstrous fangs and demonic eyes. She turned it to face Poppy.

"Wow, you're talented." The gnome pulled her pumpkin closer as if to hide it.

"Let's see yours." Marigold slid a candle across the table.

Poppy grimaced as she placed the candle inside and lit it. "Don't laugh."

When she turned the pumpkin around, Marigold couldn't help it. She burst into laughter at the lantern's small, uneven eyes. They were so far apart that the pumpkin looked surprised, and what were supposed to be fangs looked more like two snaggleteeth dangling from the top of its wide and gaping mouth.

Poppy huffed. "I told you not to laugh."

"I'm sorry." Marigold wiped a tear from her eye. "But that's too adorable."

The gnome's scowl twisted into a smile as she walked around the table to join Marigold, placing the pumpkins side by side. "It is kind of cute, isn't it?"

A loud shriek came from the shed, and they both jumped. Marigold's heart raced as she looked around. The other noises she could explain, but not this one.

"That wasn't a tree branch," she said, stepping closer to Poppy.

Poppy clutched the halfling's arm. "Then what was it?"

"Who's there?" Marigold called.

To their left, something stirred in the bushes. They both froze, and all around, objects thunked in the darkness.

The fire pit roared as something crashed into the embers, sending a plume of ash and glowing cinders into the air.

Poppy screamed, wrapping her arms around Marigold. She held the halfling so tight that Marigold could feel the gnome's heart thundering against her chest.

"Let's go inside." Marigold placed her arm around Poppy.

They turned around to see a figure in white standing on the other side of the fire.

Their screams echoed across the night as Elara tilted her head back and laughed maniacally, apples tumbling from her arms. Onyx weaved between the elf's legs, unconcerned with the chaos around him. "You should have seen the look on your faces!" she cackled. "Wait until I tell Locke about this. He's going to love it."

"You!" Poppy's voice was a mixture of terror and relief.

"Elara Moongrove, you are the most devilish person I know." Marigold wanted to be upset, but Poppy still clung to her side, making it hard to feel anything other than nervous excitement.

"I couldn't help myself." Elara walked over. "I saw you carving pumpkins, and once the clouds came out and the wind picked up, the opportunity was too good to pass up. Onyx almost gave me away traipsing through the garden."

Marigold frowned at the dire cat. "Traitor."

He let out a raspy meow and rubbed his head against her legs.

Elara approached, resting a hand on Marigold's shoulder. She leaned in and whispered, "You're welcome."

Marigold met Elara's mischievous gaze as the elf pulled away. If not for Poppy's warm body pressed against her own, she'd have been furious.

When Elara finally noticed the two pumpkins on the table, she started grinning.

"Not a word." Poppy finally let go of Marigold, crossing her arms and tilting her head up to stare down the elf.

"Alright, alright. I'll leave you to it." Elara held up her hands, slowly backing away. "Say hello to the spirits for me."

Once Elara was out of sight, Marigold turned to Poppy. "Sorry about that. She can be a child at times."

Poppy chuckled. "It's kind of funny after the fact."

"Yeah." Marigold smiled. "Kind of. Want to put our pumpkins on the porch?"

Poppy frowned, her gaze darting to the table. "You're not ashamed of mine?"

"Not in the slightest." Marigold moved her pumpkin closer to Poppy's. "I think they make a good pair."

"They do balance each other out." The gnome laughed.

As they carried their lanterns to the front porch, Marigold kept thinking about the warmth of Poppy's touch. Amidst the terror and uncertainty of the moment, the gnome had turned to her for safety.

Marigold wasn't that different from the pumpkin she carried. A flame had sparked inside her, and its glow could keep all the terrors at bay.

14. SPIRITED DISCUSSIONS

A yellow leaf tumbled down the dirt path of the inn, carried by the autumn wind. Summer had officially waned, and the timeline for harvesting the vineyard was ticking down.

Finn pulled the wagon to a stop beside the porch, and Marigold climbed inside. He flicked the reins, and Acorn Blossom took off at a slow trot toward town. The pony's mane had been braided again, Gerty's handiwork, and tied at the end with a yellow bow.

Three days had passed since the incident with the missing grapes, and they were no closer to understanding the culprit. Elara had walked the grounds every morning, but so far, it appeared to have been an isolated incident. That didn't make the crime any less mysterious, but for now, it wasn't a pressing issue.

Finn had inquired with the wardmaster two days prior, and according to his records, the wards weren't due to be recharged until next year. He was too busy to make a house call this week, so instead, Marigold and Finn were bringing the wards to his shop for an inspection.

The enchanted crystals sat in a basket at Finn's feet, wrapped in fabric, occasionally clinking as the wagon bumped along. The vineyard would be without protection from pests and certain creatures for the next few hours, but this late in the season, it wouldn't be much of an issue.

Marigold's mind was elsewhere as they rolled into town. She held a scroll case in her lap, the handwritten notice for their vineyard's grape harvest stuffed inside the wooden tube. She'd stop by Town Hall once they were finished with the wards. While Gerty would do a fine job spreading the word on her own, posting a request for volunteers at Town Hall was the best way to ensure that everyone knew about it.

The harvest was always a wonderful time of celebration and fellowship, but it meant they were that much closer to the harvest festival, and she still needed to select a wine to enter.

Even though the decision loomed like a dark cloud, a smile tugged at the corners of Marigold's mouth. She'd been preoccupied with other things of late.

At first, Marigold had been irked by Elara's antics during the pumpkin carving, but it seemed the elf was an evil genius. Some invisible wall had crumbled between Marigold and Poppy in the days that followed. The gnome worked downstairs more often than she had before, and there were times when their eyes would meet as Marigold crossed the room, followed by a sheepish smile or rosy cheeks. Yesterday, Poppy had lingered at the bar long after the other guests had retired, the two of them talking late into the night.

Marigold's fingers clenched around the scroll case. While the notice inside promised good times were on the horizon, it was also a reminder that once the festival was over, Poppy's time here would be too. Between her interviews and research, she had plenty of information on the festival. All she had to do now was experience it herself. That was the final piece of the puzzle, and then she'd be off to her fast-paced city living once again.

The halfling shook her head, pushing those thoughts from her mind. There was no point in dwelling on the future. The only time they were promised was the here and now, and she'd be grateful for every moment of it. It was like her father always said, 'cherish the moments you have, not the ones you wish for.'

Finn pulled the wagon to a stop outside of Windell's Wards. The shop was located within a moss-covered hill on one of the higher streets. A long winding path dotted with stepping stones led to a rustic wooden archway built into the hillside. There was a circular door at its center, and a window to each side. Crystals dangled from the wooden beam over the door, similar to the ones Finn carried in the basket.

A gong-like chime echoed as they entered. Amber light cast the shop in a warm glow from the enchanted glow-stones. There were displays of various wards on each side of the room, and a long counter that separated the display area from Windell's workspace.

The halfling with the frizzy, gray-hair leaned over a cerulean crystal, holding it steady beneath a magnifying glass as he etched a symbol into the side. "One moment, dears."

"Take your time," Marigold said as she perused the shop.

The majority of the wards in Windell's shop were dedicated to farming or gardening. The most common were for repelling various pests or preventing disease, but many gardeners used wards to protect their flowers from a late frost. There were also wards for certain magical creatures, pixies being the most common, but those tended to be less effective. When it came to magical beings, the smartest route was usually to hire an adventurer to root them out.

Marigold had always been fascinated by how wards worked. They came in various shapes and sizes, each one with different effect radiuses or alarm signals. Those for prevention usually functioned passively, emitting a constant aura that kept the subject at bay when it approached too close. And then there were protective or one-time-use wards that would glow when activated. Those needed to be recharged after each use.

The Bank of Aedrea was said to use some of the most complex wards in the realm, and in some of the larger cities, there were ward shops that catered almost exclusively to adventurers. She'd heard that one could buy a shrieking ward that would let out a loud scream when activated, but those were said to cost a small fortune.

Wards might not be as exciting as Runetech, but as far as Marigold was concerned, they were just as valuable, especially for someone in her situation. And if she couldn't have a druid to save her crops, then wards were the next best thing for preventing catastrophe.

She was inspecting an intruder ward when Windell approached.

The elder halfling leaned on the counter from the other side, his bushy gray eyebrows were like two furry caterpillars, nearly concealing his brown eyes. "Good to see you, Mari. Finn tells me the wards may be acting up."

She joined him by the counter. "We're not sure, to be honest." She went on to tell him about the missing grapes and the filmy residue left behind.

"Now that is strange. Sounds like it could be a slime, but we're much too far south. You don't hear about those much outside of the dwarven mountains." Windell pressed a finger to his chin. "Let's see the wards first, and then we'll go from there."

Finn placed the basket on the counter and removed the fabric.

Marigold watched with intrigue as one by one, Windell lifted the wards and closed his eyes as he sensed some hidden property within. She knew some of the theory behind wardmaking, but it was fascinating to watch it in action. Not just anyone could craft wards, and those who could were similar to mages in a way, able to tap into the arcane and infuse the stones with mana. She'd read that for repellent wards, the wardmaster needed a sample from whatever they were trying to fend off, but beyond that, it was all magic to her.

Windell inspected the last ward and placed it on the counter. "They're all still charged. Whatever has gotten into your grapes, it's not because of the wards failing." He helped return the crystals to the basket. "I wish I could be of more help."

"You've been plenty of help." Marigold tapped him on the arm. Knowing the wards were working properly was another piece of the puzzle they could fill in.

"Say…" He gave her a warm smile. "How are your folks? It's been a while since they've come through these parts."

"Still seeing the world." She returned the smile. "They send a letter every few months, and the last I heard from them, they'd just arrived in Crowhold. Pop said that Mother was excited to visit their mineral springs and try the different flavors of sparkling water."

"Your mother did always have adventurous tastes." Windell chuckled. "I'd love to chat more, but the work beckons. I hope you find your bandit."

"We'll leave you to it." Marigold handed the basket to Finn. She paused as she was about to leave. "One more thing. The harvest is coming up. Hope to see you there."

Windell looked up from the stone he was holding. "I wouldn't miss it."

Finn waited by the wagon while Marigold ventured into Town Hall to post the harvest notice. The door closed behind her, and she froze like a troll in daylight.

A tall human woman stood in front of the notice board, perusing the announcements. She had long, wavy, brown hair tinged with green and wore a wreath of fresh flowers like a crown. Her robe was a shimmering forest green, its sleeves embroidered with silver vines that sparkled as she moved. Her jeweled fingers wrapped around a polished staff topped with an emerald.

Tansy Ironvale. The druid from Darkroot Cellars.

For someone who worked amongst nature, there wasn't a stray twig or blemish on her. If not for her rounded human ears, she could have been mistaken for an elven ambassador with how spotless her attire was.

Marigold scowled. She had no desire for an interaction with Tansy or, gods forbid, Galvin. She'd come back and post the notice tomorrow. There was still plenty of time between now and the harvest, so one more day wouldn't hurt. Marigold turned to leave and collided with a thick, muscled body. The notice fell from her hands, clattering against the floor as it rolled down the hallway.

"Apologies," a familiar deep voice said as a strong hand grabbed Marigold's arm, keeping her from falling. Korin, the dwarven cleric who had healed her broken arm, held her steady as recognition dawned on his face. "Now it makes sense." He let go, smiling as he patted Marigold on the shoulder to make sure she was okay. "A wise dwarf once said, 'don't let your axe outrun your noggin', mountains crumble when you're not watchin'.'"

"S-sorry," Marigold stuttered as heat rushed to her cheeks. She prayed silently that Melora would open a hole in the wall that she could crawl into and hide. The last thing she wanted was to attract Tansy's attention.

"Excuse me." A finger tapped her on the shoulder. "I think you dropped this."

Marigold closed her eyes and took a deep breath before turning around.

Tansy towered over the halfling, smiling as she offered the scroll case. "Marigold Bramblefoot, fancy seeing you here."

As Marigold took the scroll case, the clasp on the end came undone, knocked loose by the previous fall. The notice slid out, unfurling as it fell.

Tansy's reaction was quick and graceful as she snatched the parchment from the air.

Korin whistled. "You have the reflexes of a dire cat."

Tansy glanced at the notice. "Is it the harvest already? Time flies, doesn't it?"

The druid handed the parchment to Marigold, and the two stood there silently.

Korin's gaze darted between them. "Well…" He cleared his throat. "Seeing as how you'd need an axe to cut through this tension, I'll take my leave. Ladies."

Once Korin was down the hall, Tansy spoke. There was a fake pleasantness to her voice. "Will you be competing in the harvest festival again this year?"

"Wouldn't miss it." Marigold rolled the notice and stuffed it back in the tube.

"The notice board is right there." Tansy pointed over her shoulder.

"I know that." Marigold crossed her arms. "I'll wait until you're done."

"I'm finished." Tansy sighed, her brow knitted in frustration. She started to turn away but stopped. "Actually, no, I'm not." She took a step back, narrowing her gaze as she took in Marigold's appearance. "I've never understood why you don't like me. Ten years I've worked in this town and not once have we ever had an honest conversation. To hear the townsfolk tell it, you're one of the warmest halflings they've ever known, but I've only ever felt your cold shoulder. Tell me, what have I done to upset you so? Is it because of the wine contest?"

Marigold's hands tingled and her chest tightened. For ten years, she'd avoided Tansy, but that didn't mean she hadn't thought about this moment a thousand times.

About what she'd say if she ever had the opportunity to speak her mind. "It's not what you've done. It's everything you stand for. Halflings have tended these lands for thousands of years. Our blood, sweat, and tears are baked into the soil. It was people like my father who helped build this town's reputation for good wine. And then Galvin comes along, pays you to wave your hand, and everything's perfect. You never have to wonder about a late frost, drought, or too much rain. There's no challenge, no struggle." Marigold shook her head, surprised by the emotion building in her chest. "There's no heart in it."

"Wow." Tansy blinked several times. "So according to you, because I have the ability to care for plants in a way that most do not, my heart's not in it." Her mouth curled into a sneer. "That's a load of griffin shit."

The words echoed down the hall, and several halflings turned in their direction.

"Is it?" Marigold's cheeks burned brighter at the attention, but she felt emboldened to continue. "What do you know of tradition?"

"Tradition." Tansy scoffed. "That's a loaded word too often used to stay stuck in the past. You can respect tradition while still making progress. At Darkroot Cellars, we're making halfling wines available to more homes across Aedrea than ever before. People across the realm will know about honeywine because of us. And you know what? Every time we win a contest, we sell more wine. If you don't like Galvin, that's one thing. You don't like the way he runs his business? Fine. But to tell me that my heart isn't in it, that's a slap to my face." She paused, and her lip quivered. The emerald within her staff had taken on a dull glow. This was the first time Marigold had seen the druid show anything more than cold confidence. "Do you have any idea what it means to be a druid? The responsibility that entails? I've brought plants back from the brink of death. I've listened to the sap coursing through trees older than this town. I nourish plants with the very fibers of my being, and they grow healthy and strong because of me. I listen to them in a way that you could not possibly understand. Make no mistake, just because I get paid to work the vineyard, that doesn't mean I love it any less." She sighed, and her jeweled fingers relaxed as the glow of the staff faded. "We aren't that different, you and I. Anyone can see the passion that you have for wine, and you're damned good at what you do. We may go about it in different ways, but we both want to share our love of halfling wine with the world."

At the end of the hall, the offices had emptied, and dozens of people were now watching. Marigold clenched her fist around the notice. Of all the ways she'd imagined this conversation playing out, it had never been like this. Had she misjudged Tansy all these years simply because she worked for Galvin?

"What's going on here?" Mayor Sweetwater appeared from within the crowd, his polished shoes clacking against the wooden floor as he approached. "I heard shouting. Is everything okay?"

"Everything's fine." Tansy's dark visage shifted into a welcoming smile. "We were just discussing the harvest festival, right, Marigold?"

The mayor looked to Marigold for confirmation. "Is this true?"

Marigold smiled nervously. "We were having a passionate discussion."

"I suggest you take your spirited discussions elsewhere then." He huffed. "You're causing a scene."

Marigold nodded. "Sorry, Mayor. Won't happen again."

"I should hope not." Mayor Sweetwater turned to Tansy. "Give my thanks to Galvin for the wine."

The mayor left, and the crowd dispersed as Marigold and Tansy stood in an awkward silence.

Marigold gulped. Admitting she was wrong was never an easy thing to do. Galvin may have relished the opportunity to remind Marigold that she'd never beaten Darkroot Cellars in the wine-tasting contest, but he was a pompous little rat. What had Tansy ever done aside from making great wine?

She met the druid's gaze. "It's possible that I may have misjudged you."

Tansy raised her brows, but there was a hint of amusement in her eyes.

Marigold took a breath and straightened her back. "It's also possible that I may have been a sore loser and taken out my frustrations on you."

"I appreciate the possibilities." Tansy's mouth curled into a smirk. "For what it's worth, I respect the way you do things. There's a reason why your wine is so well-regarded, and I always look forward to the challenge of our competition." She extended a hand. "For my part, our rivalry isn't personal, it's professional."

Marigold looked at the well-manicured hand. Even Gerty, with all of her creams and ointments, would have been jealous. There wasn't a callous to be seen, and yet these were the hands that had bested her for ten years.

She shook Tansy's hand. "I'm sorry for the way I've treated you."

"Water under the bridge." Tansy tapped her staff against the floor. "Good luck with the harvest. See you around, Marigold." The druid disappeared through the door, her robe fluttering as if she were walking on air.

Marigold leaned against the wall and closed her eyes, taking a moment to recenter herself. For so long, she'd had nothing but disdain for Tansy, all of it built from a narrative she'd created in her mind. But underneath the glitz and glamor, the two of them were more similar than she'd have ever believed. While they came from different backgrounds, it was clear that they shared the same love of the craft. In another life, they may have even been friends.

Maybe that was the key to it all. Not revenge or pride or proving that the old way was better, but the spirit of competition. Wasn't that why her father loved the challenge? He'd competed against his friends, and in the end, the contest was a celebration of wine from first to last place.

She unrolled the notice, reading over it a final time.

Calling All Helping Hands!

The annual grape harvest is upon us, and we need strong backs, nimble fingers, and cheerful hearts to bring in this year's crop.
The vines are ripe with promise, so join us for a bit of work followed by a hearty feast, flowing wine, song, dance, and above all, great company.

Bring your shears and prepare for a day of laughter, hard work, and continued tradition!

When: *Next Sorden*
Where: *Dew Drop Vineyard*

-Marigold Bramblefoot, and the Dew Drop Staff

Marigold posted the notice on the board and hurried outside. The harvest festival was around the corner, and there was work to do.

15. WORDS OF WISDOM

Upon returning to the inn, Marigold found Elara in the cellar, preparing a shipment. As the elf worked, Marigold told her about the exchange with Tansy in town.

"You did what now?" Elara looked up from the wine she'd just placed in the crate, her blue eyes fixed and unblinking. "Inside Town Hall?"

Marigold leaned against a barrel and recounted the rest of the story. When she was finished, she let out a long sigh. "I don't know what came over me. I'd been holding onto this grudge for ten years, and I don't know, I just snapped. Everything I've wanted to say to Galvin, I said to Tansy." She grimaced at the memory. "I feel terrible about it."

"Pssh. She made her choice." Elara banished the idea with a flick of her wrist. "Besides, ten years is nothing. My father once held a grudge for a century because his brother borrowed a hairpin without asking."

"Really? A hundred years?"

Elara nodded. "To be fair, it was a family heirloom,

and Uncle Thalion lost it while venturing into the wilds. But that's beside the point. What I'm saying is that she's been your main competition for ten years. A little grudge is healthy."

"Is it, though? What has it gotten me besides disappointment?" Marigold paced down the row of wine. "With Galvin, it's one thing. He and I grew up together, but I don't even know the woman and yet I've carried this burden inside of me. I don't recall my father ever talking bad about the competition. Maybe it's time to let it go."

"Your father never had to compete against a druid." Elara shrugged. "I guess you need to take a look inside and see what motivates you. For me, a little spite goes a long way."

"Yeah, I think you're right. Regardless, something needs to change." Marigold stopped next to the elf. "I can finish this up if you want to take a break. Packing bottles always gives me time to think."

"Don't beat yourself up too much." Elara wrapped an arm around Marigold. "Whatever you decide, I'll support you. We all will. I'll be in the kitchen pestering Locke if you need me."

Marigold watched the glow of the enchanted lights reflecting off Elara's golden hair before she disappeared up the stairs. For a moment, Marigold stood there, basking in the cool, musty air of the cellar. She looked across the room, where dozens of blue ribbons adorned the wall.

Her father had made his legacy, but what would hers be?

After today, she knew what she didn't want it to become. A druid on the other side or not, Marigold didn't want to hold on to that bitterness anymore. She located the packing list and started pulling wine from the racks, letting her mind wander as she worked.

Growing up, the winery and inn had been two sides of the same coin. They'd both brought happiness and joy to her father, and in turn, Marigold had adopted his passions as her own. Even to this day, there was magic in watching the morning dew glisten upon the vines, and in hearing laughter from the common area late into the night. But somewhere along the way, Marigold had lost the joy of the harvest festival. It was supposed to be a celebration of life's simple pleasures with hearty feasts, flowing wine, and warm hospitality. It was a time for thankfulness and community. But in truth, it had become a burden. The annual wine contest was a weight around her neck that grew heavier with each failure, year after year.

She could skip the wine contest, but that hardly seemed fair to Elara and the rest of the staff. They'd invested just as much of themselves into the vineyard as she had.

Tears brimmed in Marigold's eyes as she pulled a bottle of honeywine from the shelf. She sank to her knees on the cold stone floor, holding the bottle to her chest.

"What am I going to do?" Her gaze fell upon a portrait of her father on the wall. In it, he stood in front of the vineyard, a wide smile on his face and a barrel of wine at his side. "What would you do?"

Marigold wiped the tears from her eyes and placed the final bottle in the crate. After fastening the lid, she went to the cellar office, staring at shelves filled with crates of journals, invoices, and ledgers that dated all the way back to when her father first bought the property. Marigold pulled one at random. It was dated before Marigold had been born.

She sat at the desk and opened the journal, smiling at Wilbur Bramblefoot's familiar handwriting etched into the parchment. The pages were filled with commentary on prunings, weather, tasting notes, and more. She flipped through the pages until she found one that was dated around the typical harvest time. There was a list of the current varietals and the order in which they'd be harvested. At the very bottom, her father had made another entry.

The harvest is only days away, and it is always my favorite time of year. There's no occasion when our people are at their best than when we gather and share our love for wine, song, and dance. As much as I love the harvest festival that will follow, this is true prosperity.

Marigold flipped forward until she came to an entry that was dated after the harvest festival.

We gave it our best, and took home third place as a result. As much as I loved the honeywine our vineyard submitted, I'd be lying if I said that Tobin's wasn't better. He entered a blend of sunburst and emberfruit so divine that I bought six bottles for the inn. And even old Samlin surprised us all this year, taking second place with his moonshadow wine. I've never been much for robust reds, but after tasting his vintage, I'm tempted to add a few rows of my own.

As much as I want to win, I do my best to remember why we have the contest to begin with. It's not so that one can lord their wines above the others, but to showcase the breadth of wine that halflings have to offer. It is with that in mind that I set my eyes and heart upon next year, where I hope to cement my name among the great winemakers of Willowbrook's storied history.

A lump formed in Marigold's throat as she read the entry several times. Even in defeat, her father was gracious.

No, that wasn't true. He hadn't lost. He'd won third place and while he may have been disappointed, he'd been happy with the showing. More than that, he'd been happy for his competitors.

Marigold closed the notebook and thought back to the countless letters she'd received from her father over the years. After every festival, she'd apologize for not winning first place, but his replies never focused on the results. Instead, he'd question why she'd chosen to submit a certain wine and what made it special. He'd always ask about the others competing and how their vineyards were doing. Not once was he disappointed in her. How had it taken Marigold so long to realize that it was she who carried the loss like a burden? She was the one who'd become so enamored with winning that she had forgotten the true meaning of the festival. In recent years, she'd do anything to keep the thoughts from her mind. She'd let her rivalry with Galvin consume her, so much so that it had sapped the joy from the process.

A knock on the door startled her, and Marigold dropped the notebook onto the desk.

Poppy stood in the doorframe, biting her lip as if she

was unsure whether a smile was acceptable. "Elara said you were down here. I thought I would check on you. Gerty told me what happened."

"Gerty?" Marigold chuckled to herself. "She wasn't even there."

"You'd never know it by the way she tells it. Mind if I come in?"

Marigold opened the door the rest of the way and gestured toward a stool. The space was cozy for one person, but with two, it was downright intimate.

Poppy took a seat, and her leg brushed against Marigold's. "Want to talk about it?"

"Not particularly." Marigold scrunched her nose, the memory of the encounter was one of the few things that was more distracting than their thighs touching. "I made a fool of myself."

Poppy gave Marigold's hand a reassuring squeeze. "Who hasn't?"

"It's not all bad, though." Marigold tapped the journal. "Between all the facts and figures, there's a surprising amount of wisdom in these pages."

"Is that so?" Poppy's mouth curled at the edges. "Who would have thought?"

"Sometimes, people have a hard time seeing what's right in front of them." Marigold took Poppy's hand, savoring the warmth of the gnome's touch. Their eyes locked, and in that moment, the stress of the day didn't matter. "For the first time in a while, I'm actually looking forward to picking out a wine for the harvest festival."

16. FAMILY LEGACIES

"Three cases of emberfruit from the 1848 harvest. Only two bottles left from 1847," Marigold called out the inventory to Elara as she sorted through the cellar shelves.

Between selling wine to those visiting the vineyard and stocking the bar upstairs, bottles were always disappearing from the cellar, so each week, Elara and Marigold took inventory to manage the stock for outgoing shipments.

The elf scribbled in her notebook. "We can save those last two for the harvest. I'll go ahead and mark them out of stock."

Marigold set the wine aside. Under the enchanted lights, the layer of dust gave the older bottles a frosty appearance.

"Today's the day." She moved to the shelves of honey-wine. "I'm finally going to decide on a wine for the festival."

"Really?" Elara looked up from the checklist. "I

thought we were going to have to force you at sword-point. Why the change of heart?"

"I think it was a mixture of your advice and my father's wisdom." Marigold turned around to face the elf. "I've been so caught up in trying to win that I lost sight of what would actually make him proud. The contest is an opportunity for us to connect with the community and showcase our hard work."

"I'm glad you've found some peace about it all." Elara smiled. "Though, winning would still be nice."

"You're not wrong." Marigold laughed. "That's still the goal, but it's not the motivation."

The door to the stairwell opened from upstairs, followed by a patter of feet. Gerty smiled sheepishly as she entered the cellar.

Marigold rolled her eyes. "Well, if it isn't the Hearsay Halfling."

"You mean the Mouthy Meadowlark." Elara smirked.

"Some call her Gossiping Gertrude."

"She goes by many names—" Elara waggled her brows. "—but this much is certain… In the town of Willowbrook, no secret is safe, no action unnoticed, no—"

"I get it." Gerty held up her hands in apology. "I'm a gossip. I'm sorry. It's just, well, sometimes I can't help myself. Finn was telling me what happened, and I got excited, and, well, you know the rest."

"A tale as old as time." Marigold let out an exasperated sigh. "What is it you need?"

"Oh, don't be mad." Gerty gave her best innocent face as she batted her eyelashes and twisted a golden ringlet of hair around her finger. "There's a man upstairs. Says he's a wine trader."

Elara and Marigold exchanged a glance. The elf pressed a finger to her nose a moment before Marigold did the same.

"Not it!" Elara did her best evil laugh.

"Curse your elven reflexes." Marigold shook her fist at the elf. "Guess you'll have to finish up on your own."

"Fine by me." Elara grinned. "I find the wine to be better company than most merchants. I've never had a bottle try and haggle me for a better deal."

Marigold rolled her eyes. "If you put half of the wit you use antagonizing us toward selling wine, we'd be the most popular vineyard in Tyne."

"What can I say? I'm a grower, not a shower." Elara shrugged. "Give me the vineyard and cellar and I'll leave the people-pleasing to you."

"You're a pain in my backside is what you are." Marigold laughed as she turned to Gerty. "I'll be up in a moment."

Upstairs, a few guests sat in the common area. An older halfling woman sat in the corner reading a book, and two middle-aged halflings played a board game while sharing a bottle of wine.

Aldric had staked his claim to the highbacked chair near the hearth. The mage was knitting a scarf that had passed comical length and was now more mystifying than anything. Splinter was probably buried somewhere within the mass of fabric.

At the bar, a blonde man sat on a stool, his gaze focused on the various bottles on the shelves. He wore a burgundy cloak over a purple tunic, both of fine quality, and an eye-catching satchel sat at his feet. The leather bag was dyed a rich burgundy, and the metal buckles and clasps were engraved with grape clusters. Whoever he was, he certainly had expensive tastes.

Marigold pulled her shoulders back and smiled. "Welcome to the Dew Drop Inn and Vineyard." She extended her hand. "I'm the proprietor, Marigold Bramblefoot."

The man stood, smiling broadly with an excitement that traveled all the way to his eyes. "I'm so pleased to meet you, Marigold." He wrapped both hands around the halfling's, and she was surprised by how soft they were. "Name's Eris. I'm a trader of fine wines and spirits, mainly dwarven reds, but I'm looking to add some halfling wines to our offerings. I've always had a soft spot for honeywine."

"Well, you came to the right place." She tried to release the handshake, but Eris kept his hold.

"I should hope so. You come highly recommended by the merchants in town." He finally let go and looked around the room. "Lovely place you have. The moment I stepped inside, there was warmness and a sense of welcoming that you don't find in a lot of establishments."

"Thank you." Marigold wasn't sure if he was flattering her or if his personality was truly this earnest. Either way, it was a bit disarming. "My father started the business, and it's been mine for a decade now."

"Good on you! There's nothing better than a family legacy. My grandfather was the one to get us into the trading business." Eris took a seat at the bar and continued. "He was a diplomat for King Lyle of Warminster. One day, he was sent to Rockdale on a stately visit, and he fell in love with their wine. He wanted to share it with the world, and our family has been in the trading business ever since. I've got two young boys myself, and there's nothing I would love more than for them to continue the tradition."

"Sounds to me like you know your wine." Marigold gathered that Eris was a talker, which was an unsurprisingly common trait among many traders and merchants. If she didn't steer the conversation back to business, the man might talk her ears off for the entire evening. "How about we do a tasting and you can tell me what it is you're looking for?"

Eris grinned. "I'd be lying if I said I didn't enjoy this part of the job."

Marigold pulled some of their most popular wines from the shelf while Eris launched into another story.

"Normally, I do most of my trading across Mount Tor. There's just something about dwarven wines that resonate with the mountain folk of Warminster. Probably because we share the same frigid winters. Not so much in Whitehaven, but Silverpeak and Stormrest are mountain cities. The dwarven red wines have been our most popular, but lately, we've been thinking of expanding our offerings. My brother is sailing to Aethervale to try and acquire some of their icewine, and I just finished touring some of the vineyards in Honeydale. Someone suggested I make a stop by Willowbrook on the way to Whitblossum. After that, I'll be heading north to try some of the lowland dwarf wines in Hillside and Bearmouth. With a little luck, I'll be home before the first snow."

The man was certainly a mouthful. By the time he'd stop to take a breath, Marigold had uncorked four bottles of wine and poured samples into eight glasses so that they could both do a tasting. She knew all their flavor profiles by heart, but it always helped to share a drink with a prospective business acquaintance.

"Sounds like you've got quite the adventure ahead of you, so I'll get straight to it." She gestured to the bottles. "These are our four main grape varietals—emberfruit, dreamcatcher, honey, and moonshadow. I'm sure it's no surprise that the honeywine is our most popular."

Eris went down the line of glasses, lifting each one and examining the color. For the first time since they'd met, the man was actually quiet. After Eris set the glass of moonshadow wine on the bar, he finally spoke. "Beautiful coloring, especially the moonshadow. It reminds me of the ironroot varietal. There aren't many grapes that can achieve such a deep hue." He picked up the glass and admired it again. "I honestly didn't know that halflings were known for their reds."

"We're not, really, but my father loved to try new things." She smiled as she recalled the journal entry detailing the wine contest he'd lost. "He decided to grow moonshadow grapes after tasting it at the local harvest festival. Speaking of which, we'll be harvesting our own grapes soon, if you're going to be around for a while. The inn is all booked up, but you're more than welcome to join us."

"That is mighty kind of you. I've always wanted to experience a halfling harvest. Unfortunately, I'm only passing through. I still have three cities to visit, and I'm sure you know as well as I that if something can slow you down, it will certainly try."

"You're as right as rain on a spring morning."

"I will say, I find the halfling grape stomping tradition fascinating, especially compared to the dwarves. Nowadays, most of them use presses, but there are still some who stick to the old way of mashing grapes with large warhammers."

"There's a lot to be said for the old ways. They may not be the fastest, but there's something special in doing things in the same way as your ancestors." Marigold picked up the first glass of wine. "This is our emberfruit wine. It's a lovely summer wine. The nose is very citrusy with a hint of elderflower, and the flavor profile is a nice balance between sweet and tart."

Eris raised the glass to his nose, sniffed, swirled, and then sniffed again. "Delightful."

They clinked their glasses and sipped the wine. The emberfruit had a sweet, fruity beginning that transitioned to the tartness of lime and grapefruit.

"Very vibrant." Eris swirled the wine and drank again. "I love how the citrus lingers, encouraging another taste."

Marigold moved to the next glass. "This one is our dreamcatcher wine. It's our most floral wine and has a wonderfully crisp finish."

Eris repeated his process, lifting the wine glass and examining the golden hue. He swirled, sniffed, and then sipped.

Marigold did the same, inhaling the notes of jasmine and rose petals, followed by a mineral-taste that gave the wine a much drier profile than the other white wines.

"Surprisingly refreshing for being so dry." Eris licked his lips. "Definitely bolder than the last."

Marigold nodded. "Occasionally, we'll age the dreamcatcher wine to mellow it out. The oak will often soften the palate and give it a creamier finish."

"That sounds lovely." Eris pulled a piece of parchment from within his cloak and made a note.

Next, Marigold moved to the honeywine. "This is what you came for." She raised the glass and swirled the straw-colored wine. "There's not a vineyard across Tyne that doesn't grow honey grapes."

Eris smiled from ear to ear as he took in the aroma of honeysuckle and citrus blossom. "This makes me want to lay in a meadow."

Marigold chuckled. "Watch out or you'll discover what it truly means to be a halfling." She closed her eyes, savoring the sweet blend of honey and peach on her tongue.

"This is divine." He turned the glass up, not letting a single drop go to waste.

Marigold placed her hand on the base of the last glass, swirling the moonshadow wine without lifting it off the bar. "I saved this one for last, since it's the heaviest of our offerings."

The moonshadow was deep and full-bodied, with aromas of blackberry and vanilla. The flavor profile was bold with notes of dark berries, oak, and leather. It was the perfect complement for a heavy stew or roast.

"Wow." After tasting the wine, Eris shook his head as he sat back on the stool. "I'm impressed. This rivals many of the reds I've tasted across Mount Tor. Rich. Robust. I can imagine sipping this by a warm fire with a hearty steak. If you told me this was produced by the Crimson Anvil Winery, I would have believed it."

"I appreciate the kind words." Marigold bowed

slightly. It warmed her heart to have someone appreciate the red wine with the same fervor as her father. "Like I said, these are our four main products. We do experiment with blends, but since we produce those in much smaller quantities, we only offer them locally."

"Understandable." Eris made a few more notes before returning his attention to Marigold. "If you're able to supply us, I'd love to order cases of both the honeywine and the aged dreamcatcher, if you have it. If this bottle is anything to go by, then I trust it will be superb."

Marigold tapped her chin. "Honeywine won't be a problem. I'll have to check our records, but I believe we have a few barrels of five-year dreamcatcher we're due to bottle in the spring. If you want to place the order with one of the wine merchants in town, I'll let them know once it's ready and they can manage the shipments for you."

"Perfect." He clapped his hands together softly. "Would you mind if I toured the cellar while I'm here? I always love to peek into the dragon's lair when I have the chance."

"Not at all." Marigold gathered the empty wine glasses and set them behind the bar. "It's actually right beneath us."

She led him down to the cellar, where Eris once again became a chatterbox. Elara was nowhere to be seen. Either she'd finished up with inventory, or she'd heard footsteps and decided to bolt. With her, there was no telling.

"What a quaint little cellar." He looked around in wonder. "And connected to the inn, too. You've got yourself something special here, Marigold. If more people had your father's vision, the world would be a much better place."

"He believed that a good wine and a full belly could bring anyone together."

Eris nodded his approval as he inspected various barrels. "He sounds like a wise man."

"He is." Marigold thought about where he might be at this very moment. Probably sitting in a tavern somewhere with her mother, chatting away with the locals over a platter of food. "I've never met another halfling quite like him. He has an adventurous spirit and a zest for life's experiences."

Eris stopped in front of the wall of ribbons. "And a decorated history, it seems."

"He's certainly left his mark on this town." Marigold smiled as she looked at the awards. Not long ago, she'd thought that they were his greatest accomplishments. Every part of her had wanted to achieve that same level of greatness. But in truth, Wilbur Bramblefoot's legacy wasn't the awards he'd won, but the joy he'd created. This vineyard, the inn, and the wine they'd created had brought so many people together. That was his true legacy.

Once they finished with the cellar, Marigold gave a tour of the winery uphill and then they walked some of the vineyard. Their conversation consisted mostly of Marigold explaining something and then Eris delving into a story about his travels or past that was only tangentially related. The man was a book that refused to close once it was open. Marigold was certain Poppy could fill entire notebooks with his escapades.

"So that's the vineyard." Marigold stopped at the end

of a row of honey grapes and turned to face Eris. "I truly appreciate your interest in our wine. I get a sense that you have a similar passion as my father, and I look forward to doing business together." She shook the man's hand. "You're more than welcome to stay for dinner tonight. Locke is an amazing cook, and I can have Finn give you a ride back to town afterward."

"That's very hospitable of you. I wish I could stay, but I do have a prior commitment to meet with another vintner for dinner."

"Let me guess." She tried to hide the annoyance in her voice. "Darkroot Cellars?"

Eris grinned. "How'd you know?"

"Just a hunch." Marigold forced a smile. While she may have made peace with Tansy, she wasn't there with Galvin, even if she was trying to separate professional rivalries from personal.

Her momentary frustration vanished when she noticed a flash of blue by the inn. Aldric stood on the porch, peeking around the corner like he was trying not to be seen. He hurried around the edge, almost comically, glancing this way and that as he went to the wagon he kept parked beside the inn.

Marigold pulled Eris back into the row of vines, hiding among the leaves.

"What's going on?" His brow knitted with confusion.

"Shh." Marigold held a finger to her lips, watching the mage as he pulled an apple from his pocket and placed it inside the cart.

From where they were standing, she couldn't see what was inside, but Aldric was saying something as he wagged his finger before closing the cart door.

Marigold frowned. Had Aldric put Splinter in the cart? And if so, why the apple? Did a stick golem even need to eat? "Sorry, that was strange."

"Everything okay?"

Marigold was surprised by the man's genuine concern. "Yeah, I'm sure it was nothing. Mages go by the beat of their own drum."

And so, as they made their way back to the inn, Eris launched into another story about an earth mage he'd met while visiting Durendreg.

17. PUMPKIN PIES

"It's happened again!" Elara stood in the doorframe, frowning and arms crossed. "This time, the bastards got into the moonshadow grapes."

"Bastards?" Marigold raised a brow. "Plural?"

"There's no way a single person or animal cleaned out half a row of grapes by themselves. Not unless Melora herself decided to take a sample." The elf's scowl deepened. "Why are you not more upset about this?"

Marigold blew on her tea, savoring the warmth of the mug in her hands before answering. "We're harvesting the grapes tomorrow. What would you have me do?"

"I don't know." Elara placed her hands on her hips. "If we don't get to the bottom of this now, how do we know it won't happen again next year?"

"We don't." Marigold took a sip. That was a problem for another time.

"Exactly!" Elara waved her index finger vigorously, then she stormed out of the office.

Marigold leaned back in her chair and let out a

contented sigh. The incident with the grapes was concerning, especially since it had happened twice this week, but she refused to let it rile her up. Not today. There was too much to be grateful for.

For the first time in nine years, she was looking forward to the harvest festival. She'd already decided on a wine for the contest, though she hadn't told anyone yet. That probably added to Elara's annoyance, but Marigold wanted to share the news with Poppy first. With prep for the harvest and Poppy's research, the two hadn't had a chance for any one-on-one time the past week, but today, that would change.

With tomorrow's harvest, and everything that came after, today was the last chance Marigold would have to take a moment to herself until the festival was over. So, she'd decided to do something she hadn't done in ages— bake a pie. And Poppy had agreed to join her.

Locke was already in the kitchen when Marigold and Poppy arrived. He stood over the center island, his braided beard tucked into his apron as he chopped vegetables for a stew. The dwarf was usually very protective of his workspace, but he had no hesitation about welcoming Marigold into the kitchen.

"There she is!" He looked up and grinned, still chopping with expert precision. "It's always a joy to watch Mari put her talents to use."

Poppy gave Marigold a look of surprise. "You didn't tell me you were a talented baker."

The halfling's cheeks flushed. "I'm not. Locke is just being gracious."

"That's a lie if I've ever heard one." Locke scoffed as he scooped chunks of potato into a bowl. "She learned her way around the kitchen from her mother and inherited her skills for baking and cooking. A real shame she doesn't use them more often."

Marigold narrowed her eyes at the dwarf. "I suppose the inn will just run itself while I make pies all day."

"I'm not saying yer not busy." He set the knife aside and stretched his arms overhead. "But I know it makes you happy. Besides, I like having you around."

Marigold walked over to the dwarf and hugged him. "Don't let Finn hear you say that."

Locke grunted. "Don't even get me started on that little rascal." He gestured to the empty counter space against the wall. "I cleared a spot for you lot to work."

On the counter, there were two cutting boards with several bowls neatly stacked to each side, along with whisks and a variety of measuring spoons positioned in a line from largest to smallest. Marigold grinned at Locke's compulsive orderliness.

She turned to Poppy. "Ready to get started?"

"You know I've never baked anything in all my life." Poppy shifted her weight as she looked over all of the bowls and spoons. "I can't be held responsible if this turns out poorly."

"There's a first time for everything." Marigold took Poppy's hand. "I'll be holding your hand the whole time."

"That's a terrible way to work," Locke chimed in from across the kitchen.

"It's an expression, Locke." Marigold chuckled as she

let go of the gnome and pulled her mother's recipe book from a shelf above the counter. She handed the book to Poppy. "Books are involved, so it can't be that bad, right?"

"That is a valid point." Poppy opened it up and flipped through the pages. There were recipes for bread, pie, puddings, and all manner of dishes inside.

Marigold stood beside Poppy, watching as the gnome perused the recipes. Her shoulders relaxed with each turn of the page. When she found the recipe for pumpkin pie, she handed the book back to Marigold.

"The first thing we want to make is the filling." Marigold had made pumpkin pie with her mother so many times growing up that she didn't actually need the recipe. It was etched into her memory, but for Poppy's first time in a kitchen, it would be helpful to visualize the steps. "I'll grab a pumpkin from the pantry."

She came back a moment later with an orange pumpkin the size of her head and set it on the island. "Locke, would you be a dear?"

The dwarf looked up from the food he was prepping and grunted. He slammed his knife into the pumpkin with enough force that the blade passed through the gourd like butter. The blade hit the wood with a loud clack, startling the gnome, and the two halves fell aside. Poppy jumped, letting out a tiny yelp of surprise. Locke grinned as he returned his attention to the ingredients before him.

Marigold handed half of the pumpkin to Poppy. "Half for you and half for me."

"Is he mad?" Poppy whispered.

"He likes to pretend." Marigold couldn't hide her smile. "It's something he learned from his mentor."

"Oh, good." Poppy relaxed, setting the pumpkin on her cutting board. "I didn't want to be an imposition."

"This first part isn't that different from the spirit lanterns we carved." She took a spoon and started scooping out seeds and stringy portions. "Remove everything but the flesh and put it in this bowl here. Locke can use it for something else later."

They worked side by side, with Marigold sharing her technique and Poppy imitating it the best she could. The gnome watched her like a hawk, likely analyzing every movement the halfling made.

"Remember, this is supposed to be fun." Marigold gave Poppy a warm smile. "Worst-case scenario, we feed it to Finn. He'll eat anything."

"How encouraging." Poppy snickered.

Once the seeds were removed, they cut the pumpkin flesh into chunks and placed them in a large pan.

Marigold tossed a few logs beneath the stove and placed the pan in the oven. "We'll let this cook for about an hour or so. We want the flesh soft enough to mash into a puree."

"What do we do while we wait?" asked Poppy.

"We can start on the dough for the pie crust." She handed a bowl to Poppy. "This is the part where my mother always put me to work. Grab a bowl and we'll mix the flour and salt."

Poppy read the steps twice before carefully measuring out the correct amount of each ingredient and stirring them together.

Marigold nodded with approval as she mixed her flour. "Good, now we want to add in the butter. We'll use this pastry blender to cut through the butter and blend it together. Mash it until it has a crumbly consistency."

"This thing?" Poppy held the pastry blender like it was a foreign object. "It looks like a weapon."

Locke snorted and then pretended to cover it with a cough.

"It is, in a sense. It's the weapon of bakers across the realm to fight against soggy crusts." Marigold took the tool and wielded it like a pair of armored knuckles. It was a simple piece of wood with four curved wires in the shape of a crescent that was used to press through butter and flour. "It's very difficult to get butter and flour to mix by hand, but with this, you can cut the butter into the flour, making a mixture of coarse crumbs perfect for a pie crust. It has this curved shape you can use to rock it back and forth on a flat surface or press against the curved edges of a mixing bowl."

Marigold showed Poppy how to use it, then handed it to the gnome.

Poppy admired the tool. "They say necessity is the mother of invention. Let's give it a go." She grunted as she pressed through the butter again and again until it began to crumble into the flour. After about a minute of work, she wiped her forehead with the back of her hand. "Now I see why bakers have such strong hands."

"Working with dough is a lot of work. Your arms will probably be sore tomorrow, but it will all be worth it." Marigold held out her hand for the tool. "Here, let me help."

Marigold rolled up her sleeves and started pressing through the butter until she had a bowl of crumbly flour.

"Next, we'll add in some water, just a little at a time, until the dough is moist enough to hold together."

She added the water by the spoonful, molding the dough by hand until it was the desired consistency. Poppy tested Marigold's method and repeated the process. Once they both had a ball of dough, they placed it on the cutting board and rolled it with a pin until it was flat.

"Now, we'll take a bowl slightly bigger than the pan we plan to use and place it upside down on the dough, like this. Use your knife to trim off all of the excess pieces." Once Poppy finished, she continued. "Here's a little trick for getting the dough into the pan." Marigold took the rolling pin and rolled it across the circle of pastry, wrapping it around the pin as she did so. "Now you set the pin over the pan and unroll it. Use your fingers to gently press the dough into the pan." She watched Poppy repeat the process. "Excellent!"

Poppy beamed with pride. "Maybe I'm not hopeless after all."

"You're a natural." Marigold bumped her shoulder into the gnome's. "This next part is mostly for decoration, but presentation is just as important as taste."

Locke grunted his approval.

Marigold took the crust and used one hand to pinch the dough around her finger, making a ridge around the rim. "Take the dough around the top edge of the pan and fold it around your finger like this."

Poppy's ridges weren't as symmetrical as Marigold's but for her first time in the kitchen, she'd done well. At least Marigold hadn't burst with uncontrollable laughter like she had with the spirit lantern.

"Now we wait for the pumpkin to finish cooking." Marigold turned and leaned her backside against the counter. "What do you think so far?"

"I think cooking is a lot of work." Poppy massaged her forearm. "But it's nice to make something yourself."

"It is." Marigold smiled as she noticed a smudge of white on the gnome's face.

"What's so funny?"

"You have a little flour on your cheek." Marigold reached up and gently wiped away the flour with her thumb.

Her hand lingered for a moment, cradling Poppy's face against her palm. The gnome closed her eyes and leaned into Marigold's touch. The sounds of Locke working and the sizzle of pumpkin roasting drifted away. There was only Poppy, and Marigold's racing heart.

Poppy opened her eyes, biting her lip as she met the halfling's gaze. Marigold let out a shaky breath.

"Is it just me or is it hot in here?" She dropped her hand as heat rushed to her cheeks.

"Oh, it's you all right," Locke mumbled.

Marigold turned to see the dwarf grinning like a wolf.

Poppy took Marigold's hand, interlacing her fingers with the halfling's and drawing Marigold's attention back to her. "I've been wondering what your mother is like? You've told me a lot about your father, and I've gathered bits and pieces of your mother's personality from the journals, but I'd love to hear it from you."

"She's amazing." Marigold basked in the warmth of Poppy's touch. "Kind. Welcoming. She's the personification of halfling values, and I don't think my father would have ever taken on the challenge of running an inn without her by his side. For all the credit he receives for the wine and vineyard, my mother's touch runs just as deep. She never hesitated to get her hands dirty around the property. She's a phenomenal cook, and she always seems to know how to make someone feel at ease. Most of all, she's incredibly loving. I always wanted to be just like my father because I didn't think anyone could be as great as my mother."

Marigold's chest swelled with emotion. It had been far too long since she'd been able to hug either of them. They deserved their adventures, but it would be nice to spend an evening together in front of the hearth, telling stories and sharing a bottle of wine.

Poppy squeezed her hand. "She sounds like a lovely person."

"I really miss her. Both of them. But it's days like today that remind me of how lucky I am. Because missing someone is part of loving them. And just like the wine is a connection to my father, every time I use her recipes, I can feel my mother's comforting presence." Marigold noticed the smell of roasted pumpkin had filled the kitchen. "Speaking of which, I think it's time to make the filling." She removed the pan from the oven, and chunks of charred pumpkin sizzled as she set it on the counter to cool. "Luckily for those scholarly arms of yours, the hardest part is over."

"Scholarly arms?" Poppy made an exaggerated gasp. "If you weren't so cute, I might be offended."

Marigold blushed as she used the spatula to split the roasted pumpkin into two bowls and then handed Poppy a masher. "This makes the next part a lot easier."

"What do I do with this?" Poppy had a puzzled expression.

Locke chortled from behind them.

"Don't mind him." Marigold took a second masher and demonstrated for Poppy, crushing the steaming pumpkin. It was so soft and tender that it practically melted beneath the tool. "Mash it until you have a mushy consistency, then we'll start adding the ingredients."

Poppy grunted as she worked. Her features were equal parts focused and adorable, and Marigold found herself stealing glances as she pulled ingredients from around the kitchen.

"Here's where you'll want to pay careful attention to the recipe." Marigold tapped her finger against the book. "Too much salt and you'll have spent the day baking a pie for Onyx because I doubt even Finn would enjoy it."

Poppy nodded. "Got it."

"You'll want to mix all of your ingredients and whisk them together until everything is blended."

The recipe for the filling was pretty simple—two to three cups of mashed pumpkin, half a cup of honey, half a teaspoon of ground cinnamon, a quarter teaspoon of ground cloves and nutmeg, two eggs, and half a cup of cream. Finish it off with a pinch of saffron and a dash of pepper.

Poppy's brow furrowed as she stirred the ingredients, and a strand of sapphire hair fell across her nose. She blew it away and stirred harder.

"Don't tell anyone, but the secret ingredient is the pepper," Marigold said as she set her bowl aside. "Everyone thinks it's the saffron, but the pepper is the key.

There's something about the spice that brings out the best in all of the other flavors."

"That's—" Poppy grunted as she stirred vigorously. "—fascinating." She set the bowl down with a sigh. "Whew. I think I did it."

"You did great." Marigold winked. "Now, we pour the filling into the pie and let it bake."

They both carefully poured the filling into their crusts and placed them in the oven.

"That's it?" Poppy looked at the recipe again. "What do we do now?"

Marigold grinned. "Now, we have a drink."

"Ahem." Locke cleared his throat.

Marigold chuckled. "That is, after we clean up."

While Poppy and Marigold cleaned, Gerty arrived to help Locke prepare the table for lunch.

"What's going on here?" Gerty's gaze darted from Marigold to Locke and then to Poppy as the wheels of the rumor mill began to turn.

"Enjoying the calm before the storm." Marigold washed a bowl and handed it to Poppy to dry. "I thought I would spend some time in the kitchen before things get crazy."

"Do I smell a pumpkin pie?" Gerty sniffed at the air and a smile spread across her face. "I'd recognize that scent anywhere. Saffron. You're using your mother's recipe."

"I guess that nose is good for something other than sticking it where it doesn't belong," Locke said as he arranged a platter of fruits and crackers.

Gerty harrumphed as she carried the platter into the

dining room. Poppy went to return the stack of bowls to their rightful place on the shelf across the kitchen.

"For the lovebirds," Locke whispered to Marigold as he placed a smaller plate of food on the counter next to her.

"Will you stop?" Marigold playfully elbowed him in the side. "You're as bad as Elara."

"I'm teasing." He grinned. "It's nice to see you this happy, Mari. I mean it. Go enjoy yourself. I'll take out the pies when they're ready."

"Thank you." Marigold wrapped her arms around the burly dwarf. "I don't know what I did to deserve a friend like you."

"None of that now." Locke pried her arms away and gestured toward the door. "Go on before I change my mind."

Marigold held out the plate of food to Poppy when she returned. "You take this, and I'll meet you by the garden."

She hurried down to the cellar. As she was pulling a bottle from the wine rack, Marigold noticed a silvery sheen on several barrels. The normally dust-covered barrels shimmered in the light of the glowstones.

Marigold went to investigate, finding a trail about a foot wide that went from the barrels to the cellar entrance. Had someone forgotten to close the door last night?

She scooped some of the film and rubbed it between her fingers. It was the same consistency that had been on the vines each time the grapes had gone missing. Not slimy or sticky, but clearly a trail of some kind. She searched for more but whatever had been in the cellar was gone. The corks hadn't been touched, but she knocked on the barrels anyways to check. They were still full.

Marigold shook her head. This was a problem for another time. Right now, there was a lovely gnome waiting for her by the garden.

By the time she found Poppy, Marigold had all but forgotten about the mystery in the cellar. She held the bottle of wine behind her back as she approached the picnic table.

"Should I be worried?" Poppy narrowed her gaze as she tried to peek behind the halfling.

"Not this time." Marigold stopped a few feet from the table. "I decided on a wine for this year's harvest festival, and I wanted to tell you first."

Poppy's eyes widened. "Really? Why me?"

"Because you've helped me remember why I wanted to follow in my father's footsteps to begin with. I love making wine and sharing it with the world. For so long, it was like I was wound so tight that I couldn't feel anything other than pressure. Since you came into my life, I've felt that tension slowly release." She looked into the endless purple of Poppy's gaze. "It doesn't matter if we win. What matters is that we show up."

"That's wonderful, Marigold." Poppy's eyes glistened with emotion. "I'm so happy for you."

"This year, I've decided to enter something non-traditional." Marigold revealed the bottle of dark red wine. "I was looking through father's old journals when I discovered the reason he'd planted the moonshadow vines to begin with. It wasn't born of envy or pride, but a celebration of what someone else had accomplished. When I enter this wine, I want to remind everyone that even though we may be rivals, we're still a community."

"That's beautiful."

"Want to have a taste?"

Marigold opened the bottle, and they spent the next few hours in one another's company, sipping wine as they shared stories and laughed. She savored every moment.

Once again, her father was right. The only thing better than good wine was good company.

18. SUSPICIONS

Marigold awoke with a smile, the memories from the previous day fresh in her mind. From cooking with Poppy in the kitchen to an afternoon sipping wine by the garden, yesterday had been truly wonderful. Even Poppy's pumpkin pie had been a hit at dinner.

Now, she was as ready to take on the harvest as she could be.

Therein lay the challenge. Keeping halflings on task when there was food and wine involved was like trying to herd rabbits. They were always disappearing, lying about, or losing themselves in conversation, song, or dance. But what her people lacked in diligence, they more than made up for with sheer numbers.

There were last-minute tasks to complete around the vineyard and winery, not to mention that hosting over one hundred townsfolk was an undertaking in itself. That was why she was up as the first rays of sunlight streamed through the windows.

Most of the volunteers would arrive around mid-morning, while the rest would trickle in as the day unfolded, and there was plenty of prep work to do beforehand.

Marigold made her way downstairs. Aldric was slumped over in his chair by the fire, wearing the purple nightgown patterned with yellow moons and stars. His matching nightcap sat askew. The scarf he'd been working on since his arrival filled his lap and draped to the floor like a coiled snake. He must have fallen asleep while knitting late into the night.

The mage stirred at the sound of Marigold's footsteps. Aldric grumbled as he wiped the sleep from his eyes and adjusted his hat. For a moment, he looked lost, until his gaze fell upon Marigold. He smiled. "Sorry, I must have dozed off."

Something moved beneath the pile of yarn, and a wooden head emerged. Splinter waved his twig hand before scaling the scarf and climbing into Aldric's lap.

"Today's the harvest." Marigold stopped midway across the room. "I hope to see you there."

"There's nothing quite like the fellowship of halflings." He set the scarf aside and stood, stretching his arms over head. Splinter mirrored the movement. "I wouldn't miss it."

"We'll see you later, then." Marigold headed to the kitchen, where Locke was already hard at work.

Elara stood behind the dwarf, massaging his shoulders. Locke groaned with pleasure as he kneaded bread.

"Good morning." Marigold took a scone from the platter on the counter. The flaky pastry was topped with a maple glaze and chunks of pecan. She took a bite, savoring the sweet, buttery flavor as it crumbled in her mouth. "Everyone ready for today?"

"We will be." Locke continued to knead the bread. "The hog is already on the spit. Should be ready in time for dinner. For lunch, I'll have sandwiches, cheese, bread, and fruits for everyone."

Marigold licked glaze from her fingers. "How long have you been up?"

He looked over his shoulder at Elara. "This one wanted to catch the culprit of your missing grapes, so let's just say a lot longer than I would have liked."

"And?" Marigold looked at Elara.

The elf frowned. "We lost another half-row of moon-shadow grapes but I'm no closer to solving this mystery than on day one." She shook her head. "It's like the grapes just up and vanished off the vine. The only evidence left behind are the seeds and a shimmery trail."

"I almost forgot!" Marigold pressed her hand to her forehead. "Yesterday, I was grabbing wine from the cellar and noticed a similar trail around some of the barrels, only it was a lot wider, like something had come in from outside. I was so excited to tell Poppy about the wine I'd picked for the festival that I completely forgot to tell you."

"You decided on a wine and haven't told us?" Elara raised her brows. She held up a finger as if she had more to say but paused. "Wait, no. That will most certainly be a discussion for another time, but first, let's go to the cellar." She kissed Locke on the head. "Sorry, love, but there's a mystery to solve."

Locke chuckled. "I can already tell this is going to be a harvest for the ages."

Marigold followed Elara down to the cellar. Even in

the dim light of the glowstones, the elf was radiant, her blonde hair catching the light.

Elara turned around, her face set with determination. "Show me."

"By the barrels of moonshadow wine." Marigold pointed to the row. "They were covered in the stuff, and there was a trail that led out the cellar door. I assumed someone had forgotten to close it the night before."

"Finn." Elara scoffed as she knelt beside the barrels.

Marigold looked over the elf's shoulder. Whatever substance had been covering the barrels was gone, but there were streaks from where something had traveled over the dust-covered wood.

"Whatever was here was at least a foot wide. I've never seen a snail that big. Are dire snails a thing?" Elara ran her finger through the dust and shook her head. "I can't believe you didn't tell me. This could have been the missing clue, and probably our last chance at discovering the culprit before next year."

"Sorry. Like I said, I was a bit preoccupied." Marigold offered her best apologetic face. "I wanted to tell you, but Poppy helped me out of the rut I was in. I felt I owed it to her. I hope you're not mad."

"I'm talking about the trail, not the wine. If Poppy is important to you, I understand telling her first. I'm glad you've found someone you want to share your special moments with." Elara's expression softened. "You've always been a beacon of positivity but lately, something has changed. You seem more, I don't know, free. It's a good thing."

"So you're not upset?"

"Not in the least." Elara crossed her arms expectantly. "Now, spill it. What's it going to be this year?"

"Moonshadow." Marigold waited for a reaction from Elara, but the elf just stared. "I thought it might be time to submit something unexpected. Everyone knows we make moonshadow wine, but not even my father has ever entered it."

"Hmm." The elf tapped her chin.

"What?" Marigold suddenly felt nervous. She ran her fingers along the hem of her apron. Had she made a mistake with her choice? It was their least popular wine after all.

"It's bold." Elara paced down the row of wine muttering to herself. "Not many vineyards produce red wine around here, so I doubt anyone will expect it. But then again, a red wine has never won as far as I know, and halflings are creatures of tradition, after all." She stopped, her brow furrowed as she pressed a finger to her lips. "I like it."

"Really?" Marigold's insides felt like she'd been pushed down a hill in a horseless carriage.

"Really." Elara placed her hands on Marigold's shoulder, and looked the halfling in the eyes. "It's a great wine, and I think it's high time we shake things up a bit."

Marigold let out a sigh of relief. She trusted Elara's opinion more than just about anyone in the world.

The elf's attention returned to the wine barrels. "When you were here yesterday, you didn't check to see where the trail came from?"

Marigold shook her head. "I followed it to the door, but that's it."

"This is going to vex me all winter, I can feel it." Elara

walked to the cellar entrance and removed the bar from the twin doors before pushing them open. "Nothing we can do now, so I guess we should get to work."

Outside, it was a beautiful, crisp morning. Dew covered the grass, and fluffy clouds made for a picturesque view among the rolling hills. The trees were tinged with yellows, oranges, and reds. It was the perfect day for a harvest.

A raspy meow came from beside the inn as Onyx appeared around the corner, his paws wet from the dew. He might not give a damn about horned rabbits or whatever was terrorizing the vineyard in his old age, but he always had a sixth sense for where Marigold was.

She knelt, waiting for the milky-eyed cat to approach when she noticed Aldric's cart parked in its usual spot beside the inn. She suddenly remembered the mage's suspicious activity from the day she'd been showing Eris around the vineyard. "Huh."

"What?" Elara followed Marigold's line of sight.

"It might be nothing, but I think I may have our first suspect." Marigold scratched Onyx behind the ears. "The other day, I saw Aldric putting an apple into the cart, and it looked like he was talking to something inside it. I thought maybe it was Splinter, but that doesn't make sense. It's not as if the construct can eat." She stood, her brow knitted as she tried to piece it all together. "I was across the vineyard, so I couldn't get a good look, but it seemed suspicious at the time."

"And if he was feeding something apples, it's logical to assume that whatever it was eats grapes as well." Elara grinned wickedly. "We've got a mage to interrogate."

The elf walked with purpose, practically leaping up the

stairs as they entered the inn. Aldric was at the bar, having changed from his nightgown into his blue robe. He sat on a stool, talking to another guest while Splinter played with a toothpick like it was a small sword.

"You!" Elara raised her voice and pointed at Aldric from across the room. "We need to talk. Now."

The inn fell silent as heads turned in Elara's direction.

"Easy there." Marigold grabbed the elf by the arm. "He's still a guest, and we don't know anything yet."

Aldric frowned as he turned around on the barstool. "What's the meaning of this?"

"Sorry about that." Marigold stepped in front of Elara. "There's been a bit of a situation around the vineyard. Can we speak to you for a minute in my office? It's about your cart."

The mage's eyes went wide. "Has something happened to Ol' Bertha?"

"She's fine. We just have a few questions."

Aldric turned to the human he had been chatting with. "Excuse me for a moment."

Elara shut the door once they were all three inside the office.

"I must admit, this is most irregular." Aldric looked from Marigold to Elara before taking a seat. "What seems to be the problem?"

"Why don't you tell us?" Elara leaned forward, finger pointed at the mage.

"Enough with the finger pointing, Elara." Marigold sighed. "I'll handle it from here."

"Fine." The elf crossed her arms and leaned against the wall, her gaze fixed on the mage.

"We just have a few questions." Marigold drummed

her fingers on the desk as she pondered how to broach the subject. "Right around the time you arrived, grapes started to disappear from some of our vines in a strange manner. The other day, I noticed you placing an apple inside your cart. We were wondering if the two might be connected."

"I see." Aldric stroked his beard. "You think I have something to do with your missing grapes."

"It's the only lead we have at the moment." Marigold shrugged. "Our wards are working fine, and we've never had an incident like this happen before."

"Hmm." The mage rubbed the embroidered edges of his robe between his fingers.

"Why were you putting an apple in the cart?" Elara asked.

Marigold narrowed her gaze at the elf but said nothing. She waited for Aldric to respond.

Aldric rested his hands in his lap. "Sometimes, I store food for when I'm on the road."

"Marigold said you were talking to something."

"I give life to inanimate objects, what do you expect?" Aldric laughed. "But if it makes you feel better, I'll say it. I haven't touched your grapes."

"Then I suppose you wouldn't mind if we looked inside your cart?"

Elara had taken control of the interrogation, but Marigold didn't have any better questions and let it continue.

Aldric stood. "If that will put this to rest, then by all means."

On the way to the cart, he picked up Splinter from the bar and grabbed his staff, which was resting in the corner.

Onyx was waiting on the porch when they stepped outside. The dire cat nuzzled his massive head against Marigold's thigh, and his chest rumbled.

A knot formed in Marigold's stomach as she followed Aldric and Elara. Reprimanding a guest was never a fun prospect. If Aldric wasn't involved, then she'd just insulted him for no reason, but if it turned out that he was involved, what would she do? That possibility opened an even greater host of questions. Whatever was in there, this was a no-win situation.

Aldric set Splinter on top of the cart and turned to face Marigold and Elara. "Here you go." He tapped his staff against the wood, and the door on the side of the cart popped open.

Onyx sniffed at the air, his hackles raised as he approached the open cart. A low growl emanated from the dire cat as he peeked inside. Marigold knelt beside the cat and stroked his back. He was as tense as the day Aldric had first arrived. Elara crouched beside them, peering inside.

There were two shelves. The bottom was empty, and a jar filled with a pink substance sat on the other.

"What's in the jar?" asked Elara.

"It's for the firelight display." Aldric frowned.

Onyx continued to moan his displeasure while Marigold and Elara exchanged a glance. Something was clearly amiss, but there was no evidence against the mage.

"You're welcome to check the drawers on the other side if you wish." He tapped the cart again, and the drawers whooshed open. "They're filled with supplies for the firelight show as well."

Marigold walked to the other side. The drawers were

filled with jars of powders in a myriad of colors along with papers, tubes, fuses, and other components.

"I'm sorry to have bothered you." Marigold held both her hands together at her chest. "Something had been infesting our grapes, and we're at our wit's end trying to find out what."

"It's okay. I don't take it personally." Aldric tapped the cart, and all of the drawers and doors closed with a snap. Onyx's growling immediately stopped. "I am sorry to disappoint you. I've found that when something can't be explained, magic is often where people first look for answers."

"I appreciate your understanding. Again, we're sorry for disturbing you." Marigold nudged the elf in the side. "Right, Elara?"

"Yep." The elf nodded. "So sorry."

They waited beside the inn until the mage had returned inside.

"He's hiding something." Elara glowered at the cart.

Marigold shrugged. "Unless it's a gluttonous appetite for grapes, I don't know what it could be. He's certainly acting suspicious, but there's nothing to link him to the vineyard." She looked down as Onyx threaded between her legs. "If only he could talk."

Elara examined the cart again, looking at it from all angles and then dropping to her knees to view it from underneath. "I don't know, but I don't trust this cart one bit."

"That's a mystery for another time." Marigold set off for the shed. "For now, we still have a harvest to prepare for."

19. THE HARVEST

Marigold pushed the incident with Aldric from her thoughts as the townsfolk began to arrive at the inn. Whether or not the mage had anything to do with the missing grapes would be a moot point once the harvest was over and all of the juice was left to ferment. For now, there was plenty of work to do.

Elara was uphill at the winery, making sure the stomping trough was clean and the clay pots were prepared for the fermentation process. Finn had moved the wagon by the vineyard and was unloading crates, baskets, and wheelbarrows for collecting grapes.

Locke monitored the hog as it roasted on the spit. It sizzled and crackled as he basted it with his signature sauce—a mixture of apple cider vinegar, butter, and spices. Where most recipes called for a splash of apple juice, Locke's secret ingredient was the juice from ember-fruit grapes.

A crowd of halflings had gathered around the dwarf's

workspace, lured by the heavenly smell of the roasting pork. They looked as ravenous as Onyx, who was now underfoot, voicing his hunger with raspy meows as he nuzzled the dwarf's legs. Nearby, there was a table with food and beverages, where a second crowd was lurking while Gerty brought out platters of food.

So far, everything was coming together nicely.

Gerty returned with plates of butter-toasted bread bites and crispy potato fritters with apple chutney. There was grumbling as someone pushed to the front of the line. A trail of pipe smoke followed Elmwood as the gray-haired halfling nudged his way through his neighbors like a kitten searching for a teat. He picked up a carafe of apple cider from the table and sniffed it. "Mari!" he called out. "When do we get the good stuff?"

Marigold joined Gerty behind the table. "We go over this every year, Elmwood. Nobody gets wine until the first stomping." She gave him a knowing look. "It's safer for everyone that way."

Elmwood's cheeks flushed as the crowd laughed.

"It was one time, Mari. One time!" He sucked on his pipe and blew smoke from his nostrils as he stormed away, followed by more laughter.

Marigold held her hand in the air, gathering everyone's attention. "If you need a bite to eat before we get started, now's your chance. The harvest will begin shortly."

She saw Poppy out of the corner of her eye as the gnome finally arrived. She had her satchel and an armful of notebooks.

"Where do you want me?" Poppy asked with a grin.

By my side, the halfling wanted to say, but they both

had duties to uphold. "Find a spot you like. I'll let everyone know you're here once we get started."

"Thanks again for doing this." Poppy's hands were full, so she leaned her shoulder into Marigold. "It'll be nice to meet some of the faces that don't come into town as much."

"I'm happy to help." Marigold touched the gnome's arm. "I hope you'll take some time to enjoy the harvest and get your feet dirty."

"Of course." Poppy smiled. "I'm learning there's nothing better than first-hand experience when research is concerned."

"That's the spirit." Marigold chuckled. "I'll see you in a few. I still need to make another round."

Marigold ventured toward the vineyard, helping Finn spread out the equipment. Afterward, she made a final check-in with Elara.

Everything was nearly ready.

Some of the townsfolk had brought their instruments, and the sound of music drifted up the hill. Marigold took a second to appreciate the moment. It warmed her heart to see so many halflings gathered around the inn, all coming together in the name of community. As much as things were changing in the world, it was comforting to know that some things stayed the same.

She turned to Elara. "We've worked all year for this moment. Are you ready?"

The elf placed a hand on Marigold's shoulder and gazed upon the vineyard. "Let the fun begin."

When Marigold made it back to the inn, more familiar faces had arrived, some of which were attending the harvest for the first time. She made her rounds, welcoming everyone and thanking them for their attendance.

Korin, the dwarven cleric who had healed her arm, was talking with Hamlen, the cleric banker from Stormrest, both wearing the gray robes of the Order of Clerics. Rosie, the baker from Hearth & Honey Bakery, had brought pastries and was fighting off Elmwood with a pair of tongs as he tried to take two. Windell the wardmaster was in a deep conversation with Aldric, and a crowd of curious children had gathered around the mage to watch Splinter dance upon his shoulder.

Marigold climbed atop one of the picnic tables, and the music and chatter faded as all eyes fell upon her.

"Welcome once again to the Dew Drop Vineyard's annual harvest. Though our vineyard is relatively new in the long history of Tyne, the harvest tradition dates back farther than our written records. Once a year, we all come together to work a little and drink a lot." Someone strummed their lute, echoed by a round of cheers. "Gatherings like this are what set us apart from the other kingdoms. We relish in the simple pleasures of life—good food, good drinks, and good company. When you have that, what else could you possibly need?"

"Hear, hear!" someone shouted.

"Before we get started, I want to thank you all for coming out. There will be plenty of food and drink to go around this evening, but first, a few ground rules." She reached into her apron and pulled out a pair of shears. "I don't know if there's a halfling in Willowbrook who doesn't own a good pair of shears, but in the event that you need a pair, Finn will have some on hand. Baskets and crates are already waiting around the vineyard. Elara and

I will explain the best way to cut the clusters for those who haven't participated before. Also, we have a very special guest with us this year." She gestured to the table where Poppy was sitting. "Many of you have already met Poppy Deepspring. She's a scholar for the Gnomish Historical Society here to research the history of the harvest festival. For the past few weeks, she's been conducting interviews with many of you. If you haven't had a chance to meet her, she's lovely company. So stop by and tell her about your fondest memories."

"Like the time Elmwood cut off his finger," someone shouted.

"*Almost* cut off my finger!" Elmwood corrected them, holding his hands in the air for everyone to see.

"On a final note, I just want to say how grateful I am for each and every one of you." She swallowed hard as she met Poppy's gaze. "This time of year is a reminder of how lucky we all are. In addition to a wonderful and supportive community, I've been blessed with an incredible staff that keeps this place running. Today would not be possible without all of their hard work. To Elara, there's not another vintner in all of Tyne that I would trust as my cellar master more than you. Locke, you are the rock that anchors all of us with your steady presence. And to Finn and Gerty, no matter how much you may rattle my nerves, I love you like siblings." Marigold paused, waiting for the applause to die down. "Now, let's go harvest some grapes."

The music picked up as about half of the crowd made their way to the vineyard. The harvest tended to start slow as people socialized, and the rest would join them in time.

For those that followed, Marigold gave her usual speech, demonstrating the best way to prune the grape clusters. She and Elara walked among the rows, monitoring people as they worked. Once she was satisfied with the progress, Marigold joined in as well. It was always important to be a part of the process. Not only that, she enjoyed it.

She held a bunch of honey grapes in her palm, feeling their waxy exterior and the weight of the fruit. How amazing it was that such a small thing could bring so many together. She snipped the stem and placed the grapes in her basket.

Chatter and song carried through the vineyard while they worked. Before long, it was time for lunch. Locke had prepared the ingredients for sandwiches early in the morning, so all Gerty had to do was set them out.

Marigold found Poppy at a table surrounded by Elmwood, Rosie, and a few other townsfolk. The gnome scribbled intently in her journal as the group rambled on. Marigold grabbed two sandwiches and took a seat next to the gnome.

"Mind if I steal her away for a bit?" Marigold asked.

"By all means." Elmwood rubbed his hands together. "All this work is making me hungry."

He reached for one of the sandwiches, and Rosie slapped away his hand.

"Work?" Rosie scrunched her nose. "You've been here the entire time."

"I suppose the research will just write itself, will it?" Elmwood scoffed as he left to go find food.

"Always the curmudgeon, that one." Rosie shook her

head, and then she winked at Poppy. "We'll continue our story later."

Marigold placed a plate in front of Poppy. "What was that all about?"

"Thank you." Poppy set her notebook aside and picked up the sandwich. "Rosie was telling me about a dalliance she had at a harvest festival when she was younger."

"A dalliance? How scandalous." Marigold's mouth gaped as she watched Rosie take her place in line behind Elmwood. The baker wasn't quite as old as Elmwood, but she had streaks of gray in her curly blonde hair.

"Apparently, it's quite a romantic event." Poppy smirked. "There's wine, delicious food, music, dancing, and firelights."

As heat rushed to her cheeks, Marigold tried to change the subject. "After you eat, would you like to try your hand at harvesting?"

Poppy nodded as she bit into the sandwich. She answered with a full mouth. "Gotta get the full experience, right?"

"That's the spirit."

After they finished eating, Marigold led Poppy to a row of dreamcatcher grapes that was less crowded, giving them a bit of privacy.

They worked their way down the row, cutting grapes and filling the basket. Usually, harvests were hectic as Marigold tried to wrangle everyone, but this year, she was determined to take a little time to enjoy herself. This day only came around once a year, after all.

A few rows over, someone burst into a chorus of *Where the Clover Grows High*, a song about a halfling who fell asleep in a patch of clovers.

Marigold watched as Poppy cradled a cluster of grapes like they were made of glass and carefully snipped the stem. "You're a natural."

"I had a good teacher." Poppy smiled as she regarded the fruit in her palm. "They're so beautiful."

Marigold admired the way the shades of lilac and violet perfectly complemented the gnome's purple eyes. "Yeah, they really are."

"I don't know if I've told you this enough, but I'm grateful for all the help you've provided." Poppy placed the grapes in the basket and took Marigold's hand. "When I first arrived, I assumed I'd be spending all my time in the library or at Town Hall. I thought I'd have to beg people to give me time for an interview. That's how it usually goes. But you've gone above and beyond anything I could have hoped for. I think this may be some of my best research yet."

"I'm glad I could help." She squeezed Poppy's hand, noticing the ink splotches across the gnome's fingers that had become so familiar after the past couple of months. "But I'd say we're even. I doubt I would have ever picked up my father's old journals if not for your influence. Those have been a gift."

Poppy wrapped her other hand around Marigold's, and their eyes locked. "I've enjoyed my time here. Part of me doesn't want to leave."

Then don't, Marigold wanted to say. She closed her eyes, focusing on the kindling between them.

Poppy's touch was a radiant hearth that warmed Marigold to her core, the kind of touch that left the world feeling colder in its absence. It could erupt if she let it. As much as she wanted to bask in the comfort, she knew it was fleeting. Poppy's place was elsewhere. She worked for the Gnomish Historical Society, and her passion was in research. Marigold would never be the person to stand between someone and what they loved.

"What's wrong?" Poppy's brow knit with concern.

"It's nothing." Marigold forced a smile. "The inn won't be the same without you."

Poppy's thumb caressed the back of Marigold's palm, sending a wave of tiny sparks up the halfling's arm. "I'm not leaving just yet. We still have the festival, and then I'll have to take time to gather my thoughts and write everything down. We can enjoy the time we have together."

Marigold nodded. She wouldn't let these moments pass her by, but deep down, there was a part of her that was already aching.

She took a deep breath. "You're right. We can choose to treasure the time we have."

Poppy smiled, and Marigold's gaze fell upon the gnome's lips. Their soft pink was reminiscent of the tea roses that grew alongside many of the buildings in town. She wanted nothing more than to taste their sweetness.

Marigold's heart raced as she leaned in, closing her eyes. Her body tingled with anticipation.

"Marigold!" Finn's voice cut through the moment like a banshee's shriek. "Mari, I know you're over here somewhere."

Poppy and Marigold both laughed, and their hands drifted apart. Whatever was about to happen, the moment had passed.

"What is it, Finn?" Marigold called as she waved her hand through the air above the vines.

"There you are. I've been looking all over for you." He

wiped sweat from his brow. "The wagon is loaded, and Elara's driving it up the hill for the stomping. Gerty said she'll meet you there with the guests."

"Alright, we'll be right there." Marigold picked up the basket of grapes and turned to Poppy. "Ready to get your feet wet?"

20. SLOW-DANCING

Marigold and Poppy weaved through the crowd at the top of the hill. Gerty had already gathered the inn's guests around the massive trough, and many of the townsfolk had joined to watch the Dew Drop Vineyard's tradition of having the guests participate in the first stomp.

While there were still grapes to be harvested, the majority would be finished in the next few hours. The rest of the evening would be spent stomping grapes and enjoying one another's company as they ate, sang, and danced. For Marigold and Elara, they'd be busy storing the juice in pots for fermentation.

Marigold took her place behind the huge, hollowed-out log used for the stomping. In the afternoon sun, the vibrant green honey grapes looked like a giant bowl of marbles.

"Welcome, everyone! Today is always a magical day." She smiled at Aldric, who stood at the end of the trough with Splinter on his shoulder. "The yearly grape harvest is one of my favorite halfling traditions. Not only is it a symbol of what makes our community great, it's also a time to celebrate our love for food and drink." Someone strummed a lute, and the crowd cheered. "I like to think that one of our most endearing qualities as halflings is our hospitable nature. What better way to showcase that friendly spirit than to let our guests begin the stomping?"

Including Poppy and Aldric, there were a total of eight guests staying at the inn. There was Ronan, a human adventurer who'd stayed at the inn earlier in the year while passing through on a quest. After learning about the harvest, he'd promised to return. Marigold had fully expected the man not to show, but he'd been true to his word. There were also two halflings from Whitblossum and a trio of dwarven sisters from Hillside who'd all come specifically for the harvest.

"Alright, everyone." Marigold gestured for Finn to bring the water bucket. "Rinse your feet and climb in."

After dousing his feet, Aldric held up his robes and stepped into the trough. As soon as he was over the edge, Splinter jumped from the mage's shoulder and disappeared among the sea of grapes. A moment later, his little wooden head appeared.

The three sisters climbed in next, one of whom kept stealing glances at Ronan. The adventurer had his blond hair pulled back, and his trousers were rolled up to his knees. He wore a sleeveless tunic that showcased arms painted with scars and tattoos. Despite his grizzled appearance, he was one of the nicest people Marigold had ever met. The two halflings climbed in next, followed by Marigold and Poppy.

Once they were all inside the trough, someone started a chorus of *Seven Pies for Breakfast*. The music quickly followed, and Gerty and Finn interlocked arms, skipping in a circle to the rhythm.

"Stomping is basically like it sounds," Marigold said as she began marching in place. The cool grapes exploded beneath her feet, and a mixture of juice and pulp sloshed between her toes. "Keep at it and the juice will drain down the hill."

A fruity aroma filled the air as the others joined in. The dwarven sisters giggled among themselves as they stomped vigorously, sending waves across the trough. Where most of them churned their legs through the grapes, Aldric made dainty steps, each time fully removing his feet before stomping again. He held his robes up like he was doing a curtsy, his pipe dangling precariously from his mouth. Beneath him, Splinter skewered grapes on his twig fingers as he swam around.

"This is certainly an experience." Poppy held onto Marigold's shoulder for stability. "Such a strange sensation."

Marigold smiled at the joy radiating from the gnome. Grape stomping always seemed to bring out a person's inner child, no matter the age. "You've got to admit it's fun, though."

"I can't argue with you there." Poppy laughed. "No one at the historical society is going to believe that I took part."

After a few minutes, everyone except for Ronan had started to tire. For as much fun as it was, grape stomping was equally grueling.

The guests cleaned their feet, and many of the children quickly climbed into the trough to take their places. It wouldn't be long before they were all tuckered out and napping on the hillside.

Laughter blended with music as Marigold led the guests down the hill. Along the way, she gave her customary tour of the winery and cellar, showing how the juice would be fermented and then aged. She proudly showcased her father's many accomplishments along the wall of ribbons.

As they left the cellar, the smell of roasted pork called like a gilded trap with its tantalizing aroma. Locke was standing beside the massive beast when they arrived, sharpening his knife.

Ronan closed his eyes and inhaled the savory aroma. "This has been everything you promised and more."

"Did you have your doubts?" Marigold asked.

"I never doubted you, but I did pass up a pretty lucrative quest to be here." The man tapped the coin pouch on his side. "But I'm glad to have made the trip."

"Just wait till the wine starts flowing." Locke sliced through the hog's golden-brown skin and steam wafted from the cut. "That's when the real fun begins. I hope you lot are hungry."

One of the dwarven sisters nudged Ronan in the side. "I don't know about you, but I'm ravished."

Ronan frowned. "Do you mean famished?"

"I could be both if you like." She bit her lip seductively.

Marigold exchanged a glance with Poppy, who wore an equally surprised expression. Not that it was a bad thing, but Marigold never understood how someone could be so forward with their intentions. Then again, it probably saved a lot of forlorn thoughts when you wore your intentions on your sleeve.

As if on cue, Gerty arrived with several bottles of wine. The halflings who weren't at the stomping flocked over like ants to a piece of cake.

"Guests first." Marigold raised an admonishing finger. "I promise there's enough for everyone." She turned to Poppy. "There's still work for me to do, but I've enjoyed taking a few moments away. Keep your notebook close. Once they have a few drinks in them, I'm sure you'll hear plenty of stories, some of which you'd rather not."

Poppy's eyes widened. "I can't wait."

"And one more thing..." Marigold gently squeezed Poppy's fingers. "Don't forget to enjoy yourself."

While the process of draining juice from the trough to the winery was relatively simple, and gravity took care of most of the heavy lifting, it was still a lot of work. Once the grapes were stomped, the skins and seeds would need to be scooped out so that the next batch could be loaded from the wagon. The juice filtered through a hole at the bottom of the trough and flowed down a gutter to the winery, where it would be stored to ferment. The pots were much smaller than the barrels, but each one needed to be moved by hand once they were full.

Luckily, they had plenty of help.

By the time the last wagon made its way up, the afternoon sun cast the hillside in a golden glow.

"So far, no hiccups," Elara said as she placed the stopper in the trough so that they could shovel the pomace.

"Hey, now." Marigold narrowed her eyes at the elf. "Don't you jinx us."

"I would never." Elara wore a mischievous expression. "By the way, I saw you and Poppy earlier."

"What do you mean?" Marigold's cheeks instantly burned as she shoveled a heap of pomace from the trough.

"You know exactly what I mean." The elf's eyes twinkled with amusement. "Did you forget I can see the whole vineyard from up here? Even the rows of dreamcatcher grapes." She placed a hand on Marigold's arm, stopping the halfling from working. There was a kindness to her tone when she spoke. "It'll happen. Give it time."

"Time is the one thing we don't have." Marigold swallowed at the memory of the almost… whatever it was.

Elara scoffed. "Time is a construct."

Marigold set the shovel aside. "I don't even know what that means."

"It means—" Elara rested her hands on Marigold's shoulders. "—that things will happen at their own speed. There's an elvish saying that goes 'the tranquil river can still carve through stone.' If something is meant to be, then it will happen."

"And what if it's not meant to be?" Marigold stared into the bottom of the trough. That was the question she'd been too afraid to ask herself.

"Then it's not meant to be. But look at me, Marigold." She waited for the halfling to meet her gaze. "You don't have to wait for things to come to you. There's another saying that I'm quite fond of. 'The river doesn't wait to be told where to flow.' It's a mantra I try to live by. If you want something, don't let time, fate, or the gods themselves stand in your way. You go out there and get it, because you deserve everything this world has to offer you. And most of all, you deserve to be happy."

"Thank you. I don't know how I ever found a friend like you." Marigold blinked back tears as she wrapped her arms around the elf. "Are all elvish sayings about rivers?"

Elara laughed as she patted Marigold on the back. "Not all, but there are a lot."

Marigold held onto the elf for a long moment before wiping her eyes. She got back to work, and with the help of the volunteers, the trough was soon emptied and filled with more grapes.

Wine bottles had somehow made their way uphill, and the next round of stomping was the liveliest of the day. Halflings danced in the trough, serenaded by music and song as the line between work and play blurred along with their vision.

For the next few hours, the harvest consumed Marigold's thoughts as she and Elara worked late into the evening.

"Finally." Elara stretched her arms overhead after capping the last of the clay pots. "I don't know about you, but I need a drink."

Back at the inn, torches burned as Marigold and Elara joined the gathering. Wine flowed and fellowship reigned as lively music carried across the night. There was laughter and conversation, song and dance. Empty bottles littered the tables, and Locke's hog had been trimmed to the bone. Many of the older halflings sat together near the garden, bellies full as they blew smoke rings into the stars. Onyx sat nearby, gnawing on the remains of a bone.

A giant yarn snake slithered past the indifferent dire cat, followed by a trail of giggling children.

"So that's what he's been working on." Elara raised a brow. "Better than a scarf for a giant, I suppose. Well, maybe not for Locke."

The dwarf watched the enchanted scarf with a wary eye as it weaved through the crowd.

Marigold searched for Aldric, but the mage was nowhere to be seen.

"Good work today." She smiled as the giant gray snake passed by. Splinter sat on the back of the construct, riding it like a mount as it weaved through the grass. "I couldn't have done it without you."

"I know." Elara chuckled. "We can evaluate everything tomorrow. For now, I think we've both got someone special waiting for us." She didn't wait for a response before heading to find Locke.

Marigold scanned the crowd for Poppy. She found the gnome sitting with Tobin and Prim Lightfoot, owners of Wick & Willow Candles. There were several bottles of wine on the table, and Poppy swayed back and forth as she wrote in her journal. Her movement reminded Marigold of the first night the two of them had drank together in the cellar.

"She's a lightweight, you know," Marigold said, joining the table.

"She might be." Prim winked. "But she's good company."

"Zere she is!" Poppy's words slurred as her face lit up with excitement. "I's was wond'rin' when you'd be done."

"Look at you." Marigold's smile broadened. "You certainly took my words to heart." Her gaze drifted to Poppy's notebook, where meticulous notes had devolved into scribbles. "I don't know how much of that you'll be able to read tomorrow, but we can't deny the effort."

Poppy was staring at Marigold intently. The gnome bit her lip. "You're pretty."

Marigold felt a rush of heat creeping up her neck. Tobin and Prim grinned like they had front-row seats to the traveling circus.

Luckily for Marigold, the music changed, and the bard started singing *Frost on the Morning Blossom*. Tobin and Prim stood as tables emptied for the slower-paced, romantic song. The kind of song even the elders would dance to.

Poppy's eyes glistened in the torchlight as she wrapped her hand around Marigold's. "Wanna dance?"

"I'd love to." Marigold helped Poppy from the table, and they joined the others.

Their fingers intertwined, and Marigold placed a hand on Poppy's side. The gnome stepped in close, resting her head on Marigold's shoulder as they swayed to the music. Marigold's heart pounded at their proximity, so close that she could smell the remnants of honey soap in Poppy's hair.

She closed her eyes, breathing in the moment and savoring the warmth of Poppy's body pressed against hers. She didn't listen to the words of the song, but to the rhythm of two hearts beating as one.

When Marigold opened her eyes, she saw Aldric in the corner of her vision. He stood by his cart, placing a bunch of grapes inside.

Marigold rolled her eyes. Whatever the mage was up to, he could keep his secrets. Now that the harvest was over, she didn't care anymore. She had everything she wanted right in front of her.

Poppy stirred, mumbling something about it being a good day.

Marigold rested her cheek against Poppy's head. There was nowhere in the world she'd rather be. After all this time, she finally understood what it meant to be touched by magic.

21. TRICKLE DOWN

Over the following days, cool autumn air descended on the vineyard, expunging the last vestiges of green as the hills were painted with hues of gold and crimson. The staff still had plenty of work to do, but the hardest part was over.

With the harvest festival quickly approaching, there was an uptick in visitors to the orchard and pumpkin patch. The wine contest was always the highlight for the vineyards, but for the rest of the town, the pie contest reigned supreme. Some rivalries went back decades as neighbor competed against neighbor for the elusive blue ribbon. From pumpkin to pecan, blueberry to apple, there were flavors for every palate, and from now until the festival, the scent of cinnamon, apple, and buttery crusts would linger in the streets as half the homes in Willowbrook tried their hand at one pie or another.

For Marigold, the next few weeks would be a test of patience as she waited for the juice to ferment. She and

Elara would check the pots daily, monitoring the sugar, acidity, and alcohol levels. After the juice became wine, it would need to be clarified to remove any sediment before eventually being stored in casks to age.

Even though she'd decided on a varietal for the wine contest, Marigold still needed to pick a vintage. That would involve sampling various barrels. Once she made the final decision, the wine would need to be bottled, since it was customary to bring additional cases of wine for purchase.

As attention shifted to the festival, a quiet calmness settled over the inn. Aldric was gone more often as he continued his preparations for the firelight display in earnest. Poppy spent hours in her room as she organized the numerous interviews she'd conducted.

The common area was empty as Marigold passed through on her way to the kitchen. She found Locke chopping a heap of apples on the center island. The honey aroma from the fruit was so tempting that Marigold risked his wrath by taking a slice from the bowl.

"Making a pie?" She bit into the slice, and tart sweetness gushed across her tongue.

"I'm going to pretend I didn't see that." He gave her a reproachful look. "I'm making cider."

"How lovely! There's nothing like a glass of warm cider on a cool evening."

Marigold was contemplating taking another piece when Locke slid the bowl in front of her.

"Actually, I still need a few ingredients." He shook the bowl, a hunter luring its prey, until Marigold took another slice. "We're running low on cinnamon and nutmeg. Would you be so kind as to pick up some in town?"

"Anything for you." She scooped a handful from the bowl.

Locke's mustache twitched, but to his credit, he said nothing.

While Finn hitched Acorn Blossom to the wagon, Marigold walked up to the winery to check on the fermentation.

Elara was already inside. She knelt over one of the clay pots, holding the notebook for cataloging the process. Each vessel was numbered and labeled with the varietal, and stored underground to keep it cool.

"I'm about to venture into town," Marigold said, crouching next to Elara. "Locke needs ingredients for cider. Is there anything I can pick up for you?"

"I don't think so." The elf used a ladle to scoop a small amount of juice from the open pot. She took a sip and scrunched her nose before passing it to Marigold. "You can finally taste the yeast."

Marigold took a sip. The juice was fresh and fruity, but it had taken on a distinct bread-like taste. It wasn't bad, but it wasn't pleasant either. Kind of like if someone had left a piece of bread soaking in grape juice all day.

This early in the fermentation process, the juice was still exceptionally sweet, but as the yeast began to consume the sugars and convert them into alcohol, flavors of bread, cheese, or buttermilk would become prominent. These flavors would fade as the alcohol content rose and the yeast slowly died off.

During the first week or so, they weren't tasting the wine for flavor, but to make sure the yeast wasn't over-stressed. A rotten, sulfur-like smell would indicate they'd need to aerate the pot. If that didn't correct the problem, there were additional steps they could take. Luckily, this batch was exactly as it should be.

Marigold handed the ladle back to Elara. "Seems we're right on schedule. I'll check in again later this evening."

She knew Elara could handle everything, but this part of the winemaking process only happened once a year. It was nostalgic in a way. When Marigold was a child, she'd followed her father around like a cat chasing string. She'd peek into the pots like she knew what she was doing, and he'd always let her smell the wine. She smiled at the memory as she made her way back to the wagon.

Acorn Blossom raised his head as the wagon rolled across the bridge into Willowbrook, the bell on his mane jingling as he sniffed at the scent of roasted apples and freshly baked pies that seeped through the open windows. Marigold's stomach rumbled, equally entranced by the heavenly aroma shrouding the town.

Finn turned to Marigold with a pleading expression. "If we don't stop for a bite, I'll never be able to concentrate."

"You read my mind," Marigold said as she parked the wagon by Hearth & Honey Bakery. The market would still be open for a few hours, and it was hard to resist the call of sweetness.

Inside, the bakery was surprisingly empty.

Rosie leaned against the counter, twiddling her thumbs. Her face brightened as Marigold and Finn entered. "Good to see you!" She clapped her hands together. "What can I get for you today?"

Finn looked around. "Where are all the customers?"

"Same as every year. Once the festival rolls around, the whole town thinks they can bake a pie." Rosie pursed her lips. "Give 'em a few days. They'll be back. Not everyone was meant to be a baker."

"That's the truth of it." Marigold laughed as she recalled the time Elara had tried to bake a cake for Locke's birthday. It had been so black that even Onyx wouldn't touch it. "You can't argue with the aromas, though. This is the one week a year I wish we lived closer."

Marigold perused the display of baked goods, bypassing the breads and savory pastries for the sweeter offerings. There were honey cakes drizzled with glaze, lemon poppy seed muffins, cinnamon sugar twists, and a variety of cookies and biscuits.

She tapped her chin as she decided. "I think I'll take a cinnamon sugar twist. Finn?"

"Make it two."

Rosie picked up the twists with her tongs, and crumbles of cinnamon sugar dusted the counter. "I enjoyed meeting your friend the other night. She's a real sweetheart."

"Yeah, she is." Marigold smiled as she paid for the pastry. "See you around, Rosie. Thanks for the sweets."

Outside, Marigold and Finn indulged in the delectable

pastries. There was a slight crunch from the glazed sugar as she bit into it. The inside was soft and chewy, buttery and rich with a cinnamon sweetness.

Marigold licked her fingers and sighed. "What is it about sugar that is so comforting?"

Finn shrugged, savoring the last bite. "I don't know, but I could eat an entire batch of these twists and not even feel bad about it."

***

The market was bustling when they arrived. With a little over a week until the festival, various stalls and stages were being constructed around the market square for events and contests. Not only was the festival a celebration of the end of the harvest, but it was also the biggest week of tourism for the town with many of the shops and local artisans depending on the income to see them through the winter.

Marigold spotted Mayor Sweetwater from afar as he instructed a carpenter on the stage's placement. The mayor held a piece of string, his brow deeply furrowed as he appeared to be complaining about the measurements of the steps.

She turned to tell Finn she'd meet him back here in an hour, but he'd already slipped away and was lurking about one of the stands selling sausages. Marigold pulled out her list. The spice shop should have cinnamon and nutmeg in stock and possibly honey, but they also needed bars of soap, so she'd have to stop by the general store after.

A bell jingled as Marigold opened the door to A Dash

of Spice, where an abundance of smells assaulted her senses. Compared to the mild but pleasant smell of baked goods outside, this was a full-on incursion.

For some reason, Gerty loved this place, so Marigold often sent her when they needed to replenish their stocks.

She blinked back tears and cleared her throat as she stepped inside. The shop was cozy, filled with shelves and cabinets that housed a variety of ingredients and aromatics. There were jars of finely ground spices from across Aedrea, bundles of herbs tied with twine or ribbons, and containers of exotic fruits that had been dehydrated. Braids of garlic hung on the wall along with racks of dried lavender, thyme, and rosemary. There was an entire section dedicated to mortars and pestles, clay and ceramic jars, and cloth bags in various shapes and sizes.

"Good afternoon." Marigold waved to the halfling behind the counter. He'd moved to town not too long ago, and she couldn't recall his name.

He was reading a book, a pair of round spectacles resting on the tip of his hawklike nose. His brown hair was trimmed just below his ears, and he wore a thick, olive-green cardigan with a red scarf draped across his shoulders.

"Welcome." He looked up, smiling as he placed a bookmark inside the book and closed it. "Anything I can help you with?"

"Cinnamon and nutmeg. Honey, too, if you have it."

"You're in luck." He stepped from behind the counter to showcase their offerings.

"What were you reading? If you don't mind me asking. You seemed pretty engrossed."

"Oh, I was." He chuckled. "My sister picked it up at a

bookstore in Whitblossum and insisted I read it. It's about a palace guard and a powerful mage who run away together to start a new life. They end up opening a tea shop on the edge of the kingdom."

"That sounds delightful." Marigold thought of Poppy. With the gnome's departure imminent, the prospect of running away together and starting over was undeniably tempting.

She paid for the items and set out toward the general store across the square. Halfway there, she spotted Tansy Ironvale. The tall human druid was talking to a pair of halflings who worked at Town Hall. She wore her hair in an elegant bun adorned with flowers that should have been long out of season, and her forest-green robe shimmered as she moved, her jewel-covered fingers glittering in the afternoon sun with each gesture. A small bird fluttered down from a nearby tree, landing on the druid's shoulder.

Marigold had to admit that Tansy demanded attention. Her very presence was commanding.

After their last encounter, Marigold felt comfortable approaching the woman. The bad blood was in the past, and she could be cordial. If nothing else, she could ask about the harvest at Darkroot Cellars. That was at least one thing the two vineyards had in common.

Marigold was walking over when she noticed Galvin a few steps behind the druid. She immediately stopped and turned to leave, but it was too late. He'd already noticed her.

"Marigold!" Galvin's voice carried above the crowd.

She closed her eyes, gathered herself, and forced a smile as she joined them.

"How's my competition?" Galvin grinned as he looked at her down his upturned nose. He tucked his gaudy hands into his suit pockets and rocked back and forth. "I'd wish you luck, but we all know how it's going to end."

Marigold bit her tongue. It was no use getting worked up around him.

"Good to see you, Marigold." Tansy gave her a warm smile. "I heard your harvest went well."

"It was good. It's always nice when so many of us can come together." Marigold returned Tansy's smile, ignoring Galvin. "How was yours?"

"There was no harvest this year." Galvin laughed. "Well, not in the traditional sense. We finally decided to forgo the ancient practice. Having others come to the vineyard to do our picking for us—" He made a tisking sound. "—it's a bit uncouth, wouldn't you agree?"

"Uncouth?" Marigold clenched her fist until the nails dug into her palm. "You can't be serious. The harvest is a part of our culture, a celebration of community."

Galvin's lips pursed as his chin tilted upward. "Be that as it may, with Tansy here, we can do the harvest in a fraction of the time. There's simply no need. Instead, I chose to have an intimate dinner with the mayor and other prominent Willowbrook citizens." He grinned. "And thanks to my new dwarven press, no one has to get their feet dirty." He looked Marigold up and down. "You should consider updating your operation. There's a whole world out there waiting for our honey wine. We don't have to be competition. We could be partners."

"I'll pass." Marigold shook her head, her frustration finally boiling over. "What happened to you, Galvin? You used to be a dreamy-eyed kid who was full of kindness.

We climbed trees together. We played in the stream outside of town, and you would tell me how one day, you'd take over the vineyard and throw the biggest harvest party this town had ever seen. I don't understand how you turned into—" She couldn't hide the revulsion on her face. "—this."

"I grew up, Marigold. Because a successful vineyard doesn't run on hopes and dreams." He crossed his arms, irritation evident in his features. "We've built one of the most respected vineyards across Tyne. Did you know that kings and queens buy our wines for their cellars? How is that not good for our people? The coin that our wines bring in will trickle down to all the small folk. It's good for everyone, even you, when people notice the name of Willowbrook."

"Trickle down, huh?" Marigold rolled her eyes. "Maybe when one of those rings falls off your fingers. I don't care if kings or queens drink our wine, Galvin. I care about the family that's gathered around the hearth for Midwinter. The ones celebrating their child becoming an apprentice. The romantic dinner where someone confesses their love for the first time. Wine is meant for the people, and that's who I make it for—the everyday people that make our community great."

"Congratulations, then." Galvin smirked. "I guess."

Marigold's heart thundered in her ears. She wasn't prone to violence, but the thought of wiping the smirk off his face was awfully tempting. Instead, she took a step forward, moving so close to Galvin that she could smell the perfume he'd applied way too liberally. "Save it for the contest. I'm going to enjoy the look on your face when you lose this year."

For a moment, he looked worried. Then he laughed. "I'm sure you'll try."

"Tansy." Marigold nodded to the druid and then stormed away.

Tansy and Galvin might be partners, but Marigold could have sworn she saw a grin tugging at the druid's mouth.

22. SHAKE VIGOROUSLY

Marigold spent much of the next few days in the cellar, barrel-tasting the different vintages of moonshadow wine. After her run-in with Galvin, she wanted nothing more than to wipe the smug look off his face.

A fire burned inside of her. It wasn't sparked by jealousy or pride or a desire to prove she was worthy of her father's legacy. No, this time she was fueled by something deeper, something bigger than herself.

"To not have a harvest, it's despicable." Marigold clenched her fists. It made her blood boil just thinking about it. "I wonder what his parents must think. Darkroot Cellars is one of the oldest wineries in Willowbrook. How much of their wine was picked and stomped by the people he's shunned? And for what? 'Prominent citizens?' I'd rather have the company of the so-called small folk than those pompous egos any day of the week." She turned to Elara, who was trying her best to conceal her laughter. "What's so funny?"

"You rarely get worked up like this." The elf grinned. "I quite like it."

"Oh, hush." Marigold rolled her eyes. "Just tell me what you think of the wine."

"It's good. Slightly more robust than the last one. It has a more oaky finish." She swirled the glass and tasted it again. "Though, I think I prefer the five-year. The blackberry and cherry notes will go over better with halflings."

"I agree." Marigold made a note in the journal. They'd sampled almost all of the vintages, narrowing them down to the five, eight, and ten-year barrels. "Tomorrow, we should gather everyone for a tasting and decide on the winner."

Elara raised a brow. "You want to rest your fate on their tongues?"

"Not when you put it that way." Marigold grimaced. "But it's clear the way we've done things in the past isn't working. We decided to shake things up, so we might as well shake vigorously."

The next day, Marigold watched leaves fall through the open window of the kitchen, a mug of hot apple cider steaming in her hands. She brought the mug to her nose and inhaled the warm, cozy notes of cinnamon, apple, and clove. It was like breathing in the essence of autumn. And the taste—spiced warmth and mellow tartness—blended in a way that was both comforting and nostalgic.

"Are you sure you aren't a mage?" she asked Locke. "Because this is truly magical."

"Don't flatter him too much." Elara stood beside the

dwarf as he chopped carrots. "He already thinks he was sent here by the gods."

"No, sweetheart." Locke shook his head as he continued to work. "I said I was the gods' gift to you."

"Well…" Elara leaned over and kissed him on the cheek. "I can't argue with that."

"So, Mari…" Locke set his knife aside and wrapped his arm around Elara's waist, pulling her close. "Are you finally settling on yer wine today?"

Marigold turned around, resting her backside against the counter. "That's the plan. I'm going to fill a few carafes with the final three contenders so that you can all have a taste. Once we decide on a winner, we can start bottling it for the festival."

After finishing her cider, Marigold made her way to the cellar. Midway down the stairwell, she was hit by an intense smell of wine. There was always a faint odor from the dozens of barrels, but this was different, like someone had emptied a barrel.

She cursed as she entered the glow of the cellar, where the acrid smell of stale wine grew stronger. It wasn't common for a barrel to spring a leak, but it had happened a handful of times over the years. It was always a mess to clean up.

"No," she whispered as she noticed an iridescent film trailing across the floor. "No, no, no, no." Her heart pounded as she ran toward the cellar door. She'd made certain to lock it before retiring the previous night.

The doors were still barred, but the shimmering trail clearly began beneath the doorframe. Her gaze followed the path from the door and across the cellar to the barrels of moonshadow wine, where a giant puddle spread beneath the many barrels.

Marigold screamed. The carafes fell from her hands, shattering against the stone floor.

A large, gelatinous blob stood among the barrels, nearly as tall as Marigold. It was translucent in areas, fading from a light pink at the top to a deep purple at its base. Sticks, rocks, and debris floated inside, along with a broken wine bottle and a dozen large cork stoppers that had been used to plug the wine barrels. Wine trickled from the barrels, staining the floor violet.

The giant blob glurped as it ingested the wine, darkening at the bottom as its body expanded.

Marigold was still screaming when footsteps thundered down the stairs. Locke, Elara, and Gerty ran toward her.

"What's going on?" Locke demanded.

Gerty yelled at the sight of the creature, hiding behind the dwarf for protection. All Marigold could do was point at the blob devouring her wine.

"Seven hells." Elara's eyes went wide. "What is that thing?"

More footsteps echoed through the cellar as Finn, Poppy, Ronan, and Aldric came to investigate.

"Is everyone okay?" Ronan's hair was disheveled. His eyes were alert as he held one hand on the hilt of his sword, the other on the scabbard, ready to draw.

Poppy rushed to Marigold's side, examining the halfling for injuries. "I heard screaming and came as quick as I could."

"Oh, no." Aldric's voice was full of resignation. It was so out of character that everyone turned in his direction.

Splinter stood on the mage's shoulder, his little twig hands covering his wooden face.

"What do you mean, 'oh no'?" Elara spat the words with enough venom that the mage took a step back.

Aldric's shoulders slumped, and his gaze settled on the blob. "Morbog, I told you to stay in the cart."

The blob gurgled as it ingested more wine.

"Morbog?" Locke stepped between Elara and Aldric, holding out an arm to stay the angry elf. "You mean to say that this abomination has a name?"

"*She* is not an abomination. She's a jelly." Aldric stepped protectively in front of Morbog. "More importantly, she's a friend. Morbog just happens to have an affinity for grapes."

Marigold was so shocked that she hadn't said a word. She just stood there, helplessly watching everything unfold as wine continued to spill onto the floor.

"So you bring it to a winery?" Ronan still had his hand wrapped around the hilt of his sword as he eyed the creature. "Aren't oozes predators?"

"I brought *her* to a winery," corrected Aldric. "Which I have begun to realize was a mistake. And yes, many oozes are predators, but like I said, Morbog is a jelly. They're more akin to slimes than oozes."

"I don't think we need a lesson in gelatin at the moment." Elara peered around the mage at the gurgling jelly. "You need to get her out of here, now."

"She's not dangerous. She's not even toxic." Aldric raised his hands. "If everyone can take a step back, I'll lead her outside."

Poppy guided Marigold, who still hadn't spoken, by

the elbow as they all moved away from the jelly, giving Aldric room to escort the creature out of the cellar.

"Come on, Morbog. Let's get you outside." Aldric wore a pained expression as the jelly sloshed through the red wine. The mage turned to Marigold as they passed. "I'm—"

"Not now." Elara pointed toward the exit. She followed the mage, keeping a wary eye on the jelly as she unbarred the door.

Back in the cellar, Marigold continued to stare at the wine barrels.

"Is she okay?" asked Ronan.

Poppy caressed Marigold's arm. "It's okay. The jelly is gone now."

Marigold released a shaky breath. "It's gone. It's all gone."

"Shit," Elara said when she noticed what Marigold was talking about. Every barrel of moonshadow wine had been uncorked, and years of aged wine covered the cellar. The entirety of what they were considering for the contest. She turned to the others. "Can you give us some privacy?"

"You heard the elf, let's go." Locke ushered the others toward the stairs. Once they were gone, he turned to Poppy, who hadn't left Marigold's side. "Poppy, you coming?"

"I'm not going anywhere." There was no room for argument as she stared him down.

"It's okay," Elara said. "Locke, can you go talk to Aldric, please? See if you can find out what the hells this is all about."

Locke nodded before disappearing up the stairs.

"Hey." Elara patted Marigold on the back. "We're going to figure this out."

"How?" Marigold sniffled, doing her best to hold back tears. It felt as if the cellar was closing in all around her as she walked among the barrels, her boots sloshing with each step. What little wine was left continued to trickle onto the floor, each sluggish drip like a dagger to her heart. "Every barrel of moonshadow wine is empty."

Elara sighed. "I know, but we still have the others. There's honeywine, dreamcatcher, and emberfruit. I know it wasn't what you wanted, but we make great wine. Whatever we enter will have a shot."

"This was our chance." Marigold tried to swallow away the lump in her throat. "For the first time, I felt like we really had a chance."

"Hey, now. Don't count us out just yet." Elara offered a sad smile. "We'll get this cleaned up and start from scratch. We can still decide on something truly spectacular."

"Can it wait?" Marigold stared at her feet, watching the ripples pulse across the puddle. "I just need a moment to process everything."

"Take your time." Elara gave Marigold a reassuring squeeze on the shoulder. "I'll be upstairs murdering the mage in the meantime."

Marigold nodded, recalling the look of anguish on Aldric's face. "Go easy on him."

Elara left, leaving Marigold and Poppy alone in the cellar.

Marigold's lip trembled as the drip-drip of the wine hammered through the silence, shattering the last of her facade. The dam crumbled, and tears streaked down her cheeks.

Poppy rushed over, pulling Marigold into an embrace. Emotion wracked the halfling's frame as she buried her head against Poppy's shoulder. She sobbed like she never had, as if ten years of frustration had been released at once. The gnome said nothing as she held Marigold, offering a comforting touch until the sobs eventually faded to sniffles.

"Thank you," Marigold said as she wiped her eyes. "Sorry you had to see that."

"You have nothing to be sorry for." Poppy caressed Marigold's cheek. "You have every right to be upset."

"I finally felt like I had direction, and now I'm lost again."

"You're not lost." Poppy wiped away a single tear. "This is just a detour. All the great stories have them."

Marigold laughed. "I don't know if this is a great story."

"It is." Poppy's eyes sparkled in the glow of the enchanted light. "Because it's the one where I met you." She stepped closer, their faces inches from one another as her gaze flitted between Marigold's eyes and lips.

Their eyes locked, and Marigold's heart thundered with expectation as she closed her eyes and leaned in. When their lips touched, it was a caress of warmth and tenderness as they yielded to one another. The sweet nectar of Poppy's taste blended with the salty echoes of dried tears in an intoxicating rush. Poppy curved her hand behind Marigold's neck, pulling her closer and stoking the fire as their bodies pressed together. Time slowed as they swayed with one another, each kiss deeper than the last.

When they broke apart, both were breathing heavily.

Poppy smiled sheepishly. "I've wanted to do that for a long time."

Marigold pressed her forehead against Poppy's and whispered, "Me too. Just never thought it would be like this."

Their hands intertwined, and although the halfling couldn't explain it, she somehow felt lighter.

"Elara's right, you know," Poppy said, her thumb caressing Marigold's hand.

"About what?"

"Everything is going to be okay."

Marigold took a deep breath. "Yeah, it will." She paused, straightening her back as she gathered herself. "I guess I should probably go find Aldric before Elara kills him."

23. MISTAKES

Marigold was a maelstrom of emotion as she exited the cellar. Her body still tingled with excitement from her kiss with Poppy, but underneath that joy was the disappointment of losing nearly a dozen barrels of wine. They didn't have much time to settle on a new wine for the contest, but right now, it was more important to figure out how this had all happened. The gnome was right, though. Everything would be alright.

She found Aldric outside by his cart, standing protectively in front of Morbog. Across from him, Elara had her arms crossed while Finn struggled to hold back Onyx. The dire cat was hissing and growling. Luckily, Finn was an experienced animal handler, and he was doing his best to mollify the enraged cat. Locke, Gerty, and the rest of the guests were there as well, even the dwarven sisters had come out to view the commotion. Everyone was there except for Poppy.

In the sunlight, the giant jelly was still unsettling, but there was something beautiful about the way the light refracted within her body, giving the creature an almost ethereal glow. It was like all of the wine had settled at the bottom, leaving her deep purple at her base and gradually transitioning to an almost transparent pink at the top.

Aldric looked exasperated as he talked to Elara. "Like I said, if you give us some space, I can put her away."

"So you admit that you were hiding this thing in your cart the entire time?" Elara uncrossed her arms and upon finding nothing better to do with her hands, she crossed them again. "You lied to us. Right to our faces."

"I'm sorry about that." Aldric wore a pained expression. "But you have to understand, I had my reasons."

"Are your reasons going to replace all of the wine that was destroyed?" Elara scoffed. "Marigold is having a breakdown because of what you've done, and I don't take kindly to those who hurt my friends."

Marigold tapped Elara on the elbow. "I can take it from here. Can you please get everyone inside?"

Regardless of the situation, no guest deserved to be made a spectacle of.

"You sure?" Elara's anger shifted to concern at the sight of the halfling. "I can stuff him in that cart of his, if you'd like."

Marigold smiled. "Let me try talking to him first, and I'll get back to you on that."

"You seem less upset." Elara narrowed her gaze. "What happened down there after I left?"

Heat rushed to Marigold's cheeks. "I'll tell you later."

"Alright, everyone," Elara raised her voice. "Show's over for now. Let's give these two some privacy." She waited as everyone but Marigold, Finn, and Aldric went inside, and then she turned to Marigold. "I'll be in the cellar cleaning up the mess if you need me."

"What about Onyx?" Finn asked as the cat continued to struggle against his grip.

Marigold looked to Aldric.

"If you can keep hold of him for a moment, I'll put Morbog away."

Marigold knelt next to the dire cat, stroking him behind the ears. "Easy, boy."

Onyx quit thrashing but continued to let out a threatening growl, his gaze never leaving the jelly.

Aldric tapped the cart with his staff, and one of the doors popped open. He removed a jar about the width of his hand and placed it on the ground. "Morbog, release."

There was a loud squelching sound as the jelly rippled. Wine poured from the creature, her body deflating as liquid puddled all around her.

"Oh, that's gross." Finn grimaced.

Marigold's stomach churned at the sight, and Onyx must have been equally perplexed because he went silent.

The jelly gurgled as it sloshed about. She was now a little over a foot tall, a fraction of her previous size. Debris still floated inside her but with the wine gone, she was a light pink color.

"All of it." Aldric tapped his staff on the ground beside Morbog.

There were slurping sounds as the jelly ejected the broken wine bottle, followed by rocks, twigs, corks, and other debris. What was left was a translucent pink blob that shimmered in the light. Aldric tapped the jar, and Morbog climbed inside. Once she settled at the bottom, one could hardly tell she was a living creature at all. She looked like nothing more than a jar of jelly.

The same pink jelly Marigold had seen when she and Elara investigated the cart. Morbog had been right under their noses, and they'd thought nothing of it.

Aldric placed the jar in the cart, and as soon as the door shut, the fight left Onyx. Finn released him, and the dire cat hesitantly approached the puddle of wine, sniffing at it cautiously.

Marigold waited for Finn to leave before returning her attention to Aldric. "Why would you lie to us about this?"

Aldric shuffled his feet. "I was worried. Most people don't know the differences between a jelly and an ooze, so they just assume Morbog will hurt them. I've found it's safer to keep her hidden. She normally stays inside my robe with Splinter when we travel, but after discovering that your cat could sense her presence, the cart seemed the safer option, even if she was a bit lonely. It has enchantments that conceal whatever is inside."

"She destroyed our wine, Aldric. Some of those barrels had been aging for ten years. Since I took over the winery."

"I know, and I'm deeply sorry. I'll find a way to repay you."

"It's not about that. It's about trust." Marigold sighed. "I opened my home to you, and you lied to me."

"You're right." There was a heaviness to the man's countenance as he met her eyes. "I'll gather my things and find somewhere else to stay."

"There's no need for that." Marigold let out a resigned breath. As upset as she was, Aldric was clearly distraught over the damage he'd caused. He'd had a lapse in judgement, but mistakes happened. Gods knew she'd made her fair share over the years. Perhaps part of the blame fell on her. While Aldric was aware that the jelly was eating some of the grapes, Marigold hadn't mentioned anything to him about the time the creature had invaded the cellar previously. If she had, maybe he would have done something differently. "We all make mistakes from time to time. And while we can't change the past, we can make amends and do better in the future."

The mage pulled his hands to his heart, eyes glistening. "Your generosity knows no bounds."

"And, Aldric…" Marigold noticed a bevy of faces out of the corner of her eye as the guests peered at them through the inn's window. She narrowed her eyes at the voyeurs, and curtains swished shut.

"Yes?"

"Is there a way to ensure Morbog stays out of the cellar?" Losing the moonshadow wine was bad enough, but they couldn't afford for this to happen again.

"If I can bring her inside, then yes. She and Splinter are practically inseparable when together. I thought that I was being smart by keeping her in the cart, but I should have known better."

Marigold nodded slightly. "I'd like to understand Morbog better at some point, but for now, I need to clean the cellar and focus on finding a wine to enter in the festival. In the meantime, try to stay away from Elara. She's known to hold a grudge."

"Can I help with the cleanup?" Aldric asked.

She shook her head. "For now, I think it's best if you steer clear."

"I'll make myself scarce." He tapped the cart with his

staff, and pieces slid and clanked as it shifted inside. "And, Marigold, I really am sorry."

She forced a smile. "I know."

———

Elara and Finn were in the cellar when Marigold returned. They both held mops, cleaning up the countless gallons of spilled wine.

Marigold thought of Morbog as she watched the wine slosh across the stone floor. The creature was so tiny in her natural form, small enough to fit in a jar not much bigger than Aldric's hand, and yet she'd absorbed so much wine that she had been as tall as a halfling and nearly twice as wide. Marigold shuddered at the memory of the creature expunging all of the wine into the grass.

"Here, let me help." She reached for Finn's mop.

He pulled it away. "We can handle this." Finn twisted the head of the mop, and deep red wine splashed into the bucket. "You focus on picking a new wine."

"Thank you, Finn." Marigold gave him a side-hug.

"What's the situation with Aldric?" Elara raised a brow as she continued to clean.

"It was an accident. A costly one, but an accident nonetheless." Marigold rubbed her forehead. "I can't fault him for wanting to protect his pet."

Elara huffed. "I'd hardly call that thing a pet." She squeezed wine from the mop head. "Even if it does have impeccable taste."

Marigold shrugged. "Nothing we can do now but move forward."

Elara stopped working and leaned against the mop

handle. "What happened after we left the cellar? I don't mean to be insensitive, but one moment, you're more upset than I've ever seen you, and the next, it's like losing all of our moonshadow wine is a minor inconvenience."

"I, uh…" Marigold's cheeks flushed as she recalled the gentle warmth of Poppy's lips. "I guess you can say I found some perspective." She smiled. "What's the worst that can happen? We lose the contest again."

"Because that sounds exactly like the Marigold I know." The corner of Elara's mouth curved into a smirk as she started mopping. "Fine. Keep your secrets."

Somehow, the elf always had a sense about these things. Marigold's cheeks burned brighter, but thankfully, the dim light of the cellar concealed most of it.

She walked the cellar, taking stock of the remaining wine. If a jelly was going to devour an entire varietal, they were lucky Morbog had chosen the moonshadow. It limited the variety of their offerings, but it was the wine they produced the least of.

But that had been part of the reason she'd chosen it. It was something no one would expect.

No one would be surprised if she entered honeywine. It was their most popular and had claimed second place more times than any of their other wines. Marigold loved honeywine and was proud of it, but for this year's festival, it just didn't seem right. They'd entered emberfruit and dreamcatcher previously, as well as a few blends, but none of them spoke to her in the way that the moonshadow had. There was the option of the aged dreamcatcher. That one had intrigued Eris, after all.

Marigold leaned against a barrel as she pondered, feeling the aged wood beneath her fingers. It was cool to the touch, the grain smoothed by the passage of time. How many times had this barrel been filled over the years? How many people had it brought together after the wine was bottled?

Soft footsteps pattered down the stairs, and Marigold looked up as Poppy peeked into the cellar.

"There you are." Poppy bit her lip and grinned. She was holding a journal to her chest.

Marigold met the gnome's eyes, and a familiar excitement sparked inside of her. She was keenly aware that the sound of mops sloshing had suddenly halted.

"Is that one of my father's journals?" Marigold asked.

"It is." Poppy set it on a barrel. Numerous ribbons extended from the pages where she'd marked her place. "You were pretty upset earlier, and I wanted to see if I could help. The first night I was here, you showed me the cellar and said that sometimes you experimented with blends. I don't know much about winemaking, but I know that blending white and red wine isn't common. I came across some interesting recipes in here from when your father had tried it. There was one year when he experimented with a lot of different blends. There might not be much of the moonshadow wine left, but maybe there is enough to give this a try." She held out the journal. "If you haven't already decided on a replacement."

Marigold opened the journal, flipping through the pages that Poppy had marked. The journal was dated a couple of years after Marigold's father had added moonshadow vines to the vineyard, and Poppy was right, he had experimented a lot that particular year.

He'd tried mixing moonshadow with honeywine, dreamcatcher, and emberfruit and had written detailed notes on how much of each wine he'd used, along with the resulting flavor profile. He'd been unhappy with most of them, but there was one that was circled.

Rosewine Blend
10% moonshadow
90% dreamcatcher

Notes: Due to the bold nature of the moonshadow wine, between 5-10% is optimal for bringing out the fruit flavors of the red without overpowering the more delicate floral profile of the dreamcatcher.

Color: Deep, rich raspberry

Nose: Strawberry and rose petals. Fruity, yet elegant.

Taste: Fruit forward on the front, transitions to a dry, minerally finish. Crisp and refreshing.

This was exactly what she was looking for—a wine that could bring people together. Something fun and exciting that could surprise not only the townsfolk, but the other vintners as well.

"This is amazing, Poppy." Marigold turned to the gnome. "I could kiss you."

Poppy stepped closer. "I think you meant *should.*"

Marigold obliged, wrapping her arms around Poppy's waist and pulling the gnome against her. Their lips touched, electric and intense, like climbing a tree during a thunderstorm. Marigold's skin tingled as firelights erupted through her body, heavy breaths rising and falling as they held one another.

A howl echoed through the cellar, followed by another. Marigold and Poppy broke apart to find Elara with her hands cupped around her mouth, howling like a wolf while Finn stared, open-mouthed.

"I knew it!" Elara clapped her hands and pointed, cackling with delight. "I knew it."

Marigold's cheeks were so hot she thought her head might melt. Poppy took her hand, interlacing their fingers, and a calmness washed over her.

Marigold shrugged. "I guess you were right."

The elf's smile widened as she walked across the cellar. She knelt, wrapping her arms around Marigold. "I'm happy for you." She let go and faced Poppy. "I'm happy for you, too, but if you hurt her, gods help me, this will be the last research you ever do."

Poppy stood her ground and nodded. "I believe it."

"Hey, now. Be nice." Marigold nudged Elara in the arm. "Wait until you see what Poppy found."

She showed Elara the journal and the recipe her father had circled.

Elara's brows rose higher and higher as she read through the notes. "Interesting. Some wineries' make rose-colored wine with red grapes by reducing the time the skins sit in contact with the juice. There are a few who do it by gently pressing the red grapes to extract juice, but as you can imagine, that process is very intensive, and the price reflects as much. This is something entirely different. I can't believe your father never talked about it."

"I wondered that, too." Marigold put her hands on her hips. "What do you think, though? Should we give it a try?"

"I think you two should grab a mop." Elara handed the journal back to Marigold. "We've got work to do."

24. THE HARVEST FESTIVAL

The morning of the harvest festival, a chill settled across Willowbrook. Marigold stepped outside to feel the first cold kiss of autumn against her cheeks. She rubbed her hands together for warmth, admiring the crisp layer of frost that covered the hills, sparkling like diamonds in the morning sun.

According to Locke, many dwarves believed an early frost was an ill omen—a warning of a harsh winter or difficult times ahead. For the halflings, it was less dire, a symbol of the inevitability of change, and a perfect complement to the harvest festival.

The door opened behind Marigold, and Poppy joined her, a steaming mug of tea in each hand. She handed one to Marigold. "Thought you might want something to keep you warm."

Marigold took the tea and set it on a nearby table. "That's what I have you for." She stepped behind Poppy, wrapping her arms around the gnome and resting her chin on Poppy's shoulder.

Poppy leaned into Marigold's embrace. "How are you feeling about today?"

"Good." Marigold kissed Poppy's neck before letting go. Over the past few days, she'd grown more comfortable showing her affection, even occasionally when others were watching. "We've done all we can. Nothing to do now but see how the leaves settle."

After the cellar had been cleaned, they'd collected what remained of the moonshadow wine from the barrels. There was enough to fill a handful of bottles from the various vintages. Too little to enter any single vintage in the contest by itself, but since they were only using a fraction of red for the rosewine blend, there was enough to experiment. They'd tested several iterations of Wilbur Bramblefoot's recipe, mixing ten percent of various moonshadow vintages with ninety percent dreamcatcher.

The resulting wine was good, but even so, Marigold understood why her father had never sold it. It wasn't great. On a whim, she'd decided to cut the amount of dreamcatcher wine to eighty percent while adding ten percent of emberfruit. The additional varietal brought a hint of citrus that gave the wine a nice, clean finish.

After tasting it, they'd all decided that it was the best of the bunch. There was enough moonshadow wine left over to make three dozen bottles of the blend.

Frost crunched underneath Onyx's paws as the dire cat made his way to the porch. He let out a raspy meow, nuzzling his massive head against Marigold and Poppy in turn.

Marigold scratched him under the chin, and his chest rumbled. "Who's a good boy?"

Onyx flopped to his side, paws swiping playfully at her apron.

From around the corner of the inn, Acorn Blossom whinnied, followed by the creak of wagon wheels. A few moments later, Elara pulled the wagon to a stop by the porch. It was loaded with crates of wine, apples, and pumpkins, along with a few mini barrels of Locke's cider.

"Alright, lovebirds, the wagon is loaded." Elara climbed down and tied the pony to a post. "Once Locke finishes his pies, we're heading into town to set up. You sure you don't want to ride with us?"

"We'll be fine walking." Marigold looked up. There were only a few clouds in the sprawling blue sky. "It's going to be a beautiful day."

Poppy hooked her arm through Marigold's. "I can't wait."

Willowbrook was already abuzz with excitement by the time Marigold and Poppy crossed the bridge into town. The streets were festive and jubilant, full of people celebrating another successful harvest season. Marigold could only imagine the joy Elara had navigating the wagon through the chaos.

While the majority of the crowd were halflings, there were a fair amount of humans and dwarves mixed in from the neighboring kingdoms. They even passed a few gnomes and a lone umbral elf, her ashen-gray skin and dark hair a striking contrast from Elara's.

To both sides of the bridge, there were halflings

resting on the banks of the stream. Some puffed on long pipes, blowing smoke rings across the water. Others fished or relaxed with picnics, enjoying conversation and laughter while sharing food and drink. Children giggled as they played in the cool water.

All across town, shops were open, and many of them had tables set up in the streets to sell their wares.

Marigold waved or said hello to those she knew, wishing them a happy harvest. Many offered her well wishes for the wine contest. The streets grew more densely packed as they got closer to the square, forcing Marigold and Poppy to walk that much closer together—not that either of them minded. There were entertainers from nearby towns and villages who'd come to take part in the festival. Musicians played on almost every corner. Jugglers performed to the delight of children. Artists painted portraits or drew caricatures to the onlookers' amusement, reminding Marigold of a charcoal sketch hanging in the library where a young Marigold sat between her parents, all of their heads disproportionately large and their features exaggerated.

Those days had been much simpler, when her only worries were how much candy she'd be able to take home from the festival.

She held Poppy tighter. Today was an opportunity to reclaim some of that magic.

Everywhere they passed, there was dancing, singing, and laughter. Food and drinks flowed like it was one big party, and smoke billowed in the air as many halflings partook in various forms of pipeleaf.

A family played joyous music outside the apothecary,

and Marigold and Poppy stopped to listen. The parents played lute and fiddle while a little girl enthusiastically shook a tambourine.

"This reminds me of the city," Poppy chuckled as someone accidentally bumped into her. "I can't believe the turnout. This is so much more lively and chaotic than even a few days ago."

"It's our busiest day of the year." Marigold hooked her arm through Poppy's and swayed with the music. The last thing she wanted to think about was Poppy going back to Aethervale.

The song ended, and Marigold tossed a few coins into the basket before they continued on. A few blocks down, they came upon a cart selling apples coated in a thick layer of hardened sugar. The candied apples sat upside-down on the cart, a stick protruding from each one.

Marigold bought one. The candied coating crunched as she bit into it, followed by an explosion of juicy tartness that further amplified the sweetness.

"Have you ever tried one?" She offered the apple to Poppy.

The gnome shook her head before taking a bite. "Wow, this is delicious." Flecks of hardened sugar stuck to her chin. Poppy frowned at Marigold, who wore a wide grin. "What's so funny?"

"You have a little something here." Marigold gently wiped the sugar away with her thumb, her hand lingering a moment longer than was necessary.

Poppy bit her lip. "Good thing I have you around."

The halfling's pulse quickened, and she swallowed hard. How was such a simple gesture so tempting that it threatened to unravel her?

She focused her attention on a halfling juggling wine bottles to calm her racing heart.

Poppy handed the apple back to Marigold and pulled a journal from her satchel. She scribbled a few quick notes before stuffing it back inside. "What?" Her brows raised. "I don't want to forget."

Closer to the square, a loaded wagon moved slowly down the streets, forcing the crowd to step aside as it ferried people from the town square to the edge of town. A sign reading "Corn Maze" hung from the side of the wagon.

"I have a fun fact for you." Marigold waggled her brows at Poppy as they waited for the wagon to pass. "You might think it's strange that the festival includes a corn maze located so far from the main events. That's because long ago, back when Willowbrook was more of a village than a town, there was a cornfield not far from the square. Every year, after the corn had been harvested, the farmers would cut a maze through the field for the children to play. It became one of the most popular attractions, and even as the town expanded outward, the maze continued to remain a staple of the festival."

"You're right. That is a fun fact." Poppy let go of Marigold's hand. "I should probably write it down."

"Oh, I think you'll be fine." Marigold chuckled as she stole the gnome's hand back. "One year, the old mayor suggested they cancel the maze since it was so far from the other events. My father said there was nearly a riot."

Poppy grinned. "Seems like a perfectly reasonable response."

"Woe unto anyone who tries to come between a halfling and the simple pleasures in life."

Upon arriving at the market square, they found it transformed for the festival. The entire area had been decorated for the season with pumpkins, gourds, scarecrows, wheat bundles, spirit lanterns, and a myriad of harvest-themed embellishments. Fully-grown cornstalks grew around the booths, which had definitely not been there upon Marigold's last visit. She imagined they were the handiwork of a certain female druid.

Many of the booths and tables normally reserved for farmers had been taken over by various wineries, businesses, and local artisans. Others were used for harvest activities like pumpkin carving or wreath making.

Marigold's mouth watered at the multitude of smells—the aroma of cinnamon and clove from the booth selling apple cider, the savory scent of roasted meats, buttery grilled corn, and the nuttiness of fresh bread pulled from a cart oven.

"This is amazing." Poppy clapped her hands together, a childlike grin spreading across her features. "Listening to people describe the festival is one thing, but it doesn't compare to being a part of it." She released a pleasurable sigh. "The sights, the smells. You were right about it being an experience."

Marigold's heart warmed at the gnome's reaction. No amount of reading could truly compare to the sensation of actually being here.

She spotted Elara from across the way, the elf's slender body and golden hair like a beacon among Locke and the diminutive halflings. She was in conversation with a customer, holding a bottle of what looked like honeywine. The new blend wouldn't be unveiled until after the tasting, but there were plenty of bottles of the other varietals for sale.

Smoke billowed from the booth next door, where The Smokey Burrow was showcasing its various pipes and pipeleaf. Several dwarves nodded approvingly as they passed around an elaborately carved pipe.

Two booths down, Galvin stood on a pedestal, towering above those in front of his booth as if he were the main attraction. His hands sparkled from countless rings and jewelry as he gestured. He wore an elegant cloak that wouldn't last a day in the wilderness, fastened together with a detailed emerald brooch in the shape of a grape cluster. Tansy stood behind him looking as resplendent as ever with a wreath of orange and red flowers upon her head.

Her eyes met Marigold's, and the druid waved. Despite the annoyance at the halfling standing next to Tansy, Marigold smiled and waved back.

"Look at this." Poppy tugged on Marigold's arm, drawing her attention to a sign painted with the day's schedule of events.

Willowbrook's 577th Annual Harvest Festival
Schedule of Events

Midday Bell
Opening Address
Pie Eating Contest
Apple Bobbing Contest

Largest Pumpkin Judging
Largest Non-Pumpkin Vegetable Judging

Afternoon Bell
Pumpkin Carving Contest
Wreath-making Contest
Pie Judging
Best Local Pipeleaf
Best Local Wine

Evening Bell
Performance by The Cider Barrel Band
Firelight Display

Wagons for the Corn Maze leave every half-hour

Marigold frowned. The wine contest was always the final event of the afternoon, leaving plenty of time for her anxiety to fester. Since the midday bell had yet to ring, it would be at least three hours before the contest started. With it being the final event before the evening bell, probably a lot longer.

"Hey." Poppy nudged Marigold in the side. "Just means we have more time to enjoy the festival."

She was right. Today was a day for celebration.

Marigold smiled. "Can you read minds now?"

The gnome shrugged. "Your expression was like reading a book."

"That obvious, huh?" Marigold grimaced.

"Only when you're staring daggers at the Darkroot Cellars booth."

"In that case, how about we go say hello to our people and then we can enjoy the festival like you said."

Marigold took Poppy's hand, making a concerted effort to not look Galvin's way as they crossed the market. The distinctly sweet smell of pipeleaf grew more pervasive as they approached the Dew Drop booth.

"Mari!" Locke's voice carried as he noticed her.

The booth was busy, and even though it was early, Marigold could tell they'd already made a sizable dent in the wine they'd brought to sell. Gerty was helping Elara with wine sales while Finn helped Locke with the cider. The dwarf stood behind a mini barrel ladling cider into cups while Finn passed them out.

One of the great things about the festival was that while its tourism was a boon for the local economy, there were still ways for anyone to enjoy food and drink without spending a coin. At the Dew Drop booth, bottles were for sale, but they also offered cider and honeywine samples for free until they ran out. Locke usually brewed several mini barrels of cider in preparation.

"Happy harvest!" Finn handed Marigold and Poppy each a mug of cider.

"Happy harvest, Finn!" Poppy beamed as she took it.

"Looks like a good turnout so far." Marigold raised her mug. "Cheers!"

They both took a sip. Drinking cider cold was a vastly different experience compared to when it was freshly made and still warm in the pot. After cooling, it was more refreshing and crisp with the tart flavors of the apple juice outweighing the spiced notes. The temperature had risen considerably since the frosty morning, so it was a welcome refreshment.

"Amazing as always, Locke." Marigold nodded to the dwarf. "Do you all need any help?"

Elara stopped what she was doing and narrowed her eyes at Marigold. "Marigold Bramblefoot, if you step one hairy foot behind this booth, I swear to Emton and all his justice, I'll drown you in cider." She handed a bottle of wine to a customer, wishing them a happy harvest before returning her attention to Marigold. "We can handle the booth this year. Enjoy yourself, I mean it, and we'll see you later for the wine contest."

Locke held a hand over one side of his mouth so that Elara couldn't see and whispered, "I wouldn't argue with her if I were you."

"Thank you." Marigold met each of their eyes in turn. "Truly."

She and Poppy moved to the adjacent booth and were admiring scented candles when the midday bell rang out from the temple.

Mayor Sweetwater stood on the main stage, holding a speaking trumpet at his side as he waited for the tolling to stop. The cone-shaped contraption helped project a speaker's voice over large crowds. As far as non-magical means went, it worked great. Marigold had heard that Queen Lilion of Warminster had an air mage on staff for the sole purpose of amplifying her voice when she addressed the kingdom. If the rumors were true, her speeches could be heard for miles across the mountainous terrain of Stormrest.

The mayor was sharply dressed as always, which was undoubtedly part of the reason he and Galvin got along so well, but today, he'd outdone himself. He wore a burgundy velvet coat over a golden vest with an ivory ascot tied at his neck. His trousers were cuffed a few inches above his ankles, showcasing a pair of burgundy socks embellished with golden leaves and polished leather shoes with gilded buckles. His hair was neatly parted, the graying curls nearly as bouncy as Gerty's. Unlike Galvin, the mayor kept his jewelry minimal—a gold leaf pendant pinned to his breast and a single gold ring set with a large ruby. Marigold much preferred the simplicity of a few statement pieces over the ostentation of a dragon's hoard.

When the bell finished tolling, the music and chatter faded. The mayor raised the speaking trumpet to his mouth, amplifying his voice as he spoke to the crowd. "Greetings and happy harvest! I am Mayor Sweetwater, and it is my great honor to welcome you to Willowbrook's 577th Annual Harvest Festival. I'd like to extend a hearty thank-you to everyone who has chosen to spend today with us. We are pleased as a pixie with a pocketful of pearls to have you in our fair town. As many of you know, the harvest festival is a tradition as deeply rooted in our culture as family gatherings, pumpkin pie, or a glass of honeywine." A few cheers erupted from the crowd. "It's a time to revel in all that we have achieved this year, to indulge in good company, and to savor the best drink and food across Aedrea. Today, my friends, Willowbrook is your oyster, and I hope that you find your own pearl somewhere within its borders. Many of our shops will be open until the evening bell, so please, explore our fine offerings. Aside from the corn maze, all official events will be hosted here, at the market square, starting with one of our most popular attractions, the pie-eating contest, where last year, Crispin Cloverhill managed to devour eight pumpkin pies before the time ran out. He assures me that he can fit in nine this year, so you won't want to miss it. You'll find today's schedule of events posted around the square. Whether you want to watch competitions, craft your own spirit lantern or wreath, or simply meander the streets singing and dancing as you savor delicious food and wine from across the countryside, I assure you, there is something for everyone. Wagons to the corn maze leave every half-hour, and the night will end with a performance by The Cider Barrel Band, followed by the annual firelight display over the market square. Before we adjourn, there are a few people I would like to thank for helping make today possible." The mayor gestured to the edge of the platform. As he called their names, each person joined him on the stage. "First, I would like to thank the town council for organizing the event. Without their hard work, none of this would be possible. I'd also like to give a special thanks to Galvin Darkroot and Darkroot Cellars for providing barrels of honeywine for many of today's festivities. For the past ten years, his wine has won the annual tasting contest, and he'll be competing once again later today."

Galvin climbed the steps. Marigold rolled her eyes at the crowd's applause, but she couldn't fault them. After all, who didn't love free wine? Galvin waved before taking a bow and joining the mayor. Poppy gave Marigold's hand a reassuring squeeze as the mayor continued.

"I'd also like to thank Tansy Ironvale, druid and vintner at Darkroot Cellars, for providing many of our living decorations, including the cornstalks and numerous pumpkins growing across town."

Tansy carried herself elegantly as she walked the stage, giving a royal wave before joining Galvin. Marigold still couldn't understand why she would want to work with someone as selfish and pompous as Galvin.

Mayor Sweetwater continued, doling out thanks to the volunteers, Rosie and other bakers for making pies for the contest, and several of the local farmers for their contributions. Lastly, he thanked Aldric for the firelight display.

The mage stepped onstage. He looked like a lanky giant, towering above the halflings, with his pointed blue hat adding to his already impressive stature. Even Tansy only came up to his shoulders. Around his neck, he wore the gray yarn snake that had roamed the grounds during the harvest. No longer enchanted, the comically large scarf draped around his neck several times.

He waved to the crowd, and the scarf began to twitch, slowly inflating as it uncoiled from the mage. The crowd gasped as it slithered across the stage and rose in front of Tansy, ready to strike.

The druid was unafraid as she raised her hand, touching the knit snake on the nose. Its fabric tongue flicked as a wave of green passed through it, moss forming along its back. Tiny white flowers sprouted among the moss in a diamond pattern, and two orange flowers grew from its eyes. The onlookers' worry quickly turned to laughter and applause as the snake crawled from the stage and slithered through the crowd.

With that, the two mages bowed, and the mayor thanked everyone once again. Music resumed, and the assemblage began to disperse.

While the stage was being prepared for the pie-eating contest, Marigold and Poppy perused some of the other booths.

"These are gorgeous!" Poppy said as they stopped by a booth selling quilts.

Lottie, the elder halfling behind the booth, had been a regular at the Dew Drop Vineyard's harvest for as far back as Marigold could remember. She'd been the owner of The Golden Loom for many years until she'd passed the business down to her children. Now, she made colorful and detailed quilts in her free time and would sell them at the market during festivals.

Poppy admired a piece featuring the changing seasons of a halfling burrow, while Marigold's eyes fell upon a quilt depicting a large silver tree on a midnight background. Silver stars adorned the tree's skeletal branches, and more scattered across the night sky.

Marigold recognized it immediately as the Guiding Tree from Grimaldi's Fables, the children's tale about how the moon goddess, Seluna, blessed the tree so that its light could guide travelers on their way home. So much had happened since she read the fable in front of the hearth months ago.

"You can never have too many quilts." Marigold took out her coin pouch. "I'll take this one."

Lottie folded the quilt and placed it in front of Marigold. When she tried to pay, Lottie gently pushed her hand aside. "Consider this a harvest gift."

Marigold reached into her pouch again. "Lottie, you know I can't do that."

Lottie took the quilt back. "Seems you've found yourself in a predicament then, Miss Marigold." She wore a feisty expression that reminded Marigold of Elara.

"Fine." The younger halfling chuckled. "If you insist,

but I'll be sending you a basket with all of your favorite wines and some of Locke's muffins as a token of thanks."

"I'd expect nothing less." Lottie winked, handing the quilt to Marigold. "Happy harvest."

"That was sweet of her," Poppy said as they moved on to the next booth.

"She was a good friend of my parents. When I was younger, Lottie would bring her family over in the summers. I'd play with the children, chasing horned rabbits and frolicking in the stream until the owls started hooting. We had the best time." Marigold paused to look at a table full of hand-carved ornamental bowls and other items.

"What's this?" Poppy held a strand of acorns that had been sewn together with twine.

"It's an acorn garland." Marigold took it and draped it over the gnome's shoulders. "Looks good on you."

Poppy twisted one shoulder forward and then the other as she modeled the item. "It's pretty, but what is it exactly?"

"They're supposed to bring good fortune." Marigold adjusted the garland until it hung evenly on both sides. "Some people will wear them like this. Others hang them above the door or the hearth."

"My fortune has been pretty good of late." Poppy kissed Marigold on the cheek. She removed the garland, placing it around Marigold's neck instead. "But I think you could use a little."

Marigold rubbed the smooth surface of the acorn between her fingers and smiled. Extra good fortune was never a bad thing.

As the day passed, Marigold and Poppy made the most of their free time. So much so that Poppy only took out her journal once.

True to the mayor's words, Crispin Cloverhill did eat nine pies, but a dwarven competitor managed ten to claim victory. The apple-bobbing contest had been a spectacle when a human mistakenly assumed that the goal was to eat the apple underwater instead of pulling them out using her teeth. She managed to eat two apples before someone noticed what was happening.

In between events, they roamed the streets eating, drinking, and dancing.

The winner of the largest pumpkin was nearly the size of Onyx, and so heavy that Marigold couldn't believe the farmers had managed to load it into the wagon. The largest non-pumpkin vegetable was a squash that came up to the farmer's waist. He'd been so proud of it that he'd commissioned a portrait of himself and the gourd from a local artist.

Once the afternoon bell tolled, a tightness settled in Marigold's chest as the nerves took hold. In a few short hours, the winner of the wine contest would be crowned. Even though she didn't feel the same pressure of years past, she still wanted to win.

Poppy tried her best to keep Marigold's mind off the event as much as possible. They viewed the entries for the pumpkin-carving contest, each one a work of art. One had a carving of the countryside at night that was so detailed you could see a child swinging from a tree beneath a crescent moon that glowed brightly. Another had a demonic face so lifelike that the hairs on Marigold's neck stood on end when she looked at it.

"There's something special in knowing that these amazing carvings are fleeting," Poppy said, admiring a pumpkin that depicted a halfling smoking a pipe. The creator had managed to sculpt the image from the flesh of the pumpkin without carving all the way through, except for a small hole at the end of the pipe. Something inside the lantern caused smoke to continually trail from the opening. "Unlike stone or wood that can last lifetimes or ages, we're the only ones who will be able to experience this magnificence. The pumpkin will rot, and the image will crack and crumble, never to be seen again. I think there's a beauty in that."

Marigold was taken so off-guard by the comment that she just stared at Poppy for a moment.

"What?" Poppy wore a sheepish expression.

"You." Marigold smiled. "I am continuously impressed by your depths." She wanted nothing more than to spend her days exploring those waters.

Their hands intertwined as they moved along to the wreaths, which were equally as magnificent. Many were made from evergreen branches of pine, cedar, or fir but some took more adventurous approaches, using straw or willow. The wreaths were garnished with everything from pinecones to berries, flowers, and acorns.

Soon, it was time for the pie-judging competition. Marigold and Poppy returned to the stage to support Locke.

For the selection process, all entrants were required to bake two pies, one for the elimination round earlier in the day and a second one to be used if they made the finals in the afternoon. Locke was one of the best bakers in town, so it was no surprise that he'd made it to the final ten.

One of the best parts about the pie-judging was that all of the eliminated pies could be eaten, nearly a hundred of them, allowing almost everyone in the crowd to have a slice. Of all the events, this one had the best turnout.

Marigold was given a slice of cream pie, while Poppy had blueberry. They took turns feeding one another as the contestants lined up at the side of the stage. Marigold could hardly tell that Locke and Rosie were rivals as they stood together, chatting like old friends. It made her wonder how different things might be between her and Galvin if he'd been less of a—

She banished the thought. He'd be on her mind soon enough. There was no reason to let him intrude into her thoughts just yet.

The pies were brought onstage. Each one had a flag in the crust with the number one through ten to ensure anonymity in order to avoid any potential bias.

There were three judges for the contest—Mayor Sweetwater, Council Member Lumina Cloudmane, and Merrin Slowwater, a local blacksmith.

The mayor held the speaking trumpet as he explained the judging process. "Welcome, everyone, to one of my favorite events of the harvest—the pie-judging contest. Today, myself, Lumina, and Merrin will be judging the ten best pies as voted on by the pre-selection committee to determine the best of the best for our 577th harvest festival. Each pie will be scored based on five criteria. First, appearance, the visual appeal of the crust, its color, and overall presentation. Second, the crust, including texture, flavor, and baking quality. Third, the filling, the balance of flavors, texture, and consistency. Fourth, the originality of both flavor combinations and presentation. And finally, the overall taste, because it doesn't matter how beautiful a pie is if it tastes like dirt."

The crowd laughed, and a few people clapped their agreement. Each judge held a notepad as they began the visual inspection. They circled the table, taking notes and occasionally leaning in or viewing the pie from a different angle.

Once they were satisfied, the tasting began. Each judge had ten forks to ensure they didn't accidentally mix any of the flavors. They took a minimum of three bites from each pie, tasting the crust, the filling, and then a bite of both together. Sometimes, a judge needed a fourth, fifth, or even sixth bite before moving on to the next pie.

After they had tasted all the pies, the judges retired to a booth, where they would score, discuss, and deliberate their assessments. After a few minutes, they returned, tasting three of the pies for a second time before continuing their deliberations.

"Quite the process," Poppy said, licking her fork. "How many times did you say Locke has won?"

"Twice in ten years, which is quite an accomplishment. Especially considering how many entries there are each year. There was only one time when he didn't make the final ten, and he's sworn off making rhubarb pie ever since."

The judges finally returned, and the mayor cleared his throat before giving the verdict. "This year was tougher than most to select a winner. While all ten pies could grace my table any time, three rose above the rest. So much so that we required a second tasting to rank them all. So without further ado, here are your winners. In third place, this beautiful pie ticked all of our boxes. With a golden crust, juicy filling, and intricately braided edges, this blueberry pie had it all. The ripe fruit filling was a perfect blend of sweet and tart. Congratulations to Callie Rootberry!"

A young halfling raised her hand in acknowledgment, and the mayor handed her the silver, third-place ribbon. Her cheeks were so rosy that if not for how dark her hair was, she could have passed for Gerty's sister. The crowd applauded, and she brightened even more.

"In second place," the mayor continued, "we have one of the classics. A pumpkin pie with a filling so velvety smooth and evenly set that it was almost a shame to cut through it. Almost. With a flaky crust and a harmonious blend of spices, each bite was like a comforting hug, wrapping me in a blanket of rich pumpkin flavor, warm spices, and buttery crust. Let's all give a round of applause to Rosie Underhill, owner of Hearth & Honey Bakery."

Rosie stepped forward, a smile spread from ear to ear.

"This one is no stranger to the podium." Mayor Sweetwater handed Rosie the red, second-place ribbon. He then held up the blue ribbon. "And then one remained."

Marigold knew where Locke's mind must have been as the dwarf kept crossing and uncrossing his arms. Either he'd won the contest or hadn't placed at all. In the kitchen, he could always direct his nervous energy toward the next task but up on the stage, he was out of his element.

A loud whistle cut through the crowd. Heads turned to see Elara with her fingers between her lips. She mouthed "You've got this" followed by a wink, and Locke seemed to settle down a bit.

"Well, then." The mayor looked at his notes. "Let us continue. This year's winner had everything we were looking for and then some. The appearance was practiced precision, with elegant latticework that hinted at the perfectly cooked apples underneath and decorative cutouts of leaves fitting for a harvest festival. The crust was tender and yet managed to provide a satisfying crunch, while the filling was tart and sweet, balancing the apple's natural sweetness with warm spices of cinnamon and nutmeg. Not to mention the baker's ability to craft apples that were pleasantly cooked yet still provide a slight bite. This pie was rich and layered, delivering a satisfying blend of buttery crust, spiced apples, and a touch of sweetness." He held up the ribbon. "Congratulations to Locke Stonefist, this year's pie champion!"

Locke shook Rosie's hand and then held his arms high, celebrating the applause as Mayor Sweetwater handed him the ribbon. Marigold cupped her hands around her mouth, cheering along with the crowd. If nothing else, this would be a moment to celebrate later. There was a flash of golden hair as Elara ran from the booth, hooting and hollering as she climbed the stage and lifted Locke off his feet. She spun him in a circle to the astonishment of the mayor before returning the dwarf to the stage.

"She's stronger than she looks." Poppy's eyes were wide as she watched the scene unfold.

Elara knelt to kiss Locke, and the mayor addressed the crowd. "That's one way to conclude the pie contest. Please stick around for our next event, Best Local Pipeleaf, hosted by Elmwood Brookstone, followed by the wine contest."

The wine contest. A lump formed in Marigold's throat

as she realized only one event stood between her and her fate. Her heart pounded as she was suddenly transported back to last year. Another loss. Another disappointment. One of many at that point.

Her face was suddenly hot, her brow sweaty as her gaze fixed on the stage. The world faded around her, and she couldn't see her friends in their celebration or the way Rosie congratulated Locke. All she saw was herself. Alone and ashamed for never living up to her father's greatness.

"Hey," a familiar voice called. "Take my hand. Let's walk."

The world blurred as Marigold was guided through the crowd. She took short breaths, unable to focus on anything other than the intense fear pervading her being. Her fingers trembled as she held onto the steady hand like it was a lifeline, the only thing keeping her from slipping into total darkness.

She walked, one foot in front of the other, until a door thudded shut and the chaos settled.

"Can we stay in here for a moment?" the familiar voice asked.

"Is everything okay?" Another voice she recognized but couldn't place, followed by a pause. "Take as much time as you need."

A door shut again, and there was silence. A soft hand cradled Marigold's cheek.

"Breathe," the voice said. "One breath at a time."

Marigold listened, taking one shaky breath after another. She focused on her breathing until the fog began to lift.

She was in a room, surrounded by dreary gray walls. As the fog receded, color peeked in, streams of fading daylight streaking through a sunburst mosaic across the room. She was in the temple, the statue of Melora looking down upon her from the dais, her outline emblazoned in the fading light.

Marigold reached up, fingers wrapping around Poppy's comforting hand.

"Hey," the gnome whispered, kissing Marigold's fingers.

"Hey." Marigold felt tears pooling at the edges of her eyes. She let out a shaky breath. "I don't know what happened back there."

"It's okay." Poppy sat on the temple floor next to Marigold, holding the halfling's hand like it was the most precious thing in the world. "No matter how far we think we've come, sometimes our past has a way of coming back to haunt us. You panicked, but it's over now."

Marigold leaned into Poppy, resting her head on the gnome's shoulder. For a long time, they sat in silence, the dull sounds of the crowd barely evident beyond the thick temple walls.

"Thank you," Marigold finally said, "for being there for me."

"Always." Poppy kissed the top of her head.

Marigold wasn't sure how she could believe those words, especially when Poppy's days in Willowbrook were numbered, but she did. There was an undeniable truth to them. No matter what the future held, a string of fate connected their souls.

She chuckled. "How is it you're always here when things go south for me?"

Poppy had been a comforting presence when Marigold fell from the apple tree, and again after Morbog devoured the wine. She'd put her beautiful mind to work, locating the recipe for rosewine in the old journals. And now, once more, she'd been there, a steadfast protector, as if sent by the gods.

"Just lucky, I guess." Time passed as Poppy held Marigold. Eventually, she stood and extended a hand. "If you're up to it, what do you say we go win a wine contest?"

25. THE SPECTER'S GRIP

The sun hugged the horizon by the time Marigold and Poppy left the temple, setting the sky ablaze with hues of pink and amethyst that faded to dandelion gold. Spirit lanterns lined the streets, their faces glowing against the waning light. While the moment of panic had passed, an unsteadiness remained. Had Marigold been with anyone else, she might have felt embarrassed by what happened, but Poppy had taken it all in stride. In Marigold's greatest moment of vulnerability, the gnome had been a guiding light in the darkness, showcasing only concern, never judgment.

Marigold was exhausted, body and mind, like she'd spent the entire day working the vineyard while simultaneously studying for a test. They passed a haybale, and it called to her like a siren, inviting Marigold to lay down and rest her eyes.

She pressed onward, trying to make sense of what had happened. Nerves were nothing new, she'd had them many times before—she'd even broken down a time or two—but Marigold had never experienced anything so overwhelming and all-consuming. She prayed she never would again.

Poppy had called it the Specter's Grip. In some cultures, it was known as the Fit of the Fae or Spirit Tremors. The gnome had seen it before in overworked scholars—a culmination of stress, anxiety, and past trauma. The upcoming contest provided an unhealthy dose of all three.

And now Marigold was going to meet it head-on. While she feared the possibility of another attack, she wanted to be there for Elara and to stand proudly behind the wine they'd created. Poppy offered some of the techniques and tools she'd seen work for her peers. Marigold hoped they might do the same for her.

Braziers burned around the square, providing a warm glow as heavy smoke lingered like fog in the aftermath of the pipeleaf contest. If it was anything like previous years, the contest had devolved into a showcase of who could blow the most elaborate smoke rings. More often than not, the judges abandoned the contest altogether, joining in the fun as they all cracked jokes at the others' expense.

Elmwood was exiting the stage as Marigold arrived. He clapped her on the shoulder and offered a warm smile. "Show 'em who's boss."

She hugged the old halfling. "Thanks, Elmwood."

Marigold turned to Poppy, taking a deep breath. "I guess this is it."

The gnome rested both hands on Marigold's shoulders, looking her in the eye. "You can do this. Just remember what I taught you. I'll be front and center the entire time." Poppy reached into her pocket, pulling out a yellow candy wrapped in waxed paper. She placed it in Marigold's palm. "Use this if you need it."

Marigold pressed her forehead to Poppy's. "What would I do without you?"

"Your very best. Like you always have." Poppy kissed Marigold, the gnome's lips like a calming salve. "No matter what happens, this is a moment to celebrate. When Morbog forced you to change plans, many people would have given up, but not you. You took lemons and made them into lemonade."

Marigold looked at the stage, where festival volunteers had covered the wine bottles with numbered crochet sleeves to conceal the labels. There was no way for the contestants or the judges to differentiate the bottles aside from the color of their necks. But even then, all of the glass was a similar shade of green or amber.

"We missed you after the pie judging." Elara stepped next to Marigold, her brow knitting with concern as she took in the halfling's appearance. "Everything okay? You look like you've seen a ghost."

"We can talk about it later, but I'm okay." Marigold glanced over her shoulder at the booth, where Locke was grinning like a fairy as he talked to people. She found herself smiling despite her nerves. "Locke has to be ecstatic to finally win again. I'm so proud of him."

"Me too." Elara's gaze softened as she watched the dwarf with admiration. "Three wins in ten years. Tonight, I'm going to buy him all the dwarven ale he can handle." She stepped aside, gesturing to the steps. "After you."

They were the first of the competitors onstage, but others soon followed. Most of the wineries surrounding Willowbrook were small, single-family operations similar to Dew Drop Vineyard. Marigold had spent time with all of them over the years at various town gatherings. For many of the smaller wineries, the owner and vintner were one and the same.

There was Cedric Underwood of Moonlight Vineyards. The silver-haired retiree leaned on a knobby cane, his shoulders hunched. Even though he'd retired a few years back, he still entered the contest every year. Twinkling gray eyes matched his cheerful personality, but for all of his charm, he was fiercely competitive.

Cora Tinkerfoot of Tinkerfoot Estates wasn't much older than Marigold. She had a petite frame and copper-colored hair that brought out the freckles on her nose. Always eager to prove herself, she'd won third place the previous year with a blend of starfire and sunburst grapes.

At Arcane Winery, Harlon and Reed Tealeaf gave proof to the phrase 'opposites attract.' Harlon was short and stocky, loud, jovial, and had a laugh so boisterous that Marigold swore he was part dwarf. His partner, Reed, was skinny, especially by halfling standards, and nearly a foot taller than Harlon. His soft-spoken voice was at odds with his mischievous nature. A couple of years back, Reed pranked Finn by offering him a glass of grape juice pretending it was wine. He'd also been known to switch the sugar and salt bowls at tea from time to time.

Two of the vineyards were dual-partnerships of families who had chosen to pool their resources and spread the labor. Even so, the vineyards together produced about half the wine as Darkroot Cellars.

The Barleys and Thatchshields of Barley-Thatchshield Cellars had sent their two patriarchs, Rosco Barley and

Eldon Thatchshield. Despite being from different families, the two halflings could have passed for brothers. Each had a generous belly, curly brown hair, and dark eyes.

The Gardners and Sunblossums of Primrose Vineyard always sent their youngest and oldest women to the contest. This sometimes meant both were from the same family, but this year there was one from each. Daisy Gardner had a slender build and wore her dark hair braided into a crown adorned with sprigs of rosemary. She'd just come of age this year, so this was her first time onstage. Gilly Sunblossum was one of the oldest halflings in Willowbrook, but you'd never know by looking at her. There was a youthfulness to her, both in action and appearance, only contradicted by the silver hair tied up with a yellow-and-red-patterned scarf.

These five wineries, along with Dew Drop Vineyard and Darkroot Cellars, attended the competition almost every year. In addition, there were always a few halflings who entered for fun. Most made wine as a hobby, producing enough for their families and friends, so it was an effort in itself to fill the two dozen bottle minimum required for entry.

This year, two hobbyists had made the cut, Rufus Foggins and Tobin Sweetroot, bringing the total number of entrants to nine.

While the volunteers finished setting up, Marigold and Elara said hello and exchanged pleasantries with the other winemakers. Once everything was ready, the judges joined them onstage. It was the same trio from the pie contest—Mayor Sweetwater, Council Member Lumina Cloudmane, and Merrin Slowwater the blacksmith.

Offstage, people continued to gather for the event, and just as Poppy had promised, she was front and center. She beamed at Marigold, giving her a thumbs-up.

Marigold noticed a few more friendly faces as she scanned the crowd. In an unexpected twist, Ronan and the three dwarven sisters from the inn were together. They passed around a bottle of wine, drinking it straight from the bottle. Marigold waved, and the sisters howled like wolves. Those four were certainly in for a night of fun. Near the Dew Drop booth, Finn and Gerty's parents shared a candied apple as they talked to their children. She spotted the gray robes of the two clerics, Korin and Hamlen, who seemed to have continued their friendship from the harvest. At the back, Aldric was unmistakable with his blue hat as he towered over everyone around him. Little Splinter sat on his shoulder, but Morbog was nowhere to be seen, probably hiding out in the mage's cart.

"We're just waiting on one more," the mayor said, taking his place at center stage.

"Here comes the little weasel," Elara whispered.

Galvin climbed the steps, followed by Tansy, their resplendent attire out of place among the other competitors.

"Good to see you, Galvin." The corner of Reed's mouth curved slightly as he spoke. "Did you come from a coronation or are we all underdressed?"

Galvin scoffed. "It's called making an entrance. When you've won nine years in a row, the people expect a certain panache." He looked Reed up and down. "But I wouldn't expect you to know much about that. We can't all be winners, can we?"

Behind him, Tansy's expression was unreadable as she watched the exchange.

"Now, now, Galvin." Cedric pointed with his cane. "Reed is just giving you some friendly banter. There's no need for hostilities. I don't know if you recall, but your father and I would give one another a good ribbing every year, even though we all knew we were competing for second place." The retired halfling turned to Marigold. "Speaking of, how is Wilbur these days? It feels like an age has passed since I last saw him."

"It has been." Marigold smiled. "Nearly two years since he and mom were last home. But I believe they'll be back next year."

"He always did have an adventurous spirit." Cedric chuckled. "Hope to see him again soon, and your mother, too. I'm sure they sleep easy knowing you've got a handle on things."

Mayor Sweetwater cleared his throat. "Now that everyone has arrived, shall we begin?" When there were no objections, he turned to face the crowd, introducing the judges and the competitors.

As he did so, Marigold became keenly aware of just how many people were watching the event. Her friends, her community, people from all over. She recognized some from the harvest, but many she'd never met. She swallowed. So many people. An all too familiar sense of dread enveloped her as the Specter's Grip tightened around her chest. Suddenly, it was difficult to breathe, as if a rope had been tied around her, continuously constricting as her heart thundered within. In that moment, she knew how this would end. All the effort she had poured into the past year—all the hoping, the planning, the replanning after things fell apart with Morbog—would amount to nothing. Just like before. She would lose. Again.

A shiver passed through her body as the world shifted out of focus for the second time that day.

"Are you okay?" Elara asked. She sounded far off, like she was speaking through a tunnel.

Not again. Marigold took short, fragile breaths. *Please, please, not again.* She searched the crowded front row for Poppy. Among the blurred silhouettes, she found a messy bun of sapphire-blue hair.

She tried to recall the gnome's advice, but she couldn't. Everything was jumbled in her mind as darkness continued to creep in. The Specter's Grip held firm, pulling her under.

Marigold struggled for each shallow breath, her thoughts racing. *What was it Poppy had said?*

Within the darkness, she heard the gnome's voice, fuzzy and muddled. Through the distortion, she made out one word—*breathe.*

Marigold closed her eyes, concentrating on one shaky breath at a time. Her hands pressed against her thighs, and with each inhale, she focused on the sensation of the crisp night air filling her lungs and nourishing her body. Something crinkled within her pocket.

The lemon candy. Poppy had bought it on the walk from the temple. She'd said that intense flavors, especially sour, were supposed to help with anxious thoughts by engaging the other senses.

Marigold pulled the candy from her pocket and unwrapped it. Her mouth puckered at the flavor, and more of the darkness receded. With her eyes still closed, she focused on the tangy burn as her breathing slowed. She wished she'd taken the candy the moment she stepped onstage.

Once again, she tried to recall Poppy's advice. This time, she could hear the gnome's voice more clearly. *"Acknowledge the situation. If you can recognize the emotions, then you can keep them in perspective."*

Marigold breathed. As scary as things felt right now, she knew what she was up against. She wasn't dying. This was panic, and it would pass. This was ten years of stress and self-doubt rearing its ugly head. She'd made it through before and could do it again.

The pounding in her heart eased, and when Marigold finally opened her eyes, she found Poppy. The pressure in her chest released slightly as she met the gnome's gaze. Poppy's words replayed in her mind. *"Find something to focus on, a single object to give your entire attention to until the panic passes."*

Marigold did as she'd been told, concentrating on the gnome's appearance.

She was beautiful, with skin the dusty pink of a summer sunset and hair as blue as the boundless sea. She had an adorable button nose and a laugh that could light up a room. Marigold loved the way the gnome's fingers were constantly stained with ink from writing in her journals, and how her eyes wrinkled at the edges when she smiled but couldn't hide the sparkling periwinkles. Above all, it was Poppy's kindness and intelligence that truly made her attractive. She had a thirst for knowledge that was unquenchable but if someone ever needed help, she'd put everything else aside. Perida Poppinton Deepspring was magic in its purest form.

Marigold's chest unclenched, like a knot that had finally loosened, and she took her first deep breath in what felt like ages. With it, the specter's hold was broken, and tension unraveled. Her entire body jittered with weakness, like she'd gone too long without eating. The sea of silhouettes surrounding Poppy unclouded as the world shifted back into focus. The gnome nodded, a gentle encouragement that said Marigold had made it out the other side.

She took in the rest of her surroundings, realizing that she'd missed the entire speech. The judges were already sampling the wines. Everyone onstage was focused on the proceedings, save Elara, who watched her friend intently.

Elara leaned down, whispering in the halfling's ear. "Marigold Bramblefoot, I swear to the gods, if you don't tell me what is going on right now, I'm going to lose it."

Marigold paused before answering. "I had a moment of panic." She squeezed the elf's hand. "But I'm okay now. What did I miss?"

"What'd you miss?" Elara snorted. "She slips through the veil and now she wants to know what she missed."

Marigold had no idea why, but she laughed—so loudly that the judges turned in her direction.

"Sorry." She coughed in an effort to conceal the laughter. "Something in my throat."

"The taste of defeat," Galvin muttered from across the stage.

Marigold ignored him, focusing on the burn of the sour candy in her mouth.

In front of her, the judges moved down the line and a volunteer poured samples from the next bottle. Four still remained, and it was almost impossible to tell if the rosewine had been tasted yet. In the fading light, the residual wine in the empty glasses looked almost the same.

Each judge had a distinct method to their process. The mayor swirled the glass of straw-colored wine at eye level. His brow furrowed as he brought the wine to his nose and sniffed, swirled the glass, and sniffed again. He set the glass on the table, making a note in his journal before finally taking a sip. There was a slurping sound as he let the wine settle on his tongue before swallowing, after which, he puckered his lips and had another taste before making additional notes.

The blacksmith, Merrin, did his tasting in two phases. He'd observe the color, smell the nose, and take a generous swig, swishing the wine in his mouth before spitting it into the spittoon. His second attempt was similar, except he'd actually drink the wine. Each time, he waited until he was finished before making any notes, evaluating the wine as a whole.

Lumina, on the other hand, was an extensive note-taker. Marigold imagined that Poppy appreciated the thorough approach the council member took evaluating each wine. She spent so much time making notes that the other judges were forced to wait awkwardly until she finished.

As the next bottle was poured, a murmur swept through the crowd as deep red wine settled in the glass. The mayor was the first to examine the wine. As he tilted the glass and long red legs lingered on the sides. Whoever had submitted this wine had gone for something bold and full-bodied, just as Marigold had originally intended.

Elara leaned in. "I guess we weren't the only ones thinking outside the box this year."

"I guess not. Whose do you think it is?" Marigold watched her competitors for any sign that the wine might be theirs.

Reed and Harlon were talking to one another in hushed voices, as were the ladies from Primrose Vineyards.

"I'd bet the vineyard it's not Galvin," Elara said.

Across the stage, he rolled his eyes and muttered something to Tansy. Whatever he said, she didn't seem amused.

Marigold could almost guarantee it wasn't his. For the past nine years, the only wine he'd entered was honey-wine. While he and Tansy did it fantastically, it was evident he had no imagination. There was no way he'd risk his title by changing things up this year.

She attempted to read the judges' expressions as they tasted the red wine but to their credit, they remained stoic throughout. The next wine they sampled was a deep yellow. If Marigold had to guess, it was likely an ember-fruit or sunburst varietal based on the vibrant color.

The judges moved to the final entry. As the wine poured from the bottle, Marigold had to force herself to remain calm. Pale pink wine splashed into the glass. There was a murmur of delight from the crowd and more than a few raised eyebrows onstage. Marigold's heart pounded, and she found Poppy. She took deep, steady breaths and focused on the gnome's calming presence. She sucked hard on the remnants of the candy.

There would be time to unpack everything she was

experiencing soon, but for now, she just needed to make it through the contest.

Elara's hand rested on Marigold's shoulder. "Now, we wait."

Three empty glasses sat on the table, and the judges left the stage to deliberate, leaving the contestants to sweat out the decision.

"How do you think it went?" Marigold asked.

"Hard to say." Elara shrugged. "They all did a pretty good job of concealing their expressions. I expected as much from the politicians, but even Merrin held it together." She wrapped an arm around Marigold. "I like our chances, though."

Marigold didn't expect the elf to say otherwise, but it was comforting, nonetheless.

"Shouldn't take them too long to deliberate." Galvin pulled his shoulders back, preening like a griffin.

"They say confidence is silent. It's insecurity that's loud." Heads turned toward Rufus, one of the hobbyist winemakers. He had his arms crossed, smirking in Galvin's direction. "The dragon doesn't need to roar to remind the mountain who it is."

Galvin laughed, but there was irritation in his eyes. "What would you know of confidence?"

Rufus uncrossed his arms, his attitude as calm as a windless sea. "I make wine for my friends and family. My confidence lies in knowing that it brings us together."

Marigold found herself smiling. The words reminded her of her father. She chuckled to herself, remembering the reason she was here.

"What are you laughing at?" Galvin narrowed his gaze

in Marigold's direction. "It must be real hard for you, living in the shadow of the great Wilbur Bramblefoot."

"Now, you listen here—" Elara took a step, but Marigold was quick enough to grab the elf's hand.

"I can handle it."

Elara's anger shifted to concern, but she didn't argue.

"It used to be." Although Marigold was drained from the day's events, she met Galvin's gaze. For all of his accolades, he was always so defensive, ready to attack anyone who didn't grovel at his feet. For the first time since their rivalry began, she actually felt sorry for him. "But then I remembered something. My father, he wasn't great because of how many contests he won. He enjoyed the process of winemaking, he experimented for fun, and he never entered the same wine in back-to-back years. He won so many contests because he was a great winemaker, and more than that, a great halfling. What mattered most to him was sharing his passion with others." She gestured at the other contestants. "The other winemakers were his rivals, sure, but he never viewed them as enemies. They were friends, and he looked forward to seeing what they entered every year because, at the end of the day, wine brings people together."

"Hear, hear." Cedric tapped his cane against the stage.

Behind Galvin, Tansy nodded her approval.

"That's a lovely sentiment." Galvin smirked. "After this is over, maybe you can hang it on the wall."

Perhaps it was the deliriousness of the day's events, but Marigold laughed at the insult. She laughed until her stomach muscles ached and tears glistened in the corners of her eyes. When she finally stopped, it took her a moment to gather her breath. "That's a good idea, Galvin. I might just do that."

He opened his mouth to retort, but Mayor Sweetwater returned to the stage, followed by the other judges. The mayor held a piece of folded parchment.

The mayor raised the speaking trumpet to his mouth. "When I say that this was one of the most difficult contests to judge in recent years, I mean it. There were so many delicious wines that we had a hard time narrowing them down to just three. As a reminder, all of the wineries competing today will have a limited number of this year's entry available at their booths. So, please, stop by afterward and show your support."

He glanced down at the paper. "Without further ado, the third-place finisher of this year's wine contest is Rufus Foggins, who impressed us all with his blend of shadowthorne and moonshadow. It's no secret that halflings have a special fondness for white wines. But even so, we can appreciate the complexities of a bold red, and Rufus made a statement we couldn't ignore. The notes of blackberry, leather, and vanilla were inviting, followed by a powerful punch of fig and dried cherry. I'm no stranger to the finer things in life, and the mouthfeel on this one was as luxurious as velvet. I could see this pairing perfectly with roasted mutton or a spiced stew. Congratulations, Rufus!"

There was a round of applause as Rufus joined the mayor up front, bowing to the crowd before accepting the silver ribbon.

The mayor raised the trumpet and continued. "Our second-place finisher is no stranger to the stage, and their winery is one of the most storied and accomplished in all of Willowbrook."

Marigold straightened her back and took Elara's hand for comfort. Second place was an accomplishment, one that seven other contestants would be grateful for. She held her head high. Considering everything they'd overcome in the previous week, there was no shame in their showing.

"It is with great pleasure that I announce our second-place finishers, Galvin Darkroot and Tansy Ironvale of Darkroot Cellars. As always, they've had a spectacular showing. The beautiful floral aroma of this vintage is inviting, followed by perfectly balanced notes of citrus and semi-sweetness that give way to that distinctly refreshing honey finish we all know and love. This wine is the embodiment of the varietal, and as delicious as ever. Let's give a round of applause to Galvin and Tansy!"

Galvin stood frozen, a dark scowl settling across his features. All around the stage, the other contestants wore shocked expressions. Galvin might have been insuffer-able, but there was no denying that since partnering with Tansy, their honeywine was of exceptional quality. It seemed no one, Marigold included, had expected this outcome.

Tansy nudged Galvin in the back, but he stood firm.

"Is this a joke?" Galvin sneered at the mayor. There were a few gasps from the crowd at the outburst. "It must be. To think that any of these second-rate wineries could compete with the excellence of Darkroot Cellars."

The mayor's gaze narrowed, and a rumble of disap-proval swept through the crowd. "Now, Galvin. I under-stand that you're upset, but that's no reason to belittle your opponents. Think of the example you're setting. The harvest festival is a celebration of what makes this town great. For nine years, you've worn the crown, but no reign lasts forever."

"Save it." Galvin laughed, and there was an edge of madness to it. "This is preposterous. Someone must have cheated. Or paid you off. We have a druid, for gods' sakes."

"Had," Tansy said from behind Galvin.

Galvin turned on his heels, his eyes wide with chaos. "Come again?"

Tansy stood tall, her gaze boring into the halfling. "You *had* a druid," she spoke calmly. "I quit."

"Quit? Oh, no, no, no." Galvin wagged his finger at the druid. "You can't quit. We have a contract."

"Had a contract," she corrected again. "You may not recall, but I signed on for ten years, and for the past ten years, I have given you my best. I've tended your vineyard with the utmost care because I believed that the rest of Aedrea should have the chance to experience halfling wine. But year after year, you care less about the wine and more about the money it brings in. It's corrupted you, Galvin." Tansy looked upon him with such sadness that Marigold felt it herself. "I've tried to rationalize many of your actions, but when you canceled the harvest this year, I realized you are no longer the same halfling I signed on to work with. Today has only reaffirmed it."

"Tansy, you can't be serious." His voice softened as he held his palms out. "We're one of the most successful producers of honeywine in all of Tyne. You don't want to walk away from that."

Tansy took a step closer, her face full of compassion as

she leaned forward and placed a hand on the halfling's shoulder. "I'm sorry, Galvin, but I can't."

Galvin swatted her hand away. "Fine, then. Leave. I don't need you anyways. I'll just hire another druid to take your place. You're nothing special." He stormed across the stage, and as he passed the mayor, Galvin snatched the blue, first-place ribbon from his grasp. "We all know I'm the one who deserves this."

Tansy sighed, and her hand took on a green glow as something swished beneath the stage. Vines shot through the cracks in the platform, wrapping around Galvin's ankles and holding him in place. He cursed, struggling to lift his legs, but more vines slithered through the platform, cinching around his body and pinning his arms by his side until he was encased up to his neck. He grunted, thrashing his head about.

"You can't do this!" he yelled. "Release me this instant!"

Tansy removed the crochet sleeve from one of the wine bottles and stuffed it in his mouth, stifling his protest into a dull mumble.

The crowd cheered at the display, and Marigold and Elara exchanged a look of surprise.

Elara shook her head in disbelief. "This has certainly been one of the most entertaining festivals I've ever been a part of."

Marigold had to agree. This was one for the ages.

A green aura surrounded Tansy's hand as the vines around Galvin's hand released enough for her to remove the ribbon. She handed it to the mayor. "I believe you still have a winner to announce."

"Well..." Mayor Sweetwater looked from Tansy to the ribbon and then to Galvin before finally raising the trumpet and speaking to the crowd. "Shall we continue?" There was a roar of applause. "In that case, let us return to the business at hand."

Marigold took Elara's hand once again. "Whatever happens, it's been an honor working by your side all these years."

Elara winked. "I know."

They both laughed, and as the mayor raised the trumpet to announce the winner, Marigold met Poppy's gaze. The gnome's earnest smile soothed her racing heart.

"The winner of Willowbrook's 577th Annual Harvest Festival Competition for Best Local Wine is Marigold Bramblefoot and Elara Moongrove of Dew Drop Vineyard. This year's winner was both unexpected and unique —a masterful rosewine blend of dreamcatcher, emberfruit, and just enough moonshadow to give the wine a stunning raspberry hue. The nose was fruity and refined, balancing delicate notes of strawberry and fragrant rose petals. What truly impressed the judges, however, was the wine's remarkable complexity. Its vibrant fruitiness gave way to a smooth, dry finish with a touch of minerality and a hint of citrus—leaving us craving another sip. I could see myself..."

"We did it!" Elara whisked Marigold off her feet, swinging her in a circle as the crowd applauded.

Marigold had no idea how long their celebration lasted, but when Elara finally put her down, Mayor Sweetwater was there with a blue ribbon in his outstretched hand. She'd missed the rest of his speech in her excitement.

"Congratulations to both of you. Your blend was tremendous, and I can't wait to buy a bottle for myself."

"Thank you, Mayor." Marigold accepted the ribbon, admiring the blue silk that gleamed in the firelight before passing it to Elara.

Mayor Sweetwater turned to Galvin, who was still bound in vines from feet to neck. "What are we supposed to do with him?"

"Don't worry." Tansy joined them. "He's not hurt or anything. Once he's calmed down a little, I'll release him."

"That's a relief." The mayor sighed. "What a night."

"You can say that again." Elara chuckled, her gaze fixed on the ribbon. "What a night indeed."

While the volunteers cleared the stage for The Cider Barrel Band, the other competitors stopped by to offer their congratulations. Tansy waited off to the side until they'd finished before approaching.

"Congratulations." She offered Marigold and Elara her hand in turn. "I had a taste of your wine before they cleared the table. You earned it."

Elara gave Tansy's hand a firm squeeze. "After watching you put that little worm in his place, I think I may have misjudged you."

The druid chuckled as she gave Marigold a knowing look. "Seems to be a lot of that going around."

Marigold shook Tansy's hand. "What's next for you?"

"I'm not sure." She shrugged. "I really enjoyed working at the vineyard. Maybe I'll find another that can use my help."

"I'm sure there's no shortage of prospective employers across Aedrea."

"Perhaps, but I've grown to like it here." Tansy looked out across the town. "I might not look like I belong in a place like this, but it feels like home."

"Then you should stick around." Marigold saw a flash of blue hair off to the side as Poppy stepped onstage. "In my experience, if something feels like home, it probably is."

Tansy smiled, then turned toward Galvin, shaking her head. "I should probably take care of him before the band starts playing. Enjoy your victory."

After the day she'd had, what Marigold really wanted to enjoy was a nap. She hugged Elara, promising that they would have a proper celebration back at the inn. Between the wine contest and Locke's victory, there was a lot to be thankful for, but right now, she owed her gratitude to someone else.

Poppy waited patiently by the steps. She grinned as Marigold approached, the gnome's eyes wrinkling at the edges. A familiar warmth buzzed within Marigold, and she opened her arms, enveloping Poppy like a blanket.

"I'm so proud of you." Poppy kissed Marigold's neck, sending a wave of sparks down the halfling's shoulder. "Not just for the contest, but everything. You are truly an inspiration."

"Thank you." Marigold held her tighter. "But what I really am is tired. What do you say we find some place to hide away?"

Poppy ran her thumb down Marigold's cheek. "There's no one else I'd rather hide away with."

Stars twinkled overhead as Marigold and Poppy lay on a grassy hilltop at the edge of town. The teashop located within the hill was aptly named The Hillside Burrow, and since it was a few streets back from the main thoroughfare, it had closed up shop with the evening bell. They had the hill to themselves as music from The Cider Barrel Band played in the distance.

A lively tune carried across the night. The fiddle led with a bright, sharp energy that was balanced by the steady sweetness of a lute. A flute added a bit of charm, weaving through the song like an autumn breeze while the drums kept rhythm, the heartbeat of the band, occasionally punctuated by the crash of a cymbal.

As the melody slowed, shifting to the soulful tempo of a ballad, Marigold rested her head on Poppy's chest, listening to the drum of her heart. "This is nice," Marigold said, closing her eyes.

"Better than I imagined." Poppy caressed Marigold's shoulder, her touch soft and comforting.

"Thank you—" Marigold reached for her shoulder, resting her hand on top of the gnome's. "—for earlier. What happened to me, I think it had been building up for a while. For years, if I'm being honest. I'd been holding everything in for so long, and I..." She paused, rolling over until she was face-to-face with Poppy. "I don't want to do that anymore. I want to be more honest with myself. And with you."

Poppy ran a finger along Marigold's cheek. "What's on your mind?"

"I don't want you to leave." Marigold's eyes glistened. "I know you have to, but I want you to know that I wish you didn't."

"I know." Poppy sat up, wrapping her arm around Marigold. "I'm not looking forward to that day either. But whatever happens, this isn't the end of our story."

Marigold leaned her head against the gnome's. "How can you be so sure?"

"Because we're the ones who write it."

A loud whistle shrieked through the air, followed by a burst of colorful light. Yellow and red ignited the sky in a series of sparks as the firelight display began. A trail of blue streaked beneath the moon like a shooting star, reflecting off the stream in the distance as it erupted with a crackle of blue wisps that spiraled outward, fading into darkness.

Spirals of green and yellow intertwined, followed by a circle that spread outward in continuous sparkling rings, each one bigger and brighter than the last.

Marigold and Poppy held onto one another as fire-lights fizzled and exploded in a never-ending barrage of sight and sound. They oohed and ahhed, bewitched by Aldric's spell of dazzling images of leaves, pumpkins, and brilliant showers of color.

Just when they thought the show was over, a single light shot upward and burst into the image of a tree. It was followed by a barrage of sparkling green leaves that blazed among the branches, growing bigger and brighter with each thunder. Specks of red and yellow burst within, forming giant apples among the heavens before the leaves changed color, crackling as they fell toward the earth, the empty branches still glowing against the night sky. For a moment, there was a steady sizzle as the skeletal tree remained, then a thunderous boom as silver cascaded like snowfall before everything faded away.

26. WINE BRINGS PEOPLE TOGETHER

Marigold sat in her office, looking over upcoming reservations. Now that the festival was over, there'd be fewer guests in the coming months, which suited the staff just fine. This was the time of year when they could slow down a bit. The inn and vineyard never truly came to a halt, but things trudged along slowly, leaving time for reflection and contemplation.

Elara and Locke had insisted Marigold take the day after the festival off, with the elf making some not-so-subtle threats of what would happen should she refuse. Marigold spent the day lounging in the library and reading while Poppy chronicled her experiences from the event.

It had been a much-needed change of pace, but Marigold was happy to be back at her desk. Work wasn't always work when you enjoyed it. She put the reservation book aside and reached for the notebook tracking property maintenance. Inside, she'd already begun calculating how many rows of moonshadow grapes they'd need to plant in order to produce the rosewine blend in greater quantities. That would be a task for the spring, but it was never too early to make preparations.

Someone knocked on the door, and Marigold set the notebook aside. "Come in."

The door swung inward, and Aldric stepped inside, removing his hat as he ducked to avoid the doorframe. In that brief moment, Marigold caught sight of a bald spot on his crown, marked with a tattoo of an unfamiliar symbol. The mage held a jar filled with a pink, translucent substance. Splinter waved at Marigold from his usual perch on the mage's shoulder.

"Good morning, Aldric, Splinter." She waved her fingers at the twig golem. "How can I help you?"

"We'll be heading back on the road today. I wanted to stop by to thank you for your hospitality and congratulate you before I left. Despite my interference, you proved yourself a winemaker of paramount quality."

"We both could have probably handled things better. I know you were doing what you thought was best, and in the end, I owe you and Morbog both a great deal of thanks. Our new blend was a success." She tapped a piece of parchment on the desk. "We sold every bottle at the festival, and there's a waiting list for the next batch."

He bowed his head slightly. "In that case, double congratulations."

"Thank you." She smiled. "You put on quite the show at the festival. I daresay people might be talking about it for years to come."

"I can't take all the credit." His eyes twinkled as he tapped the jar. "Morbog is a great helper."

Marigold raised a brow. "Is that so?"

Aldric gestured to the lid of the jar. "Do you mind?"

"Go ahead." She wasn't sure what to expect, but the mage deserved a chance to explain himself if he wished.

He removed the lid. There was a squelching sound as Morbog moved, the translucent pink gelatin's form constantly shifting as she climbed the edge of the jar and onto the mage's arm. Splinter gestured excitedly at the amorphous blob, and she gurgled in response.

Aldric placed the jar on the desk and ran a finger along the jelly. A ripple of what Marigold assumed was pleasure passed through the creature.

"The first thing you must understand is that jellies are not dangerous. They're remarkable creatures—playful, inquisitive—and unlike oozes and slimes, they gather all of their energy from absorbing plant life." He held his hand toward Marigold. "Would you like to pet her?"

Marigold paused. It went against her every instinct to touch something capable of absorbing its food, but when would she have another opportunity like this?

"Okay." She walked around the desk. Morbog had returned to her normal globular form, her arm-like appendages waving as she stood in Aldric's palm.

"Go ahead," Aldric said gently.

Marigold swallowed.

When Aldric noticed her hesitation, he held up a finger. "One moment." The mage reached into his pocket and pulled out two brass buttons, handing them to Morbog.

The jelly took the buttons with her appendages and absorbed them into her body. They floated within the gelatinous creature like coins in a pond, but then they began to shift, the jelly positioning them in a way so that they looked like eyes. She gurgled as she looked in Marigold's direction.

Marigold knew that nothing had actually changed, and yet strangely, Morbog appeared less threatening, almost friendly.

"It's funny how little things can influence people's perception." Aldric smiled. "Sometimes, Splinter will offer her twigs until it looks like she has a skeleton."

Marigold imagined that might not be as calming. She raised her hand, extending a single finger to touch the jelly. To her surprise, Morbog was neither wet nor slimy. Her exterior was cool to the touch, with a smoothness that resembled a frog's skin. The jelly gurgled as Marigold stroked her, deflating into a rippling puddle. Although Morbog had no discernible features aside from the buttons, there was a sense of personality as she pulsed and undulated.

"She likes it." Aldric watched her with adoration.

"I'll be honest, this is not what I was expecting."

"Jellies are magnificent creatures. And surprisingly adept at being trained. Allow me to show you something." He pointed at a spot on the floor a few feet away. "Take a step back."

Marigold did as she was told. Morbog reformed into a blob in Aldric's hand.

"Alright, now hold out your palm like this." Aldric showed her what he meant with his free hand, turning it face up. Once Marigold obliged, he commanded Morbog to jump.

The jelly compressed herself and then elongated, her body springing forward as she launched across the room. Morbog landed in Marigold's palm with a squelch.

"She's amazing." Marigold laughed as Morbog moved around her hand and forearm. She was even more light-weight than Marigold had imagined. And yet, this creature had been bigger than her not even a week prior. "I have to admit, I had no idea that jellies were so extraordinary."

"Most people don't." Aldric scooped Morbog from Marigold's palm. "Oozes are the reason most people fear gelatins, even though they're incredibly rare. But we can thank the Adventurer's Guild for that bit of propaganda. They're ripe with tales of unsuspecting adventurers who were devoured by oozes." He shook his head. "If you ask me, maybe the guild needs better training protocols if they want their members to live longer. It's not that hard to tell the difference. Oozes are predators, and you can always tell them apart by their murky appearance. They're naturally drawn to mana-rich areas, and this sometimes results in them developing magical properties. So if you ever see one, the best course of action is to stay far away." He stroked Morbog, and she relaxed into a puddle. "Slimes are the most common type of gelatin, mostly found in the high altitudes of mountains. They're translucent like jellies, but slow and sticky. They can be danger-ous, since they're omnivores, but they're rarely known to attack creatures bigger than themselves. I heard tales of some eccentric club in Eastborne that decided to eat them." He grimaced. "There's not enough gold in Aedrea for me to consider that."

"I'm with you there." Marigold nearly gagged at the thought. "I appreciate you enlightening me on gelatins, but I'm not exactly sure I understand how any of this relates to Morbog helping you with the firelights?"

"Like I said, jellies are remarkable creatures." Aldric quit petting the jelly. "Morbog, bubble."

There was a suctioning sound as she inflated. Her body stretched thin, forming into a hollowed-out sphere with an opening the size of a small pumpkin on one side. The two buttons that had been her eyes rested on the bottom of the bubble. If Aldric had wanted, he could probably have worn the jelly over his head like a helmet.

"All gelatins are resilient creatures. They're almost impossible to kill without tremendous effort and can continue to function after being cut in half or torn apart. That's what makes oozes so dangerous. As long as the creature's core remains intact, the pieces can be resorbed." Aldric turned Morbog around so that Marigold could see the opening. "Alchemy is a dangerous profession, and creating firelights is even more so. Morbog allows me a safe space to work when I'm blending unstable compounds."

Marigold tapped Morbog's spherical form. She was firm, but still flexible. "If something exploded, would it not hurt her?"

Aldric laughed. "Believe it or not, she enjoys it. Gelatins don't feel pain in the same way we do. Though I try to avoid such things for my own safety."

"This is fascinating." Marigold gazed upon the creature with awe. "You really are more than meets the eye. I wish I had gotten to see more of you." She returned her attention to Aldric. "What's next for you?"

His mouth curled into a smile. "Wizard business."

"Meaning none of mine." Marigold grinned. "In that case, I'll wish you good fortune, wherever the road leads you. And if you ever find yourself back in Willowbrook, know that you, Splinter, and Morbog will have a place to stay."

"That means more than you know." The mage's eyes glistened. "I know you haven't asked for recompense regarding the wine that was destroyed, but even so, a debt is owed. I intend to make things right one day. Until then, take care of yourself." He placed Morbog back in her container, and as he stepped out the door, he paused and turned around. "One more thing."

"Yes?"

"I'm happy you found your magic." He winked.

"Me too," she said, though he was already gone.

***

Over the next few days, the guests who had stayed for the festival filtered out. Ronan and the dwarven sisters had enjoyed one another's company so much that they all made advanced reservations for next year's harvest.

At the winery, the fermentation process was well underway. Elara and Marigold kept an eye on the pots, tasting them each day to gauge when the wine would be ready for racking. In the meantime, Marigold spent as much time with Poppy as possible.

The gnome was diligent in her work, but she made time for Marigold. Every afternoon, they would take a long walk through the hills, Onyx traipsing behind them as they enjoyed the cool autumn breeze and colorful leaves. Each evening, they would sit at the bar, sharing wine and talking late into the night. Sometimes, Marigold would help with Poppy's research, clarifying any questions the gnome might have. While they hadn't broached the subject of Poppy's inevitable departure since the festival, it loomed with every stolen glance, every caress, every passionate kiss.

Late one evening, they were sitting at the bar when Marigold heard the crunch of wagon wheels down the driveway. The front door opened a few minutes later, but it wasn't a guest checking in for the night. Instead, Finn stepped inside wearing a mischievous grin.

"You were in town late." Marigold turned around, resting her shoulders against the bar. "Everything okay?"

"Just running a few errands." His smile widened.

Locke appeared in the kitchen doorway, Elara and Gerty standing behind him. The dwarf looked at Finn. "Did you get it?"

"Get what?" Marigold frowned. She'd been around them long enough to know when something was up.

Finn nodded, ignoring Marigold's question. "It's in the wagon. Should we do it now?"

"Do what now? And what's in the wagon?" Marigold asked. When Poppy giggled, she turned to the gnome. "Do you know what's going on?"

Elara joined them, batting her eyelashes at Marigold uncharacteristically before Poppy could answer. "Can you do us a favor and close your eyes?"

"Close my eyes?" Marigold pointed at each of her staff. "With this energy, I'm not sure that's a good idea."

Poppy rested her hand on Marigold's forearm. "Just let it happen."

"So you're in on it too? Alright." Marigold finished off her glass of wine. "But if this is another prank, I'm holding you responsible."

"Attagirl, Mari," Locke said as he headed toward the porch.

Poppy offered Marigold her hand. "You can hold my hand if it makes you feel better."

"It would." Marigold took Poppy's hand and kissed it, then she closed her eyes.

"You two are precious," Elara said warmly. "And I'll fight anyone who says otherwise."

"Somehow, I don't doubt that." Poppy chuckled.

Outside, footsteps thudded against the porch, followed by Locke cursing and shouting at Finn to 'hold it steady.' The door opened, and the footsteps moved inside.

"Easy," Locke said, the footsteps moving closer until they were right beside Marigold. "Shit. Can you…"

"I've got it, dear." Elara moved silently. The next time she spoke her voice came from behind the bar. "Keep your eyes closed."

A barstool slid across the floor, followed by the crack of a hammer that caused Marigold to jump. She squeezed Poppy's hand.

"Almost done," the gnome whispered, her thumb's caress gentle and enticing.

Behind the bar, there was heaving and grunting, along with several noises she couldn't make out.

"Alright, turn around, but keep your eyes closed," Elara said.

Marigold did as she was told, swiveling until she felt the bar in front of her.

"Open your eyes," Gerty said excitedly.

Marigold did. Locke, Finn, Gerty, and Elara all stood behind the bar, each one grinning. Above them, a wooden sign hung on the wall just above the wine bottles. The words "wine brings people together" were engraved into the wood, along with an image of a wine glass on one side and a grape cluster on the other. An ornamental trim had been carved around the edge, and the wood had been polished to perfection, with the engravings stained so that they could be read from across the room.

Marigold swallowed back the lump in her throat. "It's amazing."

"It's true." Elara smiled.

Locke nodded. "We all chipped in to have it made."

"Worth it just to see the look on Galvin's face." Finn grinned devilishly.

Marigold arched a brow. "How would he ever find out?" Galvin Darkroot setting foot inside the Dew Drop Inn was about as likely as a summer snow.

They all looked at Gerty.

"What?" Her cheeks reddened, but there wasn't an ounce of shame to her. "After how he acted, you expect me not to tell anyone?"

No one could argue with that.

"You know..." Finn looked up at the sign. "I always thought we could do with a good motto."

"Dew Drop Vineyard, where wine brings people together." Gerty twisted a curl around her finger. "It is catchy."

"Hmm." Locke stroked his beard. "What do you think, Mari?"

Marigold grinned. "It does have a nice ring to it."

27. FIND YOUR WAY HOME

"You still haven't talked to her about it?" Elara's arms flexed as she pulled on the rope, using a pulley to hoist a clay pot of fermented wine from the ground.

Racking was a delicate process, one of the most consequential steps in ensuring the wine tasted as the winemaker intended. Without it, the leftover sediment would give the wine an unpleasant, yogurt-like taste as it aged. To prevent this, the wine needed to be carefully poured from the fermentation pots into barrels, leaving dead yeast and remnants of seeds, pulp, and skins behind. The key was to avoid disturbing the sediment that had settled to the bottom in the process.

"We talked at the festival." Marigold guided the pot away from the hole. "I told Poppy I didn't want her to leave, but we both know it's inevitable. She has to go back to Aethervale to present her research."

Elara grunted, slowly releasing the tension until the pot rested on the platform. "And then what?"

Marigold had wondered that a lot the past couple of weeks. "I don't know."

"And you're content with that?" Elara wiped sweat from her brow. "The unknown?"

"I don't know that we have much of a choice. She's found her calling, the same as I've found mine." Marigold sighed, her gaze focusing on the empty hole. "I've never met anyone who loves research and learning new things as much as her. I could never ask her to give that up. Just like she'd never ask me to step away from the winery. It's like Rosie says, 'some things only last a season.'"

"I know you don't believe that. There has to be something that can be done." Elara wore a sympathetic expression. "You deserve to be happy. Both of you."

If only it were that easy.

Elara gestured toward a nearby cart. "Can you bring the barrel over?"

Marigold pushed the cart loaded with an empty cask next to the platform. Once it was in position, Elara pulled a lever and the platform tilted, spilling clear white wine from the pot into a funnel that drained into the barrel. They watched the flow carefully, stopping once the sediment became visible.

The mostly empty pot was set aside so that it could be cleaned later, and they moved on to the next one. A silence lingered as they worked, and Marigold ruminated on Elara's words. Was there something that could be done, or were the past few weeks simply a fond memory that Marigold would carry through her life?

Only time would tell.

Together, they emptied three more pots before the

barrel was full. Marigold hammered a cork stopper into the bunghole, and then they rolled the cart to the cellar, where it would stay until spring.

Around midday, Poppy came up from the inn. "Ready for our walk?"

"I thought you'd never ask." Marigold hugged the gnome, inhaling the scent of honey soap in her hair. She turned to Elara. "Mind if we take a break?"

"Go ahead." Elara smiled devilishly. "I'll go ruffle Locke's feathers for a bit."

Hand-in-hand, Marigold and Poppy walked to the top of the hill with Onyx following. They came to a stop beneath the stomping tree. Nearly half of its leaves had fallen, painting the hillside and the trough with splotches of red, yellow, and orange.

Onyx laid down with a huff at Poppy's feet, closing his eyes as sunlight warmed his dark fur. Poppy gazed across the rolling hills, strands of sapphire hair whipping in the autumn breeze.

"Something on your mind?" asked Marigold.

"It's time." The gnome's eyes sparkled, tears brimming at the edges.

Marigold's stomach dropped, and she wrapped her arm around Poppy, pulling her close. There was no need for further explanation.

Poppy leaned into Marigold's embrace. "I'm sorry."

Marigold turned to face Poppy, both hands cradling the gnome's face. "You have nothing to be sorry for." She looked into the unfathomable depths of those endless purple eyes. "We both knew this day was coming eventually. And yes, it's going to hurt, and there will be a gnome-shaped hole in my heart, but don't think for a moment that I regret our time together."

Poppy sniffled. "You promise?"

"With my entire heart." She pulled Poppy closer.

Their lips touched, igniting that familiar spark that had been a source of comfort over the past few weeks. Beneath the passion, there was a longing as they held one another, a desire to stop time and live in that moment for eternity.

Poppy pulled away, the echoes of tears staining her cheeks as she pressed her forehead to Marigold's. "I'll write you every week, and I'll visit the first opportunity I have." She wiped a solitary tear from the halfling's cheek. "I promise you, this isn't good-bye."

Marigold released a shaky breath. "I'll hold you to that."

Two days later, Poppy waited downstairs, her bags sitting by the door while Finn readied the wagon. Marigold, Locke, Elara, and Gerty were all there to see her off. Finn was taking Poppy to town so that she could handle a final piece of business with the mayor, and then a carriage would take her to the port near Whitblossum. From there, she'd book passage to Aethervale by ship.

Locke shoved a basket full of food at the gnome, his lip trembling beneath his beard. The basket was stuffed with muffins, bread, scones, cookies, apples, and cheeses. Enough to feed a single person for weeks.

He blinked back tears, clearing his throat. "In case you get hungry."

"This is very kind. Thank you, Locke." Poppy hugged him, and he started sobbing.

Elara rubbed the dwarf's shoulder. "He's got a gruff exterior, but he's soft on the inside." She winked at Poppy. "We're going to miss having you around. Don't stay gone too long, or I'll have to come track you down."

"Something tells me you're not joking." Poppy took Marigold's hand and kissed her knuckles. "Keep an eye on this one while I'm gone."

Elara nodded. "Always."

Gerty pulled a jar of the honey cream ointment from her apron. "Just because you're traveling, it doesn't mean you can't take care of yourself."

Poppy chuckled. "Thank you, Gerty."

The others looked at Marigold, who hadn't said much all morning.

"Locke, honey..." Elara gave him a knowing look. "Didn't you say you needed Gerty and me to help you in the kitchen?"

"Help in the kitchen?" He frowned in confusion before noticing Elara's expression. "Er, right. Yes. I suppose I did say that."

"Safe travels, Poppy," Elara said as she ushered the others away, leaving Marigold and Poppy alone.

"This is harder than I thought it would be," Marigold said.

Poppy moved in front of her. "We always knew it would be."

"Yeah." Marigold placed her hands on the gnome's waist. "Doesn't make it hurt any less, though, does it?"

Poppy shook her head. "Not at all."

"I'm going to miss you, Perida Poppinton Deepspring." She kissed her gently. "Like I've never missed anything before."

"The feeling is mutual, Marigold Bramblefoot." Poppy smiled.

The wagon ground to a stop out front, and Marigold pulled Poppy closer, holding her with all the strength she had, as if that might be enough to keep her from leaving.

They broke apart as Finn opened the door.

"Ready?" he asked.

Poppy took a deep breath. "Ready as I'll ever be."

"Wait!" Marigold looked around the room, searching for where she'd placed the gift. "I almost forgot. I got you something."

She found the quilt on a nearby chair, holding it up to let the image unfold.

"Is that…" Poppy's mouth hung open.

"The Guiding Tree." Marigold smiled. It was the quilt she'd picked up at the festival. "So you can always find your way home."

Poppy embraced Marigold, quilt and all. "I love it."

They loaded Poppy's belongings into the back of the wagon, and after a final kiss that neither wanted to end, Marigold watched as the wagon rolled down the driveway. Onyx nuzzled against her legs as she stood there, transfixed on the wagon until it disappeared beyond the hills.

The longing came quickly, a hollowness that settled in her chest like a block of ice.

Marigold embraced it, as much as it hurt, because it meant a piece of her had left that day. Its absence had left room for something else, something unexpected—joy. Joy for having known something so precious. And though it might be covered in ink stains, and occasionally clumsy, it was beautiful. It was intelligent. It was funny. It was kind. Above all, it was love.

28. NEW BEGINNINGS

The Following Summer

Marigold knelt at the vineyard's edge, inspecting the newly plowed row. She scooped fresh soil into her palm. There was a color to it that only existed for a moment, ephemeral and fleeting, when the earth was still cool and moist, life teeming within as worms and beetles squirmed to escape. It offered a glimpse into another world that lurked below the surface.

Moments like this always reminded her of Poppy. Though their time together had been brief, it had left an indelible mark. As much as she still missed the gnome, she wouldn't trade those moments for anything in the world.

They wrote to one another frequently. Just as Poppy had promised, a new letter arrived at the inn every week. The gnome's research had been a success. So much so that she was in the process of formatting the content for a book that would be shared with libraries across Aedrea. This meant that there was no definite timeline for when she'd be back to visit.

Marigold was happy for Poppy's success, and proud of everything she'd accomplished, but that didn't make her absence any easier. While time might heal all wounds, Marigold's heart wasn't broken. There was nothing to mend, only a gnome-sized hole to fill. And as long as that void remained, she kept hope that it would one day be made whole again.

Sweat trickled down Marigold's forehead. Overhead, the sun beamed from a cloudless sky, sharing its warmth with the land. She stood, letting the soil fall from her fingers as she removed her straw hat, using the back of her hand to wipe the sweat from her brow.

Nearby, Acorn Blossom munched on grass, his work done for the day, while horned rabbits hopped around Onyx, the dire cat oblivious to their presence as he bathed in the sun.

"You ready?" Tansy called from behind. Her outfit was a stark contrast to her normally lavish attire. She wore trousers that had been patched at the knees, scuffed boots, a loose-fitting tunic, and an apron. Her green-tinged brown hair was pulled into a bun adorned with white flowers. Bees fluttered nearby, occasionally tasting their nectar. She wore no jewelry and if not for her polished staff, topped with a vibrant emerald, Marigold would have had a hard time recognizing her as the fashionable woman she'd encountered in town.

Marigold turned, grinning at the druid. "I still can't get over your work clothes."

Tansy shrugged. "I'm a mule in the fields but a phoenix at the feasts."

"That's one way to describe it." Marigold laughed as she picked up the basket of cuttings from the moonshadow vines. "Let's get to work."

With the increased interest in the rosewine blend after the festival, Marigold had planned to plant new cuttings in the spring. The problem was that it would take anywhere from one to three years for those vines to bear fruit. While the current vines would produce enough to blend a fair amount, it would mean waiting years before they could increase production. When Tansy found out, she offered to help speed the process along.

"I think it's really great what you've been doing," Marigold said as she planted one of the cuttings in the ground, piling soil around it. "You're helping out a lot of families."

"Thanks, but I don't do it for the praise." Tansy knelt beside the vine as Marigold planted the next one. She leaned forward, cupping her hands around the soil. "I wanted to give back, to cement myself as part of the community."

"You've more than done that." Marigold looked over, meeting the druid's gaze. Since leaving her position at Darkroot Cellars, Tansy had decided to spend a year among the community, offering her services to local farmers and winemakers free of charge. No job was too big or too small. She'd even helped Elmwood repair his flowerbed after he'd drunkenly stepped on his tulips.

Marigold watched in awe as a green aura surrounded the druid's hands, the soil shifting as roots took hold. Beads of perspiration speckled Tansy's brow as the cutting twitched, shoots sprouting from the vine and climbing up the trellis. It continued to grow, the verdant green trunk hardening into brown bark. Vines spread until small clusters of grapes burgeoned on them. Once it was a similar size to the others in the vineyard, she pulled her hands away.

"That's one down." Tansy's breaths came heavy.

They continued to work throughout the day. Elara and Finn had gone into town, acting secretive and mentioning something about needing to price lumber and other items, leaving Marigold and Tansy to work alone. They chatted during the moments the druid needed to regain her energy, and they shared a late lunch and glass of wine in the cellar. By the end of the day, they'd added an additional two rows of moonshadow grapes that would be ready to harvest in the coming autumn.

"I appreciate your help today." Marigold offered Tansy a bottle of honeywine as a token of thanks. "I wish it hadn't taken us ten years to get to know one another."

Tansy accepted the wine. "Better late than never."

Marigold chuckled. Whether it had been friendship, wine contests, or something deeper, those words had never been truer than they were this past year.

Elara and Finn were late to return, so Marigold waited until the next morning to show them the progress they'd made.

"All of this in one day." The elf ran her slender fingers along the vines. "Now I understand how Galvin beat us every year." She plucked a grape and tossed it in her mouth. "Damn, that's good. Makes it all the more impressive that we won this past year."

Marigold crossed her arms, narrowing her eyes at Elara. "Do you plan on telling me what has you and Finn acting so secretive?"

"Soon enough." She smirked. "I actually need you to go back with me today for a final confirmation on something."

Marigold rolled her eyes. "You know I hate it when you're vague."

"I know." Elara's grin widened. "That's what makes it fun."

Not long after, Finn brought the wagon around, refusing to meet Marigold's gaze as he handed the reins to Elara and disappeared inside the inn.

Marigold sighed, but she climbed into the wagon, resigning herself to her fate. If they'd gone through this much trouble, there was no way she was getting out of it.

The wagon bumped along the road as birds chirped from the trees and insects trilled among the fields. Marigold closed her eyes, losing herself in the songs of summer.

Soon, they crossed the bridge into town, where the scent of Rosie's bakery welcomed them with promises of sweet delight. Elara drove the wagon on by without slowing. They passed the market square and then Town Hall, followed by the blacksmith and general store. As they came upon the lumberyard, the wagon slowed, only for Elara to pass it by and turn onto the next street.

Marigold turned to the elf. "Where are you taking me?"

"We're almost there," Elara said without taking her eyes off the road.

They made another turn, passing more shops and a few homes built into the hillside. Just when Marigold thought this might all be some elaborate prank to distract her while the real surprise was happening back home, the wagon came to a halt in front of a tea shop nestled into the hill.

The Hillside Burrow.

Marigold's throat tightened at the memory of her and Poppy sitting on the hill, listening to The Cider Barrel Band and watching the firelight display above the town.

"What are we doing here?" She stared at the patio of the tea shop where customers were laughing and chatting over steaming mugs of tea.

Elara patted Marigold on the leg. "There's something I wanted to show you."

Marigold hesitated a moment before nodding. She trusted Elara. The elf only ever had the best intentions.

She climbed from the wagon and started walking toward the teashop.

"This way," Elara called, pointing toward the building next door.

Marigold frowned at the small, wooden fence separating the yard from the street, wondering why Elara would have brought her here. A stone pathway led to a porch about half the size of the tea shop's. It had a grass-covered roof that blended into the hill, held up by two wooden columns.

Her gaze fell upon the sign on the wall, and she froze. In freshly-painted letters, it read, "Willowbrook Historical Society."

"What's this?" Marigold asked, her voice barely a whisper.

The door opened, and someone stepped outside. The blue-haired gnome wore a pair of trousers and a form-fitting tunic. They were both stained with paint, along with the gnome's hands and fingers.

Poppy bit her lip, eyes wrinkling as she smiled. "Surprise."

Marigold blinked back tears as she looked upon the face that had frequented her dreams night after night. "What are… How are…" She looked to Elara and then back to Poppy, unable to believe this was real. Then she opened the gate, running down the path and nearly tackling Poppy to the ground.

"How is this possible?" Marigold asked as they embraced. She held Poppy tight, burying her face against the gnome's shoulder.

Poppy kissed the side of Marigold's head. "I told you I'd be back."

Marigold lifted her head, cheeks stained with tears as she met Poppy's gaze. "I know, but what about your work?"

"This is where I work now." Poppy wiped a thumb across Marigold's cheek.

Marigold looked at the sign again, her confusion only deepening. "But there's no such thing as the Willowbrook Historical Society."

"There is now." Poppy grinned. "I asked the mayor about the possibility before I left, and he thought it was a great idea. We just had to wait for a building to open up in town. Elara and Finn helped me unpack all of my books and research materials yesterday."

"So many books..." Elara's voice was caked with disbelief.

Marigold turned to the elf, eyes wide. "You knew?"

"Only for about a week." Elara smiled sheepishly. "I received a letter telling me that Poppy was on her way, and another when she arrived. I wanted to tell you, but I wanted to see this more."

Marigold sniffled. "So, this is real?"

"As real as you and me." Poppy squeezed her hand. "Can I show you around?"

"I'd love that." Marigold turned to Elara, who was still standing outside the gate. "You coming?"

"I think my work here is done." She waggled her brows. "You two kids have fun."

Marigold spent the rest of the day helping Poppy organize her new workspace. It was a quaint space, divided into three rooms. Poppy had chosen to use the largest for the welcome and display area and the two smaller rooms for her office and storage. In time, she'd fill the building with historical items and rotating features on different points of interest. Willowbrook had a trove of history aside from the harvest festival, and she was excited to discover it all.

Once the sun set, Poppy decided they'd toiled enough. For Marigold's part, she would have worked through the night if it meant spending more time with the gnome. Now that Poppy was back, she never wanted to let her go.

Poppy pulled a blanket from her luggage. "I hear there's a nice view from above."

Marigold laughed. "You don't say?"

They went outside, laying claim to the hillside. From their vantage, lamps speckled the streets below and windows glowed with golden light. At the edge of town, the moon and starry sky reflected off the stream.

Poppy spread the quilt across the grass, the silver thread of the Guiding Tree gleaming in the moonlight.

"It worked," she said, patting the blanket for Marigold to join her. "I found my way home."

Marigold sat beside her, resting her head against the gnome's shoulder. "I'm glad you're back." She kissed Poppy's shoulder and laid down, pulling the gnome with her until they were both gazing up at the stars.

They lay there, hands intertwined, serenaded by the hoot of an owl and the bark of the distant bullfrogs. Somewhere below, a horse clopped down the street and laughter rang out from a nearby tavern.

Marigold rolled over, propping herself up with her arm. "I couldn't help but notice you don't have a bedroom."

Poppy grabbed Marigold's shoulder, pulling her close until they were inches from one another. She grinned. "I thought I might find an inn. Some place nice and cozy with lots of history. Bonus points if they have good wine."

Marigold kissed her, slow at first, a gentle brush of lips as their breaths teased one another. Then more, deeper, passionate, filled with months of tension and longing. Her heart pounded with desire as Poppy held her tight, feeling the curves of her body. Just when she thought she might unravel, Marigold broke away, breathless and melting under Poppy's ravenous gaze. "I know just the place."

EPILOGUE: GOOD WINE, GOOD COMPANY

Some time later...

Marigold pulled the bottle of rosewine from the rack in the cellar, wiping away the dust that had gathered on the label over the past year. The new vintage would be bottled in the coming weeks, but this was the last of the wine that had won the harvest festival, a single bottle she'd saved for just this moment.

She paused halfway up the stairs to the inn, listening to the muffled chatter from the common area, where Elara was recounting the wine contest to Marigold's parents.

"—so then Tansy takes the wine sleeve, and she shoves it in his mouth."

Locke unleashed a volley of deep laughs that carried over the others. "That certainly shut him up."

Marigold's heart raced, and she chuckled at the absurdity of it. Why was she so nervous? This was the wine that had won the competition, after all. Her father was as likely to sprout wings as he was to critique her accomplishments.

Closing her eyes, she breathed deeply until the fluttering pixies in her stomach settled. With that sorted, she climbed the final stair into the inn.

Locke noticed Marigold as he wiped a tear from his eye. "Mari, you missed the best part."

She smiled, patting the bottle of wine. "I'd hardly say that was the best part."

"Aye. You've got me there." The dwarf waggled his brows. "Still, it's a fond memory."

In the aftermath of the festival, Galvin had made himself scarce around town. Whether it was due to anger or embarrassment, Marigold couldn't say, but she'd only seen him once in the past year. Despite his adamancy that Tansy could easily be replaced, he'd yet to find another druid to work for Darkroot Cellars. And with his outburst at the festival, the townsfolk weren't exactly eager to work for someone with such an attitude.

Marigold had considered paying him a visit. Perhaps a bit of kindness might be what he needed after his fall from grace. Maybe somewhere beneath all the ostentatiousness, there was a remnant of the playful, earnest halfling she'd known as a child.

A chair sliding across the floor pulled Marigold's attention. Thoughts of Galvin could wait.

Across from Locke, Marigold's parents watched her from the table. Wilbur Bramblefoot's expression was curious as he eyed the bottle of rose-colored wine Marigold carried. Her father hadn't changed much in the years since they'd last returned home. The buttons on his green vest were pulled a little tighter now that he no longer worked the vineyard every day, and there was more gray streaked through his curly, chestnut hair, but his eyes were as inquisitive and hungry as ever.

He raised his bushy eyebrows. "Is this the one?"

"This is the last of it." Marigold presented the bottle, her hands shaking slightly in anticipation. "I saved this one just for you."

Next to Wilbur, Marigold's mother, Gardenia, smiled as she wrapped her hands around his forearm. Her silvery-blonde hair was braided in a style similar to her daughter's and tied at the end with a green bow, the plait draping across the front of her shoulder. Her round face was speckled with freckles, and her blue eyes twinkled as her gaze fell upon her husband. She wore a floral-patterned dress and a necklace made of river stones that she'd bought during their travels in Wolfwater.

Wilbur took the bottle, holding it to the light. "This is special. You never forget your first blue ribbon." He met Marigold's gaze, a sparkle in his eye. "Want to know something funny?"

Marigold nodded. "Always."

"Out of all the ribbons I've won, you'd be surprised to know that none of my favorites are first place."

Marigold arched her brow. "Really?"

"It's true." He grinned as he ran his fingers across the label. "Winning was always nice, but the ones that stuck with me were the times I lost."

Marigold pressed her lips together, then sighed. "I can relate to that."

"It wasn't because they were bad memories." Wilbur's features softened as his jaw relaxed. "It's because those were the moments that challenged me. They allowed me to be better. Winning is nice. It reaffirms that what you've done is working. But losing, that's where the real growth happens. I became a better winemaker with every loss because I was forced to see what my competitors had done better than me. It's the reason I grew moonshadow grapes and why I tried my hand at blends." He returned to the newest blue ribbon at the end of the row. "It's not our accomplishments that build character, but our struggles. I'm proud of you, Mari."

Marigold narrowed her eyes playfully at her father. "How'd you get so wise?"

"A lifetime of experiences." He offered the bottle back to Marigold. "Will you do the honors?"

She stared at his outstretched hands. "You don't want to open it?"

"We're guests, Mari." He gestured for her to take the wine. "I think it's only fitting."

Marigold swallowed as she accepted the bottle. Even after running the inn for eleven years, it still felt like her parents' place. This was where they'd raised her, where they'd taught her the meaning of community, kindness, and passion.

"Everything okay?" Gardenia's brow was knit with concern.

"Yeah." Marigold smiled. Her parents were here, Poppy had returned to Willowbrook, and the vineyard was more popular than ever. "Everything is perfect."

She uncorked the bottle, and just as she was about to pour, her father held up a hand.

"Where'd that lady of yours get off to? And Finn and Gerty for that matter. If this is the last bottle, then everyone should be here." Wilbur looked over his shoulder, where a guest was reading a book by the hearth. The man was broad-shouldered, with thick arms and a magnificent red beard. "Excuse me. We're about to try my daughter's award-winning blend of rosewine. Would you like to join us?"

The man looked up from his book, surprised that Wilbur was talking to him. He stroked his beard. "I appreciate the offer, but I wouldn't want to intrude."

"Nonsense." Wilbur pointed to the sign hanging above the bar. "Wine brings people together. Come on over."

Elara went to gather the stragglers while Marigold made sure there were enough glasses for everyone.

Soon, they were all gathered around the table.

"One bottle for nine people." Finn raised a brow. "When you said we'd be getting a taste, you weren't lying."

Wilbur laughed. "It's not the quantity that matters, it's the quality." He gestured to the people standing before him. "I'd rather share a sip of wine with my friends and family than have an entire bottle to myself."

Poppy wrapped her arm around Marigold's waist and squeezed. "The apple didn't fall too far from the Bramble-foot tree, did it?"

"What gave it away?" Marigold grinned before kissing Poppy on the cheek. "Where'd you get off to?"

"Your mom offered to teach me how to make her famous blueberry pie later, so I was—"

"Researching," Marigold finished the sentence, and

they both laughed. Her hand shook slightly as she poured her father the first taste.

Wilbur swirled the wine, admiring the light pink color before bringing the glass to his nose. He sniffed. "That's a lovely bouquet." He took a small sip, savoring the wine on his tongue before finally swallowing. "Wow." He met his daughter's gaze. "Truly spectacular."

Pride swelled in Marigold's chest as she poured a taste for everyone before giving the last of the wine to her father. True to Finn's estimation, there wasn't a lot to go around, but this wasn't about having a drink. This was a special moment, celebrating her parents' return and what truly felt like a new chapter for the vineyard.

"Tell me, Mari…" Wilbur tilted his glass, watching the pink wine catch the light. "What inspired you to add emberfruit to the blend?"

Marigold smiled. It was like she was a kid again and her father was quizzing her on how the different varietals paired together. "Your recipe was good, but it felt like something was missing. I thought the tartness of the emberfruit could bring a little more balance to the transition."

"You were right." He raised his glass. "A toast—to good wine…"

Marigold took a moment to cherish the friends and family who were gathered around the table. Locke and Elara, who had stood by her side through all the ups and downs of the past eleven years. Gerty and Finn, who were like the siblings she'd never had. And her parents, who had given her a life and an opportunity she cherished, their support unwavering even when Marigold felt like she had let them down.

Much like her father, Marigold could finally appreciate the years of losses because they had all led her here. Somehow, the thing that had been such a black cloud had brought her and Poppy together. Marigold held Poppy's hand, savoring the warmth of the gnome's touch as she raised her glass. "And good company."

ACKNOWLEDGMENTS

Thank you for reading *The Halfling's Harvest*! If you enjoyed your time at the Dew Drop Inn, please consider rating, reviewing, and sharing your thoughts on social media using the hashtag **#TheHalflingsHarvest**. Word of mouth is the best way to support indie authors like myself.

One of the central themes of this story is community, and this book would not exist without the incredible support of my own community—friends, fellow authors, and readers who helped bring this story to life.

First, my deepest gratitude to **Caroline** for patiently listening to my endless ramblings about these characters as I pieced the story together. There was a pivotal moment when everything clicked, and it wouldn't have happened without you.

Thank you to **Cindy Koepp** for your sharp editorial eye on my earliest drafts. You've seen this story in its rawest form, like grapes in the midst of the stomping, hairy feet and all.

To my amazing **beta readers**— your feedback was invaluable, and I can't thank you enough for catching all my blunders. **Aaron Eichler, Cheryl Deal, Emma Ewert,**

Erica Nadvornik, Gregg Trotti, Janet Beane, Lance Krautlarger, Loren Foster, Morgan Byres, Nancy Ann Gazo, Paul Tuson, and **Sean Flint**.

A special thanks to my Patreon supporters—your comments, likes, and encouragement between releases mean the world to me.

Platinum Tier: Joel Southard, Willa Elliott

Gold Tier: Amanda Blackburn, Angela Fitz, Kevin Wagner, Jessica Worgo, Michael Percell, Laura Lea Davidson, Preston Leigh, Robert Schaefer

Silver Tier: Emmi Junkkari, Elise Raposa, Jess Moran, Joel Daemon, Lance Krautlarger, Nick Kelly, Rickie Brookes, Zachary Stout, Christopher Walters

Thank you for being part of this journey!

ABOUT THE AUTHOR

S.L. Rowland is a cozy fantasy and LitRPG author known for crafting immersive worlds filled with adventure, heart, and a touch of humor. A lifelong gamer and fantasy enthusiast, he draws inspiration from tabletop RPGs, video games, and the fantastical. When he's not writing, he enjoys weightlifting, hiking with his Shiba Inu, and enduring the heartbreak of being an Atlanta sports fan.

SLRowland.com

Patreon-For signed paperbacks, advanced chapters, exclusive short stories, art, merch, and more.

Newsletter: For updates on new releases, sales, and behind the scenes content!

Email: slrowlandauthor@gmail.com

Find out more at https://linktr.ee/SLRowland

ALSO BY S.L. ROWLAND

Tales of Aedrea

Cursed Cocktails

Sword & Thistle

The Halfling's Harvest

There Be Dragons Here

Pangea Online

Pangea Online: Death and Axes

Pangea Online 2: Magic and Mayhem

Pangea Online 3: Vials and Tribulations

Sentenced to Troll 1-6

Path to Villainy: An NPC Kobold's Tale

Collected Editions

Pangea Online: The Complete Trilogy

Sentenced to Troll Compendium: Books 1-3

Sentenced to Troll Compendium 2: Books 4-6

www.ingramcontent.com/pod-product-compliance
Lightning Source LLC
Chambersburg PA
CBHW020653010826
48969CB00013B/1407